Elinor's E

Book 1 of the Ch

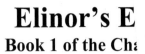

Sarah J. Waldock

ISBN-13 978-1511879460

Dedication

Dedicated to my mother, Margaret Parsons, whose
vasty experience working with children allowed me to crib
a lot about the girls from her.
Also to my friend Clio, who advised me on Jewish
matters and made sure the text was kosher

This is the first book in the Charity School Series, and it opens in early spring, 1809.

Sarah Waldock grew up in Suffolk and still resides there, in charge of a husband, and under the ownership of sundry cats. All Sarah's cats are rescue cats and many of them have special needs. They like to help her write and may be found engaging in such helpful pastimes as turning the screen display upside-down, or typing random messages in kittycode into her computer.

Sarah claims to be an artist who writes. Her degree is in art, and she got her best marks writing essays for it. She writes largely historical novels, in order to retain some hold on sanity in an increasingly insane world. There are some writers who claim to write because they have some control over their fictional worlds, but Sarah admits to being thoroughly bullied by her characters who do their own thing and often refuse to comply with her ideas. It makes life more interesting, and she enjoys the surprises they spring on her. Her characters' surprises are usually less messy [and much less noisy] than the surprises her cats spring.

Sarah has tried most of the crafts and avocations which she mentions in her books, on the principle that it is easier to write about what you know. She does not ride horses, since the Good Lord in his mercy saw fit to invent Gottleib Daimler to save her from that experience; and she has not tried blacksmithing. She would like to wave cheerily at anyone in any security services who wonder about middle aged women who read up about gunpowder and poisonous plants.

Sarah would like to note that any typos remaining in the text after several betas, an editor and proofreader have been over it are caused by the well-known phenomenon of *cat-induced editing syndrome* from the help engendered by busy little bottoms on the keyboard.

This is her excuse and you are stuck with it.

And yes, there are two more cat bums on the edge of the picture as well as the 4 on her lap/chest

You may find out more about Sarah at her blog site, at:
http://sarahs-history-place.blogspot.co.uk/
Or on Facebook for advance news of writing
https://www.facebook.com/pages/Sarah-J-Waldock-Author/520919511296291
Or particiapate as a beta reader and get an advanced look at Sarah's work in draft form at
https://mywipwriting.blogspot.com/

Early Spring, 1809.
Chapter 1

"In short, Miss Fairbrother, you are, a, er, very wealthy young woman indeed," declared Mr. Embery, the solicitor, regarding his client over his spectacles.

He saw a wan young woman, lying on a *chaise longue*. Elinor Fairbrother gave every appearance of elegant ethereal lethargy, with pale face, pale, almost silvery blonde hair, and a pale grey silken shawl around her shoulders over the customary white muslin dress. The shawl was a hasty concession to mourning, since Elinor's father had succumbed to an inflammation of the chest caught whilst hunting, which had been ignored by that erratic gentleman, and had led to fatal pleurisy.

"I had never expected to outlive father," Elinor's soft voice contained the stunned surprise she still felt. "Mr. Embery, as it is likely that I will not survive him long, I must make provision."

"Come, come, my dear young lady," said Mr. Embery, without conviction.

"Mr. Embery, my mother, my aunt, and my three sisters have all died of heart disease before they were thirty years old. I am now twenty-two and I cannot but begin to contemplate my mortality. I have no living kin; so do you not feel that it would be eminently wise to contemplate making a will?"

"Well, since you put it that way, Miss Fairbrother, I quite concur," said Mr. Embery, "but to whom might you leave such a large sum? An income of eight thousand pounds a year..."

"I know, I am not devoid of intellect, it means two hundred thousand pounds in the funds at the current interest of four percent," said Elinor, knowing that it was rude to interrupt, but resented the slightly patronising tone that had crept into Embery's voice.

"Ah … Quite," said Mr. Embery. "A considerable fortune. Your late father…." he tailed off.

"My late father terrified you by speculating on the Exchange, but only ever taking reasonable odds," said Elinor. "I know, for in more recent years I helped him make his choices."

"Good God!" said Mr. Embery, shocked out of his mind that a pretty young lady should be capable of such a thing.

"I'm not sure that the Almighty had anything to do with it," said Elinor. "I'd have said that a bold spirit and good choices were more to the case, but let it go. Some luck was involved."

"Er… Indeed," said Mr. Embery. "Well, I shall leave you to consider what you, er, want to do in terms of, er, future dispositions of your fortune."

"Oh, I know that," said Elinor. "It is something I had been considering asking Papa to do. I want to set up a school."

"I – I beg your pardon?" Mr. Embery was shocked once again. "My dear Miss Fairbrother, why?"

"Because I value the education that has enabled my weary days by to be whiled away by the joys of reading and learning," said Elinor, calmly. "And I should like to see the same joys bestowed on other girls. But I wish to help those girls who are, through no fault of their own, left orphaned and indigent with no relatives able, willing, to care for them. Those girls who have never expected to be left in such straits are those I mean to help first. Those, who are forced to become superior nursemaids, if they have not the education to become governesses, who are even forced to enter service. And I suspect that there are worse things that might happen," she added. "Papa was not mealy-mouthed."

"No, indeed," said Mr. Embery, dryly. "You wish to squander your hard-won fortune on a bunch of orphans?"

"Oh, hardly squander, I think," a hint of steel was in Elinor's voice. "I have been fortunate in my very erudite governess, Miss Freemantle, and I should like to see other girls educated to offer the same excellent services as she has done for me. And as head preceptress, she will then be assured of a job when I die, as well as an annuity which I should wish to arrange."

"Dear me!" said Mr. Embery. "You, er, appeared to have thought it out very, er, clearly."

"Yes, I have," said Elinor. "I intend to remove my living quarters to a small portion of this great pile of a house, and fit the rest out as an orphanage, which will mean I have no need to go searching for other premises. The rooms here at Swanley Court are large, so when there are large classes they will quite sufficient. The ballroom will be available to teach dancing, as any governess should be able to pass on the steps to her charges, and the air in this location near Richmond is clear and healthful."

"Good God!" said Mr. Embery again.

"What is more," said Elinor, with a martial light in her eye, "I plan to begin on a small scale so that I may enjoy some of the fruits of my endowment before I pass on. I shall be able to do so quite readily on my anticipated income, and will proceed to advertise for half a dozen orphans. I am aware that I shall require more staff, and I also intend to make the effort to visit Dame Hannah Rogers' model school set up on her endowment. *She* did not see how well it has flourished: *I* intend to live long enough to see my school blossom."

Mr. Embery took refuge in cleaning his spectacles vigorously.

"You were a trifle *peremptory* with him, my dear," said Libby Freemantle, emerging from behind a screen once Mr. Embery had taken his spluttering leave.

"He was intending to push me into a role of his own choosing," said Elinor, mulishly. "One of those men who assumes that an educated woman is like a dancing dog, whereby one does not so much marvel at how well the action is, performed, but that is it is performed at all. He needed to be told firmly."

Libby chuckled.

"You certainly told him firmly," she said.

"Libby darling, I am dying by inches. I have no intention of having what little I may have left of my life ruined by being run, for my own good of *course*, by a fatuous idiot."

"Hardly an idiot if he has his degree in law," commented Libby Freemantle. "Loose language, my dear."

Elinor made a gesture with one hand.

"It's the idiocy of a closed mind," she said, "well Libby, can you think of a better word?"

Libby considered, then laughed.

"I concede, but without considerable thought, I am unable to do so. Do you really feel that you can travel to Devon to see the model school?"

"I confess the idea is daunting," said Elinor, "but I was irritated. Perhaps you might go, if we can acquire a trustee suitable to squire you."

"Mr. Embery, following his quaint ways, is an honest man and an eminently suitable trustee," said Libby. "I would also suggest my second cousin, the Bishop of Norchester."

"Admirable," said Elinor, "though how such an excellent woman as yourself came to have a disreputable relation like a bishop I cannot imagine."

"Naughty puss," said Libby, equably. "Mr. Embery will have a shock when you provide him with the reckoning."

"Indeed. It was good of the Bishop to find out the

particulars of that endowment, and that the school runs on a little under £700 a year, including clothing the children, and a salary of £100 a year for the school mistress."

"The master who teaches them to write is paid less, but it is not so skilled a job," said Libby, "there was also, I recall, the fact that the girls there are not clad in such quality as a lady would expect, even one who is destined to be a governess, since it is a school for all indigent girls from eight to fourteen to fit them for a life of service."

"Indeed. But we have discussed this, and although I see my way to leaving monies to cover girls of all classes after I die, I fear that the excitement of having to cope with girls who lack some measure of gentility would be to wearing for my health," said Elinor.

"I agree, my love," said Libby, "and you must be mindful of your health. Moreover it is better to start small and let growth come naturally; and it is not as though there are not girls of our class who are left destitute. A boy can always go into the Navy or Army, but a girl has no such recourse, and could not cope with the rigours of factory life."

Elinor shuddered.

"I cannot see how even the most robust labourer's child can cope with the rigours of factory life," she said. "But from little acorns the mighty oak tree grows. We shall see how it goes – or at least, you will!" she added.

Libby kissed her charge on the cheek.

"You have been cherished and nurtured all your life, my dear; perhaps you may have longer than your unfortunate relations," she said stop

"It will not be for lack of determination," said Elinor.

Elinor drew up a list for a Board of Trustees, and against Libby's expostulations, added her old governess's name.

"I cannot see that a Board of Trustees can advise on school matters without the headmistress of the school also being present on the board," said Elinor.

"Part of the purpose of a Board of Trustees or Governors is to fire the head teacher if they find them inconvenient, or so I understand it," said Libby, dryly.

"Preposterous! I shall make it a condition of my will that no such thing should occur. Rather, I shall add that you should be able to remove any, who prove unsuitable," said Elinor. "Andrew Embery; that is a given. George Alsop, Bishop of Norchester. We should probably have the local vicar too, Timothy White, and we need an accountant. I believe I know just the man; Thomas Everard."

"The man who used to handle your father's investments, until he retired, and handed it over to his nephew?" asked Libby, and receiving a nod of confirmation, went on, "he should be an excellent accountant, if he will take the job. He may not wish to. I recall him saying to your father that he hoped to spend more time fishing."

"Trust me," said Elinor, "he has been out of finance long enough to feel bored. If I put up some of the endowment to be used in investment, he'll be totally happy."

"Way, my dear Elinor, you are very good at being manipulative when you try!" laughed Libby.

Elinor shrugged.

"In many ways, it is like reading the market, and buying or selling at just the right moment," she said. "Mr. Everard will appreciate that. Very well, now I must write to each of them, and ask if they will accept; and if they will, to attend a dinner party here, as an informal meeting. Please pass me my lapdesk."

"My dear, are you up to writing all those letters?" asked Libby, anxiously, carrying over the prettily-veneered little box that opened into a desk.

"I am, Libby, indeed, I feel quite invigorated by the thought," said Elinor, opening it up, all she needed for writing contained in the ingenious compartments under the sloping, plush-covered writing surface.

The dinner party passed off well enough, with all the intended trustees finding enough in each other to respect, from the unworldly vicar murmuring the odd Latin platitudes, to the very worldly Mr. Everard.

"Now, confess, Miss Fairbrother, you noticed at your father's funeral that I was disenchanted with retirement, did you not?" Mr. Everard said. "And you have snared me like a trout with the dangled fly of something to occupy me."

Elinor smiled.

"I confess it freely, Mr. Everard," she said. "You have been such a good friend to my family, I am glad to be able to give you an interest, as well as gaining for my endeavours a very able accountant."

"Mutually agreeable outcomes; the best of all deals!" Said Mr. Everard. "Now I have another, I hope, mutually agreeable proposal. You will need a doctor on hand for your girls, and I have a young nephew – well, he is some kind of cousin, but I call him nephew – who is recently qualified as a doctor. He is Scots, but you would not mind that, would you?"

"Not if he's competent," said Elinor.

"Good! Then may I send him to see you? His name is Graeme Macfarlane, and he has a lot of new ideas."

"I should be delighted to receive him at his convenience," said Elinor. "I have nothing against new ideas, providing that they are not plainly foolish, or new for the sake of newness. If the board is agreed to the engagement of a doctor, of course," she added. Her tone suggested that anyone who was not agreed must be a fool, and there were rapid murmurings of assent; though the Bishop of Norchester hid a smile. Miss Fairbrother did, he thought, use the ruthless autocracy of the weak very effectively. As it was in a good cause, the Bishop made no demur. If only Miss Fairbrother might survive a few years to see the school well and truly under way, she might achieve great things.

Elinor believed in doing things properly, and penned a letter to Dr. Macfarlane requesting that he attend an interview pending a position as school doctor at his earliest convenience.

Mr. Everard would fill in the young man as to the details; and though the doctor had, as yet, no patients, it would be good to know that even the most sickly child would be in safe hands if he was, indeed, a good doctor.

Chapter 2

"Dr. Macfarlane, Miss Fairbrother," Elinor's butler, Baxter, showed the doctor into Elinor's boudoir.

"Doctor Macfarlane! Welcome!" said Elinor.

The doctor was very tall, and Elinor had to look up from her *chaise longue* to see that he was good-looking in a craggy sort of way, but with a shock of what was undeniably red hair. Never could it be described tactfully as auburn; it was too red to be anything but fierily, gingery red. Elinor reflected that it was a stereotypical colour for a Scotsman, and hoped she could understand what he said, if his speech was very broad.

She need not have worried.

The doctor's accent when he spoke was slight, but not intrusive. Indeed, it was quite attractive; though his words were shocking.

"Miss Fairbrother! My uncle has spoken to me of your wit and cleverness, and yet he tells me that you hold to your couch for thinking yourself dying! Looking at you, I have to say that I see no signs in you of heart disease, and I fancy there is nothing wrong with you, that a good diet and plenty of fresh air and exercise will not cure."

Elinor stared at him in outrage.

"You call yourself a doctor?" she exclaimed. "Why, my aunt, my mother, and my sisters all died of heart disease!"

"Well, Miss Fairbrother, if you yourself are your aunt, your mother, and all your sisters, I must say you're a fine plurality for a man to have to meet."

"What do you mean?" Elinor almost snapped. A fine thing for the man to play with her emotions like this!

"I mean that you are not your various relatives, who may very well have died of heart disease, or who may have been killed by some quack assuming the illness to run in families as a matter of course, and giving for minor ailment doses of cures that can kill the healthy," said Graeme Macfarlane. He shrugged mentally. He had already angered her, so there was no harm in saying all that he felt. He was certain that he had lost the job with his impulsive outburst.

She stared at him, paling and clutching the side of her *chaise longue* to prevent herself fainting.

"Would such a medicine make one feel nauseous, confused, and with palpitations, and sweating?" She asked sharply.

"Classic symptoms, Miss Fairbrother," said Dr. Macfarlane. "Have you suffered such with medication?"

"Yes. I stopped taking it, and dismissed my doctor." Elinor forced herself to breathe deeply and evenly, trying to control her agitation. . "Papa was quite angry with me. But I cannot think … But maybe Arabella…" she tailed off. "I cannot speak to you immediately, Dr. Macfarlane. Pray take a walk about the grounds. I will see you in an hour."

With that, Elinor rang the bell abruptly, and her butler arrived noiselessly.

"Miss?" He asked.

"Baxter, see that the doctor has a drink; he is going to take a walk for an hour, after which you will show him back in," said Elinor.

"Very good, Miss. This way, doctor."

Graeme Macfarlane found himself being led away; but not summarily dismissed, as he had feared, at least.

"How *dare* he!" cried Elinor to Libby. She was sobbing.

"Indeed, a very discourteous young man to imply that you are malingering, my love," said Libby.

"I'm not sure that was what he was saying, I think he was saying that I am mistaken in my belief that I am prey to the fatal disease that killed poor mama and my other siblings, at least, if that is what killed them."

"You cannot suppose ... Oh, Elinor, do you really think that Dr. Robertson prescribed medicine that killed poor dear Arabella?" Libby was shocked, recalling Elinor's older sister, less than a year between the girls having made them almost as close as twins.

"Oh, Libby, I do not know what to think! Arabella was so good and patient, and when he said that the fever that so pulled her had doubtless weakened her heart, none of us questioned the pills he gave her, the same pills he gave me. And Arabella was hard put to retain food in her stomach, and she wandered in her mind, and her nightgown was wringing wet overnight with sweat. And she complained her heart felt irregular, and Dr. Robertson increased the dose, and then she died. I fear that it was not a case, as he declared, that he could not do enough, but that he had already done too much. Don't you recall how much better I got when I stopped taking those pills after he prescribed them for me?"

"Indeed, I do, my love," said Libby. "I wondered if he assumed your case to be the same as Arabella's, and made an error in judgement, but if her case was also such a serious error ... What will you do about this outspoken Dr. Macfarlane?"

"I'll ask him why, on such brief acquaintance, he thinks my heart to be unaffected," said Elinor. "Surely he cannot diagnose just by looking at me?"

"I do not know, Elinor," said Libby. She looked on her former charge with deep sympathy in her eyes; it was a cruel thing for the doctor to raise Elinor's hopes if he was wrong in this hasty diagnosis, and hard for her, too, if he were right, and poor little Arabella had died for nothing. Libby could offer no comfort, nor advice; Elinor must make her own choices, and come to a decision on her own. Libby had had it impressed in her from the moment she accepted employment that the girls were sickly, and that she was not to permit them to do too much, and now she was wondering how much of the sickliness was caused purely by paternal fears and worries, and not born out by facts. Such a waste of a childhood for Elinor, and for the life of Arabella if so! Fondness in too great a quantity might be as bad, sometimes as neglect.

Elinor stared out of the window as she pondered the doctor's words, hardly seeing the vista of the gardens sweeping down to the lake, and the carefully placed coppices of trees which had been planted by 'Capability' Brown in her grandfather's time. There was so much to consider; and also it would not do to assume that this doctor was correct, any more than any other doctor who agreed that her mother's family had heart disease. She must quiz him on what made him feel that she was healthier than her other family. She was aware but vaguely of the tall figure of the doctor in the landscape, walking in a measured fashion, seeming to count his steps.

"Dr. Macfarlane," said Elinor, when Baxter showed him back into her presence, "what makes you, on first seeing me, declare me to be free of heart disease?"

"Miss Fairbrother, I saw as I entered the room a young lady who was pale with the pallor of someone who does not get out enough into the air. However, you have perfectly normal fingernails, no excess hectic flush to the cheek, a clear and ringing voice without any defect, and if I may say so, very pretty ankles."

Elinor jerked her legs blushing.

"You may not, Sir, unless you can demonstrate good reason for mentioning them," she said.

He shrugged, and also blushed. It clashed horribly with his hair.

"It is pertinent more than it is impertinent," he said. Elinor pricked her ears up; he could manage wordplay.

"Then you may explain," she said.

"People who are suffering from a heart defect that is in their heritage often show swelling of the ankles, and sometimes other parts of the body less easy to see straight away," he said, "and often the ends of the fingers and the nail beds have a degree of blueness. These people tend to be lethargic, often short of breath, and may have a nasty tight little cough."

"I see," said Elinor. "My mother certainly suffered some of those symptoms, and my sister Abigail was quite blue when she was born. She lived a week," she added sadly. "I do not recall much about Elizabeth; she was older than I. Arabella ... I concede you may be correct that Arabella died of the medicine I stopped taking." She could scarcely speak, for emotion was choking her.

"I presume you recovered for so doing?" asked Graeme Macfarlane.

"I did. Is that another proof?"

"It is, though I could not know that when I met you. You are not well, but that is due to a lack of exercise, and probably to an invalid diet. Do you wish to be well?"

"Well that is a stupid question, Doctor!" Said Elinor, angrily. "Of course I wish to be well!"

He gave a dour smile.

"You might be surprised how many wealthy ladies are happy to be ill, for it makes them interesting, and they can have the fun of being weak domestic tyrants, with all at their beck and call for fear of providing they call a spasm," he said cynically.

"I can quite see women past their prime feeling thus, devoid of the attentions of a husband who married them only to breed from," said Elinor. "For them, I can feel compassion at such imaginary maladies. But I am only twenty-two; I am on the shelf perhaps, but still wanting life! I can hardly believe that you offer it to me."

"Aye, and I'm a fool," said Dr. Macfarlane, "for if you're a healthy creature as God intended, those poor wee orphans will lose by it."

"They will not," said Elinor firmly. "I will not go back on my word. If I am to live, then I will be able to do more for them. But I tire, Dr. Macfarlane. Please to leave me, and discuss another time such exercises as you think suitable, and what I might eat to accustom my stomach to more normal food. It cannot be good to move from an invalid diet to a rich one."

"It would be most bad for you," he agreed. "I will draw you up a regimen of exercise and a diet. And I need to assume I am hired?"

"Provisionally, certainly," said Elinor. "If your regimen makes me ill, I shall fire you."

"You can't say fairer than that," said Macfarlane. "I have already made a brief survey of the nearer aspect of your grounds, and have thought about some walks that will provide both a pleasing view, and a pleasant, healthful walk for your good health."

That, then, explained what he had been doing with such measured steps in the grounds. Elinor nodded.

"Excellent," she said.

Dr. Macfarlane was provided quarters in the school part of Swanley Court, as Elinor was already starting the separation between home, and school. It was a fine Palladian house built on the footstep of an earlier Jacobean house, with an impressive frontage and side wings, one of which did very well for Elinor's private quarters. The doctor was housed in a room on a corridor leading to the west wing where Elinor resided. Once installed, he duly drew up a list of exercises Elinor was to undertake and presented them to her.

"This doesn't seem very arduous," Elinor said, dubiously. She was dressed warmly for the cold of the weather, it having been a sharp winter that showed no signs of giving way to spring.

"If you begin with exercises that are too arduous, you will make your muscles ache with the strain," said Graeme Macfarlane, "and the heart is also a muscle. It would be a shame to make a healthy heart sick, for over using it right away, would it not?"

"I suppose so," said Elinor. "Well, I have more to think about than just my exercises. I have received a letter from a vicar in the see of Norchester about our first pupil; perhaps while I take the leisurely walk you have set me, you would be kind enough to accompany me while I tell you what I know of her?"

"Yes, if you will. Has she then any medical needs I should be aware of?"

"She has, indeed, Doctor. The child has a clubfoot. Her name is Margaret Ellis, and the vicar writes that she is never to be called Peggy, as that occasions teasing about peg-legs. She is known as Daisy."

"This vicar sounds a good and sensitive man," said Graeme Macfarlane, approvingly. "If possible, you should ignore her disability, as far as possible; misplaced solicitude can be quite as irritating as unkind remarks."

"I find I can recall instances when that has been true for me, so I understand that," said Elinor. "I, too, liked the sound of the vicar, who has written that as soon as he was advised of this school, he thought it sheer Providence for Daisy, since her situation has lately changed."

"In what way?"

"Seemingly, she was left with her grandparents when her parents went to India; her father was some clerk in the Honourable East India Company. Both parents died abroad. The vicar has been educating her, and he says she will have little trouble learning to be a governess as she has a fair grounding. Her grandfather died some months ago, and now her grandmother's sister-in-law has offered the grandmother a home. There was a proviso. That proviso is that The Child, as the wretched woman calls her, does not go."

"She'll probably be quite difficult," warned Dr. Macfarlane. "Such a set of circumstances to set up the back of a young girl! She is still grieving no doubt, for her grandfather, and this wretched old besom wrenching her grandmother away. Why doesn't the grandmother remain?"

"The house passes to some male kin of the grandfather, through an entail, and the grandmother is weak after illness following her husband's death, and cannot care for the child, or cope with hunting for a house, even if she could afford to move," said Elinor. "The vicar is unmarried, or he would adopt the child, he said. She's fourteen, so I suppose almost a young woman, not quite a child. Dear me! I should be furious, in her shoes, to be so betrayed by the adults in my life."

"Bear that in mind, my dear Miss Fairbrother, and you will be able to enter into her feelings," said Dr. Macfarlane. "But remember, too, to maintain a distance."

"But I want my pupils to love me!" said Elinor.

"Being too familiar with them when they are hurt, bewildered, and in a new place, will not achieve that end," said Dr. Macfarlane. "You must be kind, but firm, letting them know that they may bring troubles to you, or to Miss Freemantle, but that you will not accept any bad behaviour. Come, now! Do you not feel the closer to Miss Freemantle because she has contained you at need, as well as being kind and caring?"

Elinor flushed.

"You are right," she admitted unwillingly.

"I am. It's a bad habit some doctors have," said Macfarlane. "You have walked in the circle which I prescribed, and I fancy that you are ready to rest."

"I am," Elinor said. "My legs ache."

"Perhaps I have asked too much of you," he frowned.

"It is not a bad ache," said Elinor.

"Hmm. If your legs ache overnight, or feel restless, or you have trouble sleeping, let me know, and we can moderate the exercise," he said. "You are supposed to be getting well, not knocking yourself out. I wager, though, that you will be ready for more than a boiled egg for your dinner."

"I shall," said Elinor. "You will watch and see how well I eat."

He looked surprised.

"Am I then invited to dinner?"

"Why, certainly, Doctor; I do not expect you to eat in solitary splendour. You and Libby, and any other staff I accrue will dine together unless there is a reason you wish to dine alone, or have a dinner invitation. I trust that is acceptable?"

"It's generous of you," said Dr. Macfarlane. "I look forward to it. Any idea when this child, Daisy, is to arrive?"

"None whatsoever; the vicar is about as worldly as our own Reverend White, I fear," said Elinor, "though if he has put her on the stage, as he says … Dear me, the child may already be at the nearest coaching Inn!"

"Resume your cloak, Miss Fairbrother; it is not seemly that a man should meet her alone," said the doctor. "Although you are tired, I fear I must ask you to come with me, or else send your head mistress in your stead."

Elinor stared at him for such a peremptory order; the wretched man was right, of course. And Elinor was not about to have anyone else, even Libby, meet her very first pupil. She resumed her pelisse and followed the doctor meekly as he went out, bellowing on his way for the landau to be put to horse.

Libby, watching, thought it very good for dear Elinor that she had met someone she could not bend to her will. Perhaps it was unwise of Elinor to go out, but if she felt able, it might do her good.

Chapter 3

"Now, you're a fresh, pretty liddle thing, new from the country," the large woman leered at Daisy as she stood, wondering what happened next, now the Stage had gone. "Are you looking for a situation as a maid?"

"No, ma'am; I'm waiting to be picked up to go to school," said Daisy.

"School? Pretty liddle thing like you needs no schooling," said the woman, taking Daisy's arm in a grip like a vice. "You come with me, and I've a nice job waiting…" And then she suddenly bellowed with fear and pain, as a fine lady hit her hard on the head with a parasol, and a tall, red-haired gentleman hit her scientifically on her plump forearm, making her fingers fly involuntarily open from where they were grasping Daisy's wrist. Daisy stumbled, but the tall gentleman's hand was under her elbow just long enough to steady her, and was then withdrawn.

"Are you Daisy?" Elinor asked crisply.

"Can't you see the twisted foot?" asked Daisy sullenly.

"Not really, no," said Elinor. "You'd think it strange, wouldn't you, if Dr. Macfarlane and I went around lifting petticoats to peer at feet, as though it were the only way to identify someone, unless of course the people you've known before have some very odd habits."

Against her will, Daisy began to giggle.

"Good girl," said Elinor. "Laughter is a tonic against a shock. Dear me, Dr. MacFarlane, what do we do, place that creature in charge?"

"Yes, I'd like yon besom taken in charrrge, to save other young girrrls," said Dr. MacFarlane. His r's rolled rather. "Trying to kidnap a young lady on her way to school is far more likely to land this creature in hot water with the beak than is abducting poor country girls looking for work. *HEY! YOU!*" The doctor accosted mine host as that worthy came out of the inn to see what the noise was about.

"Sir? What may I do for you?"

"You can lock this … female … up somewhere, and call a constable to take away. I'll be lodging a complaint against her."

"Yes Sir," said the innkeeper, oleaginously. The woman, being still rather groggy from being hit on the head with Elinor's parasol, was more easily manhandled that if she had had all her wits about her.

"Well, Daisy, I am Miss Fairbrother, and you are the first pupil at Swanley Court School," said Elinor. "If, as I suspect, you are better educated than some of the other girls your age who come to us, you'll be able to earn some pin money teaching younger girls. As we do not know who might be joining us yet, we only have one mistress, the head mistress, Miss Freemantle, and I shall hold classes reading and discussing a selection of books. It will seem very strange to you at first, of course, and if you have been looking after your grandmother, you may find time hangs heavily, but you may have free rein of the library."

"I could have looked after her better than that horrid sister-in-law could," said Daisy.

"I'm sure you could, but I am also sure that she hated feeling a burden on you," said Elinor. "It is hard to be dependent on others."

"And speaking of being dependent, I've put you through far too much and you have taken too much exercise dealing with that creature," said Dr. Macfarlane.

"I can rest, going home," said Elinor.

"Are you ill?" asked Daisy. "… Miss Fairbrother," she added.

"I have been made ill by wrong treatments from

another doctor," Elinor temporised. It was not so far from the truth. "Dr. Macfarlane will be doctor to the school, and is helping me too. I need to make haste slowly, as they say."

Daisy gave an abrupt little nod, which might have meant almost anything, but at least was not a negative reaction. In truth, she admired this pretty lady for the prompt use of her parasol to save her; and the parasol would never be the same again.

"I might be able to mend it," she gestured to the abused parasol.

Elinor gave her a brilliant smile that filled Daisy's poor little broken heart.

"If you can, I would be so pleased," Elinor said, "but if it is beyond you, perhaps you will help me strip off the cover, and attach it to a new parasol base."

"Oh, yes, Miss Fairbrother!" said Daisy.

"Elinor, my dear, you should really have let me go with Dr. Macfarlane," said Libby, as the party returned to the new school. Elinor's pale face made her wish she had stepped forward and insisted on taking Elinor's place. "However! Daisy, my dear, I am Miss Freemantle, and if you will come with me, I will show you to your room."

A mutinous look crossed Daisy's face.

"I would rather Miss Fairbrother showed me," she said, "If you please," she added.

Libby frowned slightly.

"Miss Fairbrother has already tired herself too much in coming to collect you, leaving, as I believe, in something of a hurry, since that blessed parson who sent you had put no time of your arrival on his letter. I am sure you will not wish her to make herself ill, would you?"

"No, Ma'am," said Daisy, with poor grace.

Libby smiled.

"There's my good girl. I fear I am quite in the habit of ordering Miss Fairbrother about, too, since I have been her governess until she asked me to head this school."

"She must rate you very highly, then, Ma'am!" said Daisy, surprised into an impertinence.

"I do rate her highly, Daisy; and I am sure you will do so too," said Elinor. "Miss Freemantle is quite capable of continuing your Latin, and starting you on Greek," she added. Her voice was tired.

Daisy turned and ran with an odd, hobbling gait, to throw herself down on her knees before Elinor and hug her knees.

"I am so sorry! I am a beast to tire you!" she said.

Elinor touched the golden curls with which the child was blessed as some compensation for the club foot.

"Miss Freemantle and I understand that life seems most unfair, Daisy," she said. "Now go with her; tonight you may eat with the adults, as we have no other pupils and it seems foolish to expect you to have a nursery tea all alone. I hope soon you will have fellow students to get to know."

"Yes, Ma'am," said Daisy, relatively meekly, and got awkwardly to her feet to follow Libby, wishing that the idea of other girls did not fill her with so much trepidation.

"At least she appears to have conceived an affection for you, which must make it easier for you, and for her," said Dr. Macfarlane, when Daisy had moved out of earshot. "Her look of amazed pleasure when you imparted the news that her learning need not be confined to what is expected in a traditional Ladies' Academy was quite revealing. The child might do well to consider tutoring sickly young boys unsuited for the rigours of school."

"Or those girls whose love of learning demands

more," said Elinor. "She is young as yet; let us first give her a stable background and some joy in life."

"That is what I like to hear," said Graeme Macfarlane. "Tomorrow I shall examine her foot, in your presence, and if I think it may be strengthened or even straightened, with any kind of splint or brace, I shall recommend that she should utilise such."

"You will not order it?" asked Elinor.

"No; and what is more, I will warn her that it may hurt. How much pain she can take for a straighter foot will have to be her choice alone. I will not force it on her," he said.

Elinor nodded.

"I like your way of doing things," she said. "Though, tell me, Dr. Macfarlane, how can you be so sensitive and tender of a young girl's feelings, and sensitive of her physical courage, and yet you were quite peremptory, even rude, to me about what I should do?"

"You have moral courage that I knew before I met you, else you would not have been setting up a school as what you considered a dying act. And I hate to see a beautiful young woman waste her life," he replied. "And you were wasting it, you know. It will not cost you much pain or effort to become fit and healthy, not compared to the pain it will cost young Daisy."

"You are a paradox," said Elinor, irritably. "From sympathy for Daisy to a total lack of regard for my feelings!"

"Oh, you are over-tired and feel fractious," said Dr. Macfarlane. "You should lie down for an hour before dinner."

"*Fractious*?" Elinor's voice rose several notes.

He nodded.

"Fractious and slightly hysterical," he said.

"Let me tell you, Dr. Macfarlane, I have *never* been hysterical in my life!" declared Elinor, wrathfully.

"Then it would be a bad idea to start now," he said.

"Ah, here is Miss Freemantle, who will see you to your bed to lie down."

"I am going to sit on my *chaise longue*, Libby," said Elinor, her eyes glinting with rebellion. "I do not need my bed."

"To be sure, my dear; and I will wrap your feet in a shawl, and see to a hot brick for them too, the evenings, and even the late afternoons, are still very chill," said Libby. "There's nothing like warm feet to help to overcome a fit of the vapours."

"A fit of the vapours? Libby, you are quite as bad as that pestilential doctor, who declares that I am fractious and hysterical!"

"Why, no, dear Elinor, just that your nerves are a little overset," said Libby.

"And don't you begin to patronise me, or I won't even lie on the *chaise longue*," said Elinor, glaring at Dr. Macfarlane.

"Do as you will, woman, but don't blame me if you feel ill tomorrow," said Dr. Macfarlane, stalking off.

Libby managed to persuade Elinor to lie on her *chaise longue*, and when she came back into the room with a hot brick, it was to find Elinor fast asleep. A smile touched Libby's lips as she stealthily laid the wrapped brick by Elinor's feet.

"Well, if he's correct that you can be as healthy as any, perhaps it's as well he can curb you enough not to start running before you can walk," Libby murmured to herself.

Daisy had to admit, albeit grudgingly, that Miss Freemantle seemed nice enough; and the room she had been given was very nice too, with good furniture, not scruffy cast-offs. There were pretty counterpanes on the two beds, and velvet curtains that were not in the least worn or thin. A cheerful fire crackled in the grate.

There was plenty of coal in the hod to make it up, and a kettle on a trivet beside it. The commode for each bed was appointed with pretty chinaware, and had a mirror hung over it. While Daisy was taking all this in, she had also listened to Miss Freemantle's soothing voice saying that it was hoped that another girl Daisy's age, or thereabouts, would be able to share with her and be her friend; apparently Miss Freemantle intended to place girls together according to age. Daisy was distinctly dubious about the idea of making friends, but Miss Freemantle had not said anything to make one suppose that she considered it improper for a decent girl to share with a cripple. Daisy recalled how her grandmother's sister-in-law had said "*when my children come to stay they will not want their children associating with a cripple, no decent girl would ever want to know the creature.*"

Daisy wondered if Miss Fairbrother was right, and that the people she had known had strange habits. But Daisy also knew that most of the people who came to church either averted their eyes, or stared at her twisted foot, with a mixture of expressions. Some were sympathetic, but even they were often mixed with expressions of loathing or fear. Perhaps worst were the expressions of contempt from the squire's daughters. Daisy lay on the bed after Miss Freemantle left her to settle in, and wept. The tears were for her grandfather, whom she had not been able to mourn properly before, since she had to be strong for her grandmother; and they were for her grandmother too, too weak and ill to make decisions for herself. She also wept for herself because it was all too much. Like Elinor, she eventually slept.

When Daisy awoke, it was to see Elinor sitting on her bed. Elinor put a finger to her lips, her eyes dancing.

"Our excellent guardians, Miss Freemantle and Dr. Macfarlane, left us to sleep, but I slid up to see how you did. Do you feel better for a good cry and a sleep?"

"Yes, thank you, Miss Fairbrother," said Daisy. "I … I suppose I have to make the best of things. Since Grandfather died, everything has been all wrong."

"Well, I cannot promise to make it all right," said Elinor, "but I can promise to make a new home for you until you are grown, and to help you move out into the world. Meantime, it's almost time to dress for dinner, and I've set a kettle on your fire to warm some water for you to wash your face. As one of the older ones, you can be trusted with a kettle of your own."

"Why, thank you!" said Daisy. "It is nice to wash in warm water."

It was also nice to have someone who did not say that all would come right, or promise to make it better; a promise, essentially, to be there, and to care was far more trustworthy.

"When I have a dedicated nurse for the younger ones, she might heat water for them, but you may also earn privileges like tea and chocolate to make for yourself," said Elinor. Incentives were, she thought, always a far better way of training the young than punishments.

Elinor left Daisy washing her face, and went to dress for dinner. Daisy might be troublesome at times, being stubborn, but Elinor did not think she would be any real trouble.

Daisy, dressed for dinner in a pretty lavender gown for half-mourning, was quite quiet; but she listened to the conversation of the adults, and noted that Miss Freemantle and Miss Fairbrother were on excellent terms, and laughed together. They discussed books, and politics, and the market, and investments. They drew Dr. Macfarlane in on their discussions as well. He spoke about such things as vaccinations, as started by Dr. Jenner, and how there were probably other diseases with lesser forms besides smallpox, against which people might be protected.

"There are still a lot of old wives' tales in medicine, I fear, as well as foolish fears from lay people about the vaccinated taking on the semblance of cows," said Dr. Macfarlane. "However, there is always new research going on."

"We are fortunate to have your new knowledge and open mind," said Elinor. If her tone was a little neutral, Daisy did not notice, though the child did notice that there was more distance between the doctor and the two women than there was between the women. If Miss Freemantle had been Miss Fairbrother's governess, though, thought Daisy, it would explain how they knew each other so well.

Daisy was not sure if she was ever going to be happy, but unless any other girl, who came subsequently to the school, and was placed in her room, tormented her, she might not be unhappy.

And there was something to be said for being the first pupil, and therefore to be able to assume some air of superiority before anyone else started throwing her weight around.

Chapter 4

The next morning brought two more letters, regarding three further pupils.

The first was to Elinor, from a Squire Roberts, who wrote that a neighbour of his, one Richard Goyder, had died, leaving twelve-year-old twin daughters in straitened circumstances. Squire Roberts added that he could not, himself, take them into his household since he had younger children, and did not care to have them set a bad example by the pair.

Elinor raised an eyebrow at this, but the squire went on to explain further. He wrote that the girls' mother had died in childbed after trying unsuccessfully to bring a boy to term, and that Goyder, distraught, had allowed himself to be ruined by foolish speculations, about which he had not sought advice, and had finally shot himself, after having left the girls to run wild.

"Felicity is a vain minx who likes the sound of her own voice, and though there is no real vice in Philippa, I cannot cope with the successive stray animals she will bring home," he wrote. "The latest foundling was a gypsy child whose family I had to buy off to prevent trouble, as the foundling was no such thing – even if collecting such filthy creatures were acceptable behaviour."

Elinor read this out loud to Libby, who was breakfasting with her according to her wont, sharing a tray on Elinor's bed.

"Dear me," said Libby. "I expect that Felicity's vanity is a means to try to attract attention, if her papa was so caught up in his grief; and I cannot see that rescuing waifs to be any kind of real fault, even if it is a human waif; doubtless the gypsy brat saw a way of getting some free food and being able to steal from a wealthy household. Or if I wrong the child, to escape a hard life. Inconvenient, but Philippa seems to have her heart in the right place, even if her head does not always seem to follow."

"Indeed, her compassion is most commendable, if not very wise," said Elinor. "Oh dear, it will be easier to love a child whose fault is an excess of sensibility in such a direction than one who is in the habit of vanity and seeking attention. And that may make poor Felicity worse for seeing that Philippa has approval. Should we put them in the same room? One does not like to separate sisters, especially twins, and yet…."

"I quite take your point, Elinor, my dear," said Libby. "And here is a letter from my dear cousin, the Bishop, recommending to us a child named Hannah Loring, who at eleven years old is just a year younger than these twins. I am sorely tempted to arrange one of the larger rooms to have four beds, not two, and put the three together, with a spare bed in case there is a fourth in that sort of age range."

"Then see to it, Libby, dear; if the twins plague the other child, we might move her, or one of them, as seems fit," said Elinor. "What does His Grace say of this Hannah?"

"He says that she is the child of a reverend gentleman in his see; Hannah's mother died many years ago, and her father was accidentally killed trying to mediate in a riot. Dear me, poor child, what a shock for her!"

"Indeed!" murmured Elinor, sympathetically. "Does your cousin say anything more personal about the child?"

Libby frowned.

"Well, it does seem an odd sort of thing for a Bishop to say, to be sure," said she, "but he says that she is too religious! Ah, he adds – drat his poor handwriting – he adds that her piety, I had thought he had written poetry for a moment, is a form of vanity. He thinks it is practised for its own sake and not for a true love of God. Dear me! It will do her good to be with a pair of difficult twins, one of whom at least cares for God's creatures."

"And it might do them good too, to have to help her," said Elinor. "Have the arrangements made. The Squire said his coachman would bring the twins directly to us later this day."

"Hannah will be travelling, if I decipher Cousin George's hand correctly, with a clergyman and his wife in a day or two," said Libby. "How lowering for a Bishop to have so ill educated a hand."

"I expect he pays a secretary to write most of his correspondence, and only writes personally to family," said Elinor, "and since you are his only relative with any pretensions of close blood ties, he is sadly out of practice."

"I am sure you are right, my dear," said Libby. "Well! Just fancy, we have four girls already, almost as many as you planned to have in total for starting the school!"

Elinor's first duty of the day was to be with Daisy, whilst Dr. Macfarlane examined her foot.

He twisted it this way and that whilst Daisy suppressed cries of pain. He sat back and looked Daisy in the eyes.

"Well, my child," said the Doctor, "I believe there is a chance that if your foot were pulled into place, it may well straighten somewhat before you finish growing. Even if it does not, a heavy calliper will hold it straight enough to walk or even run without it dragging. The bad news is that it would hurt, at least at first; and whether you choose to take that pain for a straighter foot in the end, or whether you prefer to limp without pain, must be up to you."

"Why, there's no choice to be made!" Daisy said at once; and disappointment briefly clouded his eyes, which turned to a smile as she added, "of *course* I want to try it and to be straight!"

With a maid in attendance, Dr. Macfarlane took Daisy off to the local saddlery with specific instructions on making a bracing boot for the girl. The saddler was accustomed to making horse boots to assist those young horses forever throwing out a splint, and soon grasped what was required.

"And that, young Daisy, is why I asked a saddler, not a cobbler," said the Doctor as he drove her back. The boots were to be delivered as soon as they were finished. "Delicate things, horses, and their legs very prone to problems. The type of club foot you have goes by the medical name talipes equinus – don't ask me why, your foot doesn't look the least like a horse's foot to me – so there's a sort of symmetry there, hmm?"

Daisy thought the Doctor very droll, and laughed, something she never thought she would do over a discussion about her hated dragging foot.

"Are we to have any more pupils, soon, do you know, sir?" she asked politely.

"Miss Fairbrother says that twins aged twelve, and another little girl of eleven, will be coming in the next day or two," he told her. "They will all share a room. I'm afraid as yet there are no older girls to keep you company."

"I am used to my own company," said Daisy. "Other girls seem to find me embarrassing, though if I can walk better that will help. It will be nice to be the oldest so I can tick off younger ones if they cheek me about my foot, and if they learn the habit of not mentioning it, then it will be easier if an older girl comes."

"If I may suggest," said Graeme Macfarlane, "you may wish to look down your nose, as you did so nicely to that awfu' besom of a woman at the coaching inn. Then you might say, 'yes, my foot is twisted, which I prefer to having the sort of twisted mind that would comment on it.'"

Daisy was much struck.

"You are so clever, Dr. Macfarlane!" she said.

"Mind, lass, if anyone asks out of curiousity, and not sneering, then it's best to answer honestly and without hiding it," Dr. Macfarlane added. "That way, you might as well educate and inform, which is always good."

Daisy contemplated this.

"How do I tell the difference?" she asked.

"Tone of voice. Expression on face. The feeling you get – and the way it's worded," said the Doctor. "And I know a feeling is insubstantial, but our science does not explain everything, so perhaps it is a science we do not understand yet, or a message from God."

Daisy digested this; then gave him one of her queer little nods.

The antiquated carriage which pulled up outside the house later contained not two little girls, but three.

Two, who appeared to be, superficially at least, identical, must be the twins. The third, who was some years younger, looked scared. Her dress, however, was that of a gently born little girl; Philippa did not appear to be turning folk legend on its head by kidnapping gypsies again. The younger child had a fine woollen pelisse over a good quality muslin gown. One of the twins had an arm about her, whilst the other sat as far away as possible with her nose in the air.

Elinor came down the steps of the house in a hurry.

The coachman got down.

"I'm sorry, ma'am, she *would* bring the brat along. She said you'd want her in the school," he said.

"Well, you have discharged your duty; thank you," said Elinor. "If you wish to cool the horses and go in, cook will find you some refreshments before you return. Meanwhile, what can you tell me of the history of this third child?"

The coachman shrugged.

"She's some Stage coachman's brat. I don't know what's going on. I didn't want to know."

"I see," said Elinor, in a cold voice. "Your perspicacity does not seem to recognise the quality of the child's garments beyond those of a child of one of your station in life. But I have no doubt that it is more comfortable to you not to display curiosity." The vail she slipped him was not as high as she might have given had he bothered to find out more. Elinor proceeded to ignore the coachman henceforth to greet the twins, hustling them and the little girl in to the house out of the cold, biting wind.

"Felicity," she nodded to the child holding herself aloof. "Philippa," she smiled at the other. "I am Miss Fairbrother. Perhaps you can tell me something of your little friend?"

The worried look in Philippa's eyes faded.

"Oh I was right, you *are* willing to take her too!" she said.

"If she is eligible, yes," said Elinor.

"This is Phoebe Goldstone," said Philippa, "She's eight. She and her parents were moving to a smaller house, and there was a crash. The postchaise overturned, and Phoebe was the only one who survived. The Stage Coach that came along saw the crash and stopped, which I think is against regulations."

"It is, but shows a good man," said Elinor. "It is customary to render assistance to other travellers, after all."

"He took me up after he checked that my parents were…were dead, and kept me with him until he returned home to his wife," said Phoebe. "He was nice, and so was she. But he said it weren't right for a young lady to be brung up by a coachman. He said he'd have me back, though, if you wouldn't take me," she added.

Elinor's eyes filled with tears; she could too hear the kindly man in the unconscious mimicry of his intonation as well as his uncultured speech the child quoted.

"My poor little one!" she said. "We need to have my solicitor talk to you, I'm afraid, about your parents, in case you have any relatives, but certainly you will stay here for now, and continue to do so if you have nobody who will take you in. And I will see that the coachman is thanked for his care," she added.

"Mama and Papa never spoke of any," said Phoebe. "I don't think we have any money any more either."

"Not to worry; Mr. Embury will find out," said Elinor. A message must be taken to him right away, and something done to thank the stage coach driver that would not be an insult to him. Elinor went on, "there are four beds in the room we have placed the twins in, and so far we are only expecting one other girl near them in age. Would you like to be near Philippa for the present?"

Phoebe nodded, too full of impending tears to speak.

"I, however, would prefer not to share a room with a child from who knows where," said Felicity, dismounting the carriage.

Elinor regarded her.

"Very well; I believe there is a servant's room unoccupied in the attic," she said.

Felicity gasped.

"But I am not a servant!" she cried.

"Then have the manners of a lady to an unfortunate little girl recently bereaved; which you should be able to understand and so enter into her feelings," said Elinor. "And do try to use the brains the Good Lord saw fit to give you, to see that Phoebe is as well dressed as – indeed better than – you are. And even if she were not an obvious lady, a little Christian charity might not come amiss."

Elinor decided to pretend that she did not see Philippa make a face at her twin.

Felicity scowled.

"Please, ma'am, I do not see why my sister is praised for picking up waifs and strays. The girl came from a cottage; she might be wearing charitable hand-me-downs from a local lady's children. We cannot know she is gently born!" she said, with some spiteful triumph.

"My goodness, Felicity, we will need to get the doctor to find you an ear trumpet if you are so deaf that you cannot hear the child's speech and discern it as that of our own class, save when she mimicked the coachman," said Elinor. "You are out of sorts that your sister has given attention to someone other than yourself, and forgot that had you also reached out to be a friend to Phoebe, you would have had the attention of both of them. Now I expect an apology to Phoebe and to me. If, as it appears, she is an orphan without relatives as you are, and in equally straitened circumstance, then her place here is assured. My goodness, what a Friday face! You should beware in case the wind changes and it sticks like that."

"Felicity doesn't like being reminded that we are orphans living on charity," volunteered Philippa. "She never apologises."

"How unfortunate," said Elinor. "I cannot have anyone who is not a lady associating with the rest of you, and a lady always has the manners to apologise for a fault. It is most fortunate that we have that attic room, and I am sure cook can find her work in the kitchen."

Felicity went scarlet.

"I'm sorry!" she burst out.

Philippa leaned on Elinor, and whispered,

"Oh I pray you will accept that, ma'am, for it's more than she's ever done before!"

Elinor smiled at Felicity.

"There's a nice, ladylike girl," she said. It was a start.

The three girls were shown their room, and given time to settle in, which involved Philippa helping Phoebe to unpack – the coachman had saved her own trunk of clothes – while Felicity unpacked desultorily in something of a sulk.

"Cheer up, Fee," said Philippa, "It's going to be better than Mrs. Roberts flapping her hands and saying 'oh please, don't' at us all the time. And at least Phoebe hasn't horrified the mistresses like poor little Rawnie did. I suppose I did make a mistake with her," she added. "The little wretch *lied* when I asked if she had any family."

"Well, at least you realise that," said Felicity. "All right, Phoebe, you've a decent trunk of clothes. I was worried it would get us both into trouble, bringing you along."

"Oh *poor* Felicity, were the people who had you before horrid?" asked Phoebe, generous enough to forgive and sympathise.

"Well…" said Felicity.

"Squire Roberts and his wife didn't know how to cope with us," giggled Philippa. "Because he couldn't tell us apart. And sometimes we made a joke of that."

Phoebe managed a little giggle too.

"That must have been so funny!" she said.

Felicity gave a brief, half-smile.

"It was," she admitted. "Well, brat, I expect you're pretty scared by being all alone in the world, and missing your parents."

"Oh yes," said Phoebe. "And I 'spect you are too, though at least you have each other."

Felicity shrugged.

"We are older than you are, and have learned to cope

with it," she said loftily.

"Speak for yourself," said Philippa. "I miss having parents, and it isn't far to go from having everything to having nothing. But we all have to make the best of it. And I think this place is better than some we might have been sent to."

Felicity shrugged.

She agreed, but she was not going to admit it.

Chapter 5

The three girls emerged and went downstairs, where a pretty girl who was almost a young lady was coming in the door with a tall gentleman. The latter had hair red enough, as Felicity giggled, to set the school on fire.

The girl had a bit of a limp, and wore a heavy boot, for Daisy had been trying out her new boot when it arrived, under the doctor's supervision.

"Oh, have you hurt your foot?" blurted out Philippa, all compassion.

Daisy regarded her thoughtfully; read compassion and real interest in the younger girl's eyes, and managed to achieve a serene smile.

"No, I was born with it twisted. But Dr. Macfarlane believes that if I wear this ugly and heavy boot to support it, I may one day even be able to dance. You must be the twins and... Hannah? I thought Hannah was almost as old as you twins."

"Oh, this is Phoebe; we brought her with us," said Philippa, wondering if she dared ask about this Hannah who was mentioned.

"The more the merrier!" said Dr. Macfarlane. "I am, as Daisy has named me, Dr. Macfarlane, here to physick you when you are ill and threaten you with noxious medicines for fits of the vapours and bad behaviour."

Phoebe goggled, but Felicity gave him an odd look, wondering if that was a threat to her.

It had not been, and Dr. Macfarlane nodded to them all and left them to get better acquainted with Daisy.

Daisy smiled austerely.

"As I am so much older than the rest of you, and Phoebe much younger, I am sure that I shall be able to earn an allowance teaching the youngest class," she said.

"Oh, must we earn our way here?" asked Philippa,

disconcerted. "I would rather help with the horses than teach!"

"Oh, it is not required," said Daisy, "but as we will all have to make our way in the world, it is as well for those of us who are older to learn something useful, such as how to teach, as well as learning those subjects which we are to teach. And I fear ladies do not work in stables, so being a governess is really the best we can aspire to, isn't it?" Daisy was conscious of sounding pompous but was unable to think of any other way to put it, without betraying her own bitterness at the situation.

Felicity scowled, but Philippa looked thoughtful. She was aware they did have to think of the future.

"It's a shame they don't let ladies become doctors, I suppose they can't be horse doctors either," she said regretfully.

"It's better to get married," said Felicity.

"But not easy without a dowry, silly," said Philippa. "I suppose one might be a modiste like some of the émigrés."

"One might, but you never could," retorted Felicity. "You sew like...like a boy!"

Philippa laughed.

"Oh well, that's true enough," she conceded. "But we don't have to worry too much about it yet."

Daisy reflected that two years could make a lot of difference. When she had been the same age these twins were now, she did not contemplate the future either. It had taken the shock of her grandfather's death and the knowledge, the real, deep knowledge, of her utter destitution to bring home to her that somehow she must make a future for herself. Her grandparents had given her a happy childhood, though Daisy wondered if they had been truly kind to her in not pointing out that she would one day need to pay her way. Doubtless they meant to spare her that knowledge for as long as possible. There was never any question that she would have a fortune suitable to be a dowry, with her parents dead abroad, with nothing to her name worth mentioning, and an entail on her grandfather's house that meant it passed to some male cousin removed several times each way.

Daisy had every hope that she might be able to teach in this school, if she became established as a good teacher of the little ones. Apart from her club foot, which would put some people off hiring her as a governess, she was aware that she was much too pretty to be taken on in any household with older boys or an erratic father. The vicar who had taught her might have been very unworldly in many respects, but at least he had explained to her that some men, and many boys, lacked continence in the matters of virtue, and that kisses led to things that led to babies. Daisy might not be sure how this might occur, but she was not about to let herself be put in such a position, nor was she naïve enough to think that any prospective employer would wish such a situation to arise.

Elinor was wrestling with a recommendation of Dr. Macfarlane's; he suggested that she have a nursery maid, essentially to see to the day to day health of the girls. He had spoken to a colleague, and a Mrs. Rawson duly arrived. Mrs. Rawson was critical of fires in the bedrooms of young girls who were charity girls.

"How wasteful," she said, "and it encourages them to expect such luxury! And they might be careless and set fire to the house!"

"I would hope that any lady might expect the courtesy of a fire in her room wherever she might be a governess," said Elinor firmly. "These children are bereaved, and though we might hope for spring to arrive as March proceeds with the promise of dryness, the comfort of a fire is something they need to warm their bodies. People who are grieving feel the cold more," she added in a tone of finality that brooked no argument. "And the older ones shall have a kettle to heat their own water. There is something called 'trust' and one must trust in order to be trusted."

Elinor disliked Mrs. Rawson, but decided to give her a trial. As Dr. Macfarlane had organised her employment, there must be more to her than met the eye.

The new nurse fell foul of the twins and Phoebe almost immediately, declaring that their underwear was altogether too frivolous for paupers, and that they must sew plain shifts. She also decided that Phoebe should not be permitted to share a room with older girls as she required a nursery.

Phoebe burst into tears.

"*Stop* that stupid noise," said Mrs. Rawson.

"Mrs. Rawson, she saw her parents die, and she's still very upset and only a baby," said Philippa, "And Mrs. Fairchild said she was to sleep in here with us."

"I won't have any cheek from you, either," said Mrs. Rawson, slapping Philippa. Felicity promptly flew at her and slapped her back.

Mrs. Rawson grabbed her, and dragged her to the landing cupboard, thrust her inside and locked the door.

"Let us see if that teaches you a lesson," she said. "I will not take such cheek from charity brats! As for you, Phoebe, if you don't stop crying, I will give you something to cry about. You can pack two or three of your plainest gowns ready to move to a more suitable room. I will inform the housekeeper that one is to be prepared for you."

Philippa was furious, but shouting would do no good. She waited until Mrs. Rawson had left, and grabbed Phoebe by the hand.

"We'll ask Daisy what to do," she said. "Let's just tell Fee!"

Felicity was terrified and was sobbing in real earnest when Philippa knocked on the door.

"Fee, we're going to ask Daisy what to do!" she said.

"Oh get me out of here!" cried Felicity, who had a real terror of being shut in places.

They ran to find Daisy, and hid as they heard Mrs. Rawson's voice. Daisy was in the library preparing a lesson Libby had set for her. Mrs. Rawson was telling her that she would be better in a room on her own as no decent girl would want to share with a cripple. The children, squeezed behind a long curtain, heard Daisy say,

"Dr. Macfarlane told me that if I heard such attitudes, I should say that I was glad only to be twisted in my foot and not in spirit."

"Impertinence!" cried Mrs. Rawson.

"If you think the doctor impertinent, then you should take it up with him. Good day to you, I prefer to take my work elsewhere," she added, limping out of the room with her books.

"I did not say you could leave!" yelped Mrs. Rawson.

"No, you did not," said Daisy, "but I suggest that Miss Fairbrother will say that you have no say in the matter."

"You are on a diet of bread and water for that!" said Mrs. Rawson.

"I will ask the doctor to confirm that order," said Daisy. "I cannot think he will consider it conducive to the good health of his charges, I suggest you leave, the library is for the use of the students, not the servants."

She avoided the slap aimed at her and as she left, Philippa emerged briefly from the window embrasure where she and Phoebe were hiding, and pulled the older girl in.

Mrs. Rawson came stamping out, looking for Daisy to punish, but the girls were by then sitting on the broad window sill and the floor length curtains were pulled straight. Mrs. Rawson charged right past them.

"We have to see Miss Freemantle," said Daisy. "It will not do to upset Miss Fairbrother, who is not well. Miss Freemantle made the arrangements and she is the headmistress."

Libby listened to the tale the girls told with mounting horror. The livid mark on Philippa's face made her incandescently angry, and the tale of Felicity's incarceration.

"And she said she would make arrangements with the housekeeper?" Libby confirmed, thinking what contumelious presumption this would be, if the little girls had not got it wrong.

Philippa nodded, unable to speak any more, she was so close to tears.

"Go and wrap up warmly and go out for a walk," said Libby. "I will handle this."

Libby was quite well aware that most of the internal keys fitted all the locks, and soon released a sobbing, dirty Felicity.

"Felicity, my dear!" she gave the child a cuddle. "My dear, you may not have acted for the best, but I do understand!"

"Oh, am I in trouble with you?" sobbed Felicity.

"No, my dear; we shall have a talk later, and perhaps you will be able to think about how you might have handled the situation better," said Libby. "For now, I want you to go to my bedroom, wash your face, and lie down on my bed. I will have a cup of hot milk sent to you."

"If you please, I do not like hot milk, it makes me feel sick," said Felicity.

"Miss Fairbrother does not like it either," said Libby. "I will ask that a little chocolate be grated in it, however.

Not too much, that would be too rich for you, but enough to taste."

"Thank you," said Felicity.

"There! Run along!" said Libby, mentally girding up her loins for a fray.

Libby ran Mrs. Rawson to earth where she had expected to find her; in the midst of a confrontation with the housekeeper.

"What *I* say is," Mrs. Baxter, the housekeeper, was saying, "That if Miss Fairbrother and Miss Freemantle have made orders specific-like, they done it for a reason, and reverse those orders I will not do, unless Miss Fairbrother or Miss Freemantle tell me so."

"Don't be so stupid! I have been hired to see to the welfare of the girls, and so I must be able to give orders regarding that!" said Mrs. Rawson.

"You are no longer employed in any capacity," said Libby, coming into the room, "and you need not expect any reference from me or from Miss Fairbrother either. The welfare of the girls *never* includes shutting a child in a cupboard, not slapping them like a fishwife in Billingsgate, or upsetting bereaved children by planning to steal their possessions and self-respect. Nor does it include insulting those with medical needs, as though you were a guttersnipe nor depriving growing children of proper sustenance. You will pack and be ready to leave in an hour. Mrs. Baxter, you will have Tom Coachman standing by for her at that time."

"Yes, ma'am," said Mrs. Baxter, bobbing a curtsey.

"I think Miss Fairbrother might disagree," said Mrs. Rawson. "I was employed by her…"

"You were employed by *us* and I have the final veto as headmistress of this school," said Libby. "She will be very much shocked at what you have done to upset our vulnerable charges in their state of bereavement."

"Well really! They are only charity brats!" said Mrs.

Rawson.

"They are ladies, which is something you plainly are not, nor have any concept regarding that state," said Libby, coldly. "You now have only fifty minutes in which to pack. I suggest you hurry. If you leave anything behind, I cannot be bothered to forward it. And if one gown belonging to any of those little girls goes with you, I shall have Bow Street put onto you as a common thief, and you will either be hung or transported."

"Bravo, Miss Freemantle!" said Mrs. Baxter.

"How dare you call me a thief?" cried Mrs. Rawson.

"Well, you did intend to deprive those little girls of their gowns and shifts and make them sew plain ones, did you not?" said Libby. "Why else would you do that if you did not plan to make off with perfectly serviceable clothes that they might wear?"

"I – I did not think they should give themselves airs!" blustered Mrs. Rawson.

"Oh, pure spite and jealousy then? However, I shall check their belongings," said Libby, "and you have forty five minutes. Shall I ask Tom Coachman to just throw your belongings out of the window for you?"

Mrs. Rawson fled.

"Oh you did handle that besom a treat, Miss Freemantle!" said Mrs. Baxter.

"Thank you," said Libby, suppressing a sigh. She did not relish telling Elinor about this.

It had, at least, confirmed her as a force to be reckoned with in Mrs. Baxter's, and hence all the staff's eyes. As Elinor's governess, the staff had generally obeyed her requests, but now she was seen to be headmistress.

Elinor was furious, as Libby had supposed she would be, and turned quite grey. Libby quickly passed her one time charge a vinaigrette to sniff; and the sharp scent brought Elinor back to herself, her eyes sparkling with anger.

"I hope those poor children will not think that we wished such a wretched woman upon them knowingly!" she said.

"As Daisy brought the others to me to tell me, not wanting to disturb you, I think they are well enough aware of our feeling on this subject," said Libby, dryly. "I will chat to poor Felicity, and point out that rather than slapping a grown woman and putting herself in the wrong, she should have run straight away to find you, or me, or Dr. Macfarlane. I am hoping that she will have had a little sleep."

"Yes, indeed," said Elinor. "And perhaps if she understands too that people who get too much of an idea of their own righteousness can be quite unpleasant, which ought to make her less concerned with herself and how much better behaved she can appear to be than Philippa."

"At least she flew in defence of her sister, and from what I understand Philippa to say, of Phoebe as well," said Libby. "She's an odd child; she did not want Philippa to bring Phoebe along, but she will defend her twin's decision to do so against a common enemy."

"Then I suggest that her vanity is just the way she hides her grief," said Elinor.

"You could well be right, my dear," Libby agreed.

"In future we must make sure that anyone we are employing knows the limits of their powers," said Elinor, grimly. "Naturally any governesses we take on must be permitted to use discipline, but we must make clear that striking the children or locking them in cupboards is not to be permitted."

"Indeed," agreed Libby. "If a child is more than they can handle, they must come to us about her, and it made clear that this is no failure, merely an admission that some children are more creatively naughty than others."

"A good idea," said Elinor. "And I shall be having words with Dr. Macfarlane about his idea of a suitable female to be in charge of our poor little ones!"

Libby reflected that as it was a fine afternoon, if chill, it might be as well to join the children outside. There she might direct their activity with a nature walk, to look for signs of incipient springtide, since the ensuing argument was likely to be both loud and of epic proportions.

Chapter 6

"How *dare* you provide a termagant like that to upset those poor little girls?" Elinor shrieked in fury as Dr. Macfarlane came in to see her at her icily worded request via a servant.

"I have no idea what you are talking about, woman, but losh! If you don't calm down you will make yourself ill," said Dr. Macfarlane, angrily. "Now calm down and tell me what has so overset your nerves."

"What has overset my nerves? Have you no feelings you wretched dour *Scot* you? Having my children slapped and shut in cupboards is enough to overset the nerves of anyone, having Phoebe told to stop crying or she'd be given something to cry about, and having Daisy told she's not fit to associate with decent folk because she's a cripple, and trying to force them all to dress like children thrown on the parish makes my nerves more than overset, it makes me incandescent with fury and it's all your fault!"

"All *my* fault? How dare you, you totty-headed wee besom? I would have the *hide* off of anyone who acted so!" Graeme Macfarlane's own voice rose to a roar.

"So you say," flashed Elinor, "but it was you who accepted the recommendation of that Rawson woman and foisted her onto us!"

"I accepted the recommendation to send her along, it was up to you to employ her or otherwise!" he snapped. "I couldn't be expected to know you would employ anyone as wicked as that – I presume that is what she has done, that you describe!"

"And I could not be expected to realise that you would endorse the recommendation of anyone as wicked as that!" shouted Elinor. "I disliked her, but I *trusted* you to have chosen someone suitable!"

"Oh, so that's what it's all about," said Dr.

Macfarlane. "You think I betrayed your trust because you thought I was recommending her, not stopping to recall that I merely passed on the recommendation of another."

Elinor burst into tears.

He was beside her in a stride, and sitting her down firmly on her chaise longue, kneeling beside her.

"Listen, girl!" he said. "It was a misunderstanding. And I should perhaps have checked her out and not believed the word of another man that she was a canny organiser. But one trusts the word of another gentleman."

Elinor snorted through her tears.

"If by 'canny organiser' he meant someone ready to turn the lives of others upside-down it is a fair description of her," she said, grimly. "I was so upset to have put the children through that!"

"Of course you were," he said. "I am sorry, but it was not wholly my fault, and I'll not have you accusing me of betraying your trust. I'd not willingly do that."

"You are right, and I am sorry. I should not have shouted without asking for an explanation," she was contrite.

"I still recommend that you hire a good woman to bathe grazes, extract splinters and physick to minor ailments like colds in the head, sore throats and of course those female matters that they would rather not talk to a man about, even a doctor," said Dr. Macfarlane.

"Yes. Yes, I can see that," said Elinor. "Dr. Macfarlane, am I correct in my understanding that many women have served in the fleet, nursing wounded sailors? Did they not get medals at the Battle of the Nile?"

"Aye, indeed they did; and in theory women aboard were banned thereafter because the government did not like giving them medals for their gallantry," said Dr. Macfarlane. "many of them are low women; Mrs.

Rawson is supposed to be gently born, the daughter of the manse at one time, which was why she sounded eminently suitable, raised with the word of the Lord and a belief, one might assume that of Faith, Hope and Love, the greatest is Love."

"Gentle is as gentle does," said Elinor. "And she is one who does not translate the Greek as 'love' but as the common prayer book does, as 'charity' where charity is as cold as a miser's heart as may be seen in some clergymen and their families. I do not care if any good woman is rough of speech; I may wish her to refrain from its less salubrious terms in front of the children, but I would prefer a warm heart to a lady's diction. I want someone who cares. There must be some of these women left widowed, say, and because of the change in the law consequently in need. I would rather have such a woman who is rough of manner but kindly of instinct. Please will you find for me such a person yourself, without taking anyone else's word?"

He nodded.

"Aye, that I can do, Miss Fairbrother," he said. "And I'll ask them all specific questions too."

He had the chance to redeem himself; it had been wrong of him, he reflected, to make assumptions. He would not let Elinor Fairbrother nor the children down. And Charles Formby would have the rough edge of his tongue for sending a nursemaid more suitable to be a wardress in a gaol than caring for children! The only nursery she seemed fit for was one growing unfriendly looking plants like pineapples!

It only took Dr. Macfarlane a couple of days to find a motherly sort of woman who seemed eager to do whatever he asked of her. Her name was Mrs. Ashley.

"It's for my Cleo, you see," she said, indicating the child who sat quietly. "If I don't find somewhere where she can be a maid servant, respectable-like, she'll get picked up soon by the pimps and madams. She's almost eleven, you see."

"They steal them so young?" the doctor was taken aback. "Er, Clio? For the Muse of History?"

"I dunno what that might be, sir, Doctor, I should say, I called her Cleopatra, account o' how I went into labour with her right there during the Battle o' the Nile, and she's my Queen of the Nile, right enough."

"I see," said Dr. Macfarlane. "I understand now, Mrs. Ashley. Tell me, how would you cope with a child with deformity?"

The woman tapped the eyepatch she wore.

"Losing me eye was what started Cleo coming," she said. "I ain't hardly about to get uppity about deformity, am I?"

"Yours is acquired," said Dr. Macfarlane. "We have a child with a club foot."

Mrs. Ashley shrugged.

"Bein' scrog-footed affects high and low alike," she said. "If it ain't bad, I won't baby her. Reckon as how using it'll make it stronger."

"I happen to agree with you," said Graeme Macfarlane. "And Daisy wears an uncomfortable boot to pull it straighter and help her walk."

"Well, she's a brave little maid, then," said Mrs. Ashley. "Can't do no more'n your best, I say, and good luck to her!"

Mrs. Ashley duly moved into the school with Cleopatra and proceeded to suggest that it would do the girls no harm to make their own beds so they knew how to supervise servants, as well as learning how to make simple medicines, and how to bandage wounds.

"If they be destined to be governesses, ma'am, and ma'am," she said to Libby and Elinor, who were interviewing her together, "it stands to reason they'll be dealing with sickness sooner or later, and it's the person who's most like a mother to whom a sick child turns. And that's going to be who the swell cove's brats are palmed off onto, their governess. And small wounds, well, their parents won't want to be bothered with those! And naughtiness punished by the injury, not a pi-jaw from them as don't understand their own offspring. At least, if what the Young Gentlemen used to say is anything to go by; and many of them I've comforted with draughts to help settle seasickness, and salves for being struck cruel by the gunner at times."

Libby blinked. None of her charges had ever injured themselves through naughtiness, but she could readily, on reflection, understand how this might come about in a number of ways. Especially with headstrong boys. Or girls with brothers.

"It's an excellent idea," she said, "and they shall also learn how to make a bed round a sick patient, as I have learned to do, when they learn to make beds. As I have often had to do for Miss Fairbrother and her sister Arabella."

"Oh, yes, ma'am, an excellent idea!" agreed Mrs. Ashley.

"Please, ma'ams," piped up Cleo, "I don't want to be called Pattie."

"And why should you be called Pattie, Cleo?" asked Elinor. Cleo beamed at her for calling her aright.

"Because I got a job as a maid and the missus there said Cleopatra was outlandish and so was Cleo, and I should be Pattie because it was more normal, but I kept forgetting it was me when she shouted it, so she turned me off."

"She sounds a silly creature," said Elinor. "Can you read and write?"

"A little, ma'am," said Cleo. "One of the officers learned me my letters afore Pa was killed."

"Then I'll teach you a little more, and when you have no duties you may sit and listen to the lessons with the young ladies, and when you are grown, perhaps you might like to teach the very young children we may have here then," said Elinor.

"Cor, thanks, Missus, I mean Ma'am," said Cleo, forgetting the correct form of address in a surge of emotion.

The girls were not sure whether they wanted to learn how to make their own beds, but since this was endorsed by both Miss Fairbrother and Miss Freemantle, they settled down to learn with more, or in Felicity's case, less, good grace. Libby pointed out that this skill widened their options later in life, as they might consider being housekeepers, or sick nurses. Daisy, her clubfoot glanced at, acknowledged, and thence ignored by Mrs. Ashley, was ready to do her best. Mrs. Ashley must have seen such on others that were far worse, concluded Daisy. Indeed, Mrs. Ashley had seen far worse, though whether through a worse birth defect, made worse by poor diet, or even deliberately by parents to make a child a better beggar, that good woman preferred not to hazard a guess.

Felicity made something of heavy weather of the work at first, and was finally won over by Mrs. Ashley, who smiled at her, and said,

"It ain't as if you have to sleep on hammocks like sailors do, Miss Felicity, and put all your bedding away every day, where it might get carried away by French roundshot!" She added, "And at that, why, Cleo and me have had to go from what was not a bad life in the Navy to poverty, so don't go thinking I don't know something of what you're feeling. When my man was killed, and as a gunner's mate he had good wages, I had to fight for my little bit of pension. Changes ain't easy, and I ain't about to take offence when you want to gripe and bellyache about life's unfairness, and put on your parts over it."

Felicity could quite happily accept being told off for the sulks or bad behaviour, but to have her behaviour referred to as 'the gripes' and 'bellyaching' and it being inferred that it was of no moment to Mrs. Ashley, who did not mind it, was a different matter. Felicity gave up both griping and bellyaching forthwith.

Since Mrs. Ashley was a very different person to the unkind Mrs. Rawson, she was soon a prime favourite with little Phoebe, and Felicity tried very hard to behave better. Indeed, Libby's kindness to her had gone a long way towards making a change in her behaviour already, and Felicity was learning to meet people half way. Therefore, instead of raising her eyebrows and complaining when Cleo joined some of the lessons, Felicity firmly decided to take a leaf out of Philippa's book and volunteered to help her.

Libby half wondered if this seeming goodwill was merely to persuade Cleo to do more for Felicity, but there seemed to be no ulterior motive. Thus, Libby praised Felicity, and pointed out how it helped her too, in consolidating her own lessons when helping another. Felicity rather enjoyed getting attention for good behaviour, not bad!

It may also be said that Felicity did rather enjoy Phoebe's admiration for being brave enough to stand up to Mrs. Rawson, and to be praised for it; and Felicity was carelessly kind to the child, albeit without going to the lengths Philippa went to, to help her.

"Mrs. Ashley appears to be a great success; thank you, Dr. Macfarlane," said Elinor. "I hope we may get some flesh on the bones of little Cleo, too."

"I don't know that you do that child any favours in offering her education out of her class," warned Dr. Macfarlane.

"Dr. Macfarlane, how hard it must be for a child to be around other children who are receiving education, and to be starved of it! If you had seen the way her eyes lit up when I offered it, you'd surely not wonder that I permit it."

"I fear it may make her discontented with her lot; she would never be acceptable to any as a governess, not being of gentle birth, and she will be over-educated and feel resentful as a servant, knowing she knows perhaps more than her mistress," he said.

"She is assured a job here for life, and as a nanny when we take little ones, when she may teach them their letters, and read to her heart's content. And if I also decide to take in girls of lower estate, we shall then need a separate establishment, and though they will receive training suitable to their status in life, they will also need training in literacy. Perhaps by then she will be ready to be a senior mistress."

The Doctor regarded Elinor thoughtfully.

"You are looking well ahead," he said. "Does this mean you have decided to live past thirty?"

Elinor laughed.

"Already I feel better for the regimen you have prescribed for me; and yes, Dr. Macfarlane, I think I am now ready to truly believe that I will not die young. However, Libby also knows my plans and aspirations, in the unlikely event of a tree falling on me during my invigorating walks."

He chuckled.

"Good; and as you say, it is an unlikely event, since you know better than to shelter under a tree in a thunderstorm, with so many woeful events of that kind being reported in the newspapers."

"I am very excited by this whole matter, and delighted to think that potentially difficult girls like Daisy and Felicity seem to have settled down," said Elinor.

"Oh, Daisy has found a place where she is accepted, but I'd still watch Felicity if I were you. Her good behaviour is a fragile thing, and something might set off her foolishness again."

Elinor nodded.

"That, I believe, too," she said.

Hannah Loring arrived into what was fast becoming a real little community. She was delivered by hired post chaise under the protection of a vicar and his wife and their numerous progeny. The vicar had been offered a better living, through the good offices of a distant cousin, which he had gratefully accepted. Five hopeful children place a burden upon the most frugal of housekeepers when the income is meagre.

The vicar and his wife left Hannah with great relief and a sense of deliverance, and each prayed secretly to be forgiven for feeling that way.

Hannah had managed, by her comments, to alienate any sympathetic feelings the family may have initially harboured for a young girl tragically orphaned. Having first declared that anything so worldly as considering the size of a living rather than the place one might bring most spiritual comfort to be unbecoming to a man of the cloth, Hannah had added that this encouraged the children to be worldly too. As she also spent most of her time reproving the youngsters, and interfering by telling their mother how she ought to bring them up, the young couple were delighted to see the back of her, and did not restrain their older children very much when they cheered.

Libby and Elinor exchanged a dismayed look at the evident pleasure in the little family in being rid of a burden.

Chapter 7

Hannah followed meekly as Elinor showed her to her room, after welcoming her. The girl was taken aback to see that there were other beds there, and her room-mates sent for, to welcome her.

"I will have to share with three others?" Hannah asked, rather shrilly.

"Indeed, as there were three of you much of an age, it seemed much more agreeable for you all to be together and be friendly, and as Phoebe is so attached to the twins, she is here too," said Elinor, firmly.

"But... I have always been private before," said Hannah.

"The Jordan is in the little drawing room off this room, for privacy," said Philippa, the practical one. "As for washing, why, unless you are a boy in disguise, there is nothing any of us has to surprise anyone."

"It is immodest!" declared Hannah.

"Nonsense!" said Elinor. "An excess of prudery is a form of vanity, and vanity is a sin."

"But... but suppose they are not all good Christians?" said Hannah. "I am Church of England, of course."

"What on earth has the denomination of any got to do with it?" said Elinor, astonished.

"And aren't we as good Christians as you, or better, bein' good Catholics," said naughty Felicity, trying to mimic the tones of the Irish laundrymaid. "And dear little Phoebe a good Methodee into the bargain, so she is."

"No I'm not," said Phoebe. "I'm Jewish. But it doesn't matter, because God loves us and that's all that's important."

This was something of a shock; it had never occurred to Libby or Elinor to ask Phoebe, and she had obediently joined in morning prayers with the others.

Hannah actually drew back slightly.

"I cannot share with Heathens like Papists and Jews," she said.

"You can, and you will share with other little girls, some of whom are doing it rather too brown," said Elinor, giving Felicity a stern look.

Felicity perceived rapidly that Miss Fairbrother's eyes were laughing, despite the look, and realised she was not in big trouble. Miss Fairbrother understood a joke at the expense of that silly girl! Felicity gave her a beaming smile which quite transformed her.

"We are not Catholics, Hannah, but if we had been, I have to say I can't think of any comments more unchristian and uncharitable than yours!" she said.

"I don't understand. Why would you betray your faith in pretending to be something else?" asked Hannah, looking bewildered.

"To see if we could pull a Banbury Tale for someone who cares enough to make comment about it, of course, silly," said Philippa, relieved she was not going to have to attempt an Irish accent.

"So…. Is she really a….a _JEW_?" Hannah pointed at Phoebe.

"It makes no difference," said Elinor, quietly. "After all, remember that Jesus was a Jew."

"He never was!" cried Hannah, shocked.

"He was," said Elinor. "He underwent the same ceremony all Jewish baby boys undergo, and went to the temple for his entry to adulthood where he impressed the elders, do you not recall the story?"

"It's called Bar-Mitzvah," said Phoebe.

"Thank you, Phoebe," said Elinor. "And if you know your Gospels at all, you should know that Jesus was born of the line of David, and at the end of His life, Pilate dubbed him 'King of the Jews' in the sign set above him on the Holy Cross. Do you not read the

Bible?"

Hannah stammered something incoherent.

"I do wish now I'd claimed to be something really outlandish like a Hindoo or a Presbyterian," muttered Felicity.

Elinor managed to give her a quelling look, whilst suppressing laughter. She had a feeling that the Doctor might be a Presbyterian, and it would amuse him no end to be described as 'outlandish' and in the same sentence as a Hindoo.

"I'll leave you girls to help Hannah to settle in," she said. "She's bereaved too; let's have no more teasing, as you know how she feels."

"No, ma'am," chorused the twins.

After Elinor had left, Hannah said,

"If you two bully me, I shall report you."

"What peculiar ideas the little girl has," said Felicity to Philippa. "This isn't a boys' school, Hannah; and if it was, you'd probably get whipped for reporting other chaps. Squire Roberts' eldest boy said it's quite horrible, the older boys hurt the little boys and they call it 'building character'. We are ladies, Hannah; we do not bully."

"But you will please not do or say anything to upset Phoebe, or we might forget that we're ladies and just wax irritable," said Philippa.

"But she's a *JEW!*" cried Hannah in distaste. "Jews don't associate with decent Christians!"

"It's quite in order," said Phoebe, "because papa said that honest gentiles need not be considered to contaminate a Jew, so I don't mind staying with you all who are not God's chosen."

"Oh bravo, Phoebe," said Philippa. "Hannah, before you say or do anything that would make *you* into a bully, don't you think that you should consider it from Phoebe's point of view?"

Hannah turned her back deliberately on all of them,

and pretended that she did not hear Felicity mutter,

"Well *she's* going to be so much fun as taking a toss into brambles."

That the twins were plainly used to ride, emphasising their higher estate than Hannah, did not endear them to her.

Elinor meanwhile had stepped hastily over to Dr. Macfarlane's office.

"Hannah is going to be a problem," she said.

"How so?" he asked.

Elinor quickly related what had happened; and as expected, the doctor laughed over Felicity's words.

"Outlandish, eh?" he said. "Wee minx! But there's no vice in that. I'm not sure what to do about young Phoebe, though, if she was telling the truth."

"I don't think she's old enough to come up with such a creative lie," said Elinor, "and moreover she knew about Bar-Mitzvah which I did not know. And she is not a dishonest child to hold to it once the others had admitted to their Banbury Tale. And of course, it never occurred to any of us to ask when she first arrived, as we made assumptions."

"She can't be asked to attend a Church service; most improper," said Dr. Macfarlane. "I'll see if I can find a Rabbi who can come and give her spiritual guidance."

"I have to say, it is very refreshing to have a man about the place on whom one might rely," said Elinor.

A reddish brown eyebrow twitched slightly upwards as Graeme Macfarlane wondered what sort of a fool Elinor's father was. By all accounts he was a financial genius, but then, Graeme had known other men dubbed a genius in one field or another, and by and large they were unfit to be let out without a keeper in other respects.

Probably then the man was no more of a fool than most; and it seemed he would permit healthy daughters to be killed because he had blind faith in doctors. Well, many doctors encouraged the belief in them that was almost tantamount to the belief one had in the Almighty. Graeme considered such expectations to be faintly sacrilegious.

Dr. Graeme Macfarlane was as good as his word, and soon a grave young Rabbi was talking to Phoebe.

"I suppose I can't stay here?" said Phoebe, wistfully. "I do like it, and I am learning such a lot, and nobody fusses me about how I see God."

Simon Cohen sighed.

"If you were a little older, it might be in order," he said. "But you are missing out on a Jewish education. My parents are willing to welcome you into their household; my youngest sister is much of an age with the other girls you are friendly with. Perhaps I might negotiate with Miss Fairbrother, who seems a fine woman, to permit you to return, and my sister Rachel, too, for a year or two, so that a similar orphanage may be set up for Jewish orphans."

Phoebe clapped her hands.

"Oh Miss Fairbrother and Miss Freemantle will think it an excellent idea, Rabbi Cohen!" she cried. "Miss Fairbrother has mentioned how much she would like education to be available to everyone!"

"She sounds an enlightened woman," said Rabbi Cohen. "The Jewish people have always considered education to be very important. I will speak with her."

Elinor and Libby listened to the Rabbi's suggestion with great interest.

"How splendid!" said Elinor. "I should love to collaborate in such a project. And it would be good for children of different faiths to mix for lessons and only be separated for religious observances; you are very clever, Rabbi!"

This had not been at all what Rabbi Cohen had meant, but he quickly assimilated the idea that if gentile children grew up close to Jewish children, it might diminish the suspicion with which his people were viewed.

"I, too, have a suggestion," said Libby. "As Phoebe does not wish to be wrest from her friends, might she not return here during the week, and go to your parents for the weekend? And we should be delighted to take your sister, too, for a nominal fee. There is room for a fifth bed in that room until or unless another younger child arrives to share with Phoebe."

"That is very good of you," said Rabbi Cohen, who was not used to gentiles being ready to compromise. "I believe that may be acceptable, but I shall have to consult my parents, of course."

"Of course!" said Elinor. "By all means, take Phoebe on a visit too. But I shall make it plain to her, if she is not happy, she will always have a home here."

"You are what we call menschen, good people," said Rabbi Cohen.

Phoebe was glad she might come back if she wanted, and was a little scared and a little excited to be meeting the Cohen family. Her parents had not been very strict in their observances, and she was also very glad that she would be able to return to the charity school during the week, as she was somewhat afraid that a Rabbi's family might be nearly as bad as a vicar's family like Hannah's seemed to be, albeit in different ways!

Both Philippa and Felicity hugged Phoebe warmly and wished her luck in her new home.

"I'll tell Rachel Cohen all about you, she's going to love it!" said Phoebe.

Phoebe duly departed, and Philippa was feeling a little flat. It did not help that Hannah, seeing Phoebe leave, and not being privy to the other plans, smiled smugly.

"I didn't think that decent people like Miss Fairbrother would have Jews in with Christian folk. I will, of course, pray that Phoebe should be enlightened, and that she convert to Christianity."

"Why, you horrid little girl!" cried Philippa. "How would you like her to pray for you to convert to – to Jewishness?"

"It's not the same at all," said Hannah. "When Jesus came it meant Jews should become Christian."

"How stupid you are!" said Felicity. "Jesus didn't ever say any such thing!"

"Anyway, she is going to come back to her own bed after meeting Rabbi Cohen's family, and his little sister is coming here too, so put that on your needles and knit it," said Philippa rudely, borrowing an expression from Squire Roberts' housekeeper.

Hannah stared in horror.

"I won't! I won't share with two Jewish girls!" she said.

Felicity shrugged.

"Oh well, if you behave like an hysterical servant girl, I believe there's a spare servant's room in the attic you can move to," she said.

That had, after all, brought her to heel.

Hannah was a different matter.

"Very well, then, I will speak to Miss Freemantle or Miss Fairbrother about removing there; however mean a room it may be I would rather a humble abode than have luxury and associate with heathens."

"I don't think you can call Jews 'heathens'," said Philippa, frowning at the nomenclature.

"Oh never mind, let her go," said Felicity. "She's nothing but a nuisance with her – her vanity of sanctity, and we don't want her in with us anyway."

Hannah flounced out.

Libby, told tearfully that the twins did not want Hannah, came to remonstrate.

"Hannah says you don't want her to be in with you, and told her to sleep in a servant's room," she said, sternly.

"Well, if she put it like that, it's a bouncer if I ever heard one," said Philippa. "Hannah was making a fuss that Phoebe's coming back and this girl Rachel too...."

"....and so I said if she didn't want to be associated with them she could always go be in the servant's room that's spare," put in Felicity.

"And then she said she preferred that and would ask about it and acted as though it was virtuous to be martyred in a – a humble abode," said Philippa.

"And then I said good, we didn't want her," said Felicity.

"Oh, Felicity," sighed Libby. "She is such a muddled up child, it's not the most tactful thing to say."

"Well, she was being quite horrid, and I can't be expected to learn tact all in one go, Miss Freemantle," said Felicity, "though I'm sorry to disappoint *you*."

"Well, tact and discretion come with years and patience," sighed Libby, "but I could wish, my dear, that you would think before you open your mouth and say something regrettable! The damage is done, and I will place the child in a room on her own, and you twins are *not* to plague her, do I make myself clear?"

Two obedient nods and murmurs of assent showed she had made herself clear.

Libby could only hope that Hannah would miss the camaraderie of being with other girls and would come to her senses; but she found this strange, introspective child, who was so convinced that her way was the only way, very difficult. She feared that it would be long before Hannah managed to shake down with the others.

If Rachel Cohen also turned out to be as much of a religious bigot from her own perspective as Hannah was from hers, the school would cease to be the jolly place it was fast becoming.

Libby sighed.

It took all sorts; and the more children who arrived, hopefully the less any individual might upset the others.

It would remain to be seen how things went.

Chapter 8

Shortly after Phoebe's departure, Elinor received two letters, one from a girl named Abigail Meersham, and the other from the girl's lawyer.

"Dear Miss Fairbrother," Abigail had written, *"I have been orphaned for almost a year and as my funds have diminished, Mr. Cowper, my solicitor, feels that entry into your establishment would be a wiser step than attempting to find genteel employment. As I love learning and would be quite content to teach, I cannot but recognise the wisdom of his words, should you have room to take me."*

Mr. Cowper had written that Abigail's young parents had taken her to the resort of Brighthelmstone – he did not use the more accepted modern name of Brighton – the previous summer, to take the waters during the heat wave. Whilst there, Mrs. Meersham had been swept away from the bathing machine by a freak wave, and her husband, attempting to save her, had also drowned. Mr. Meersham had been a senior clerk at the Inns of Court and had had but meagre savings, much of which he spent on the holiday since the heat in the metropolis was making his wife ill. Elinor shuddered. She well remembered the enervating heat of the July of 1808; even out of London it had been oppressive in the extreme while it lasted. Many had died. How cruel to escape that and then to die by other means! Mr. Cowper wrote that he was by way of having also been a friend of Mr. Meersham, whom he had seen regularly through providing briefs to the Inn for which Meersham had worked, and had done what he could, but could only do so much for his friend's daughter.

"He could have married her," said Graeme Macfarlane, to whom Elinor was reading the letters along with Libby.

"The girl is fifteen; the age difference of twenty years must surely be repugnant if there is no love between them," said Elinor.

"He may be attracted to her and be afraid it is rather unwholesome," said Libby. "She writes a pretty hand which is full of character, yet modesty. I suggest you write to her and accept her into the school, my dear, and ask Mr. Cowper if he will discharge a final duty by bringing her to us."

Elinor nodded.

"If she has been keeping house essentially for herself for almost eight months, then she is probably a rather capable girl who might also have prospects as a housekeeper, or cataloguing and keeping a library in a large house. It is not a common activity for a woman, but not, I think, unacceptable," she said. "She might complete her education here and consider her options."

Abigail was a capable girl who had managed her father's small house quite adequately, until the need to sell it became pressing. She had, indeed, been managing it for some time since her mother was not strong. Mr. Cowper had been very kind, and so had the two servants, a married couple, whom Mr. Meersham had employed. They had stayed on with her for just their keep, and Abigail had instructed Mr. Cowper to be sure that their back wages were paid from the sale of the house. She wrote them a glowing reference in her firm handwriting, and sent them on their way with the hopes that they would find another situation quickly. Mr. Cowper had promised to help with that, too.

Abigail was a quiet, dignified girl, whose genuine interest in other people inspired loyalty, and Mr. and Mrs. Sanderson shed a tear or two on her behalf.

Abigail had no illusions about needing to make her own way in the world; she had never expected a glorious coming out and brilliant match, for her parents were gentry of courtesy by reason of distant connections. She had expected to remain a spinster, possibly becoming a governess in any case. Abigail was not plain, but had no pretensions to beauty, being sallow of complexion, though with the high colour that many associated with apple-cheeked peasant girls. Her hair was an unremarkable brown and was dead straight, resisting all efforts to curl it in any way that did not merely turn it frizzy. No dreams of love at first sight with some handsome relative of such children as she might teach had ever entered Abigail's sensible thoughts, even if perhaps, at times, she might have wished for the sort of looks that made those secret dreams possible to exist.

When Abigail arrived at the school she was greeted by Miss Fairbrother and Miss Freemantle, and a girl with a slight limp, called Daisy, with whom Miss Freemantle invited her to go into the cloakroom to hang up her pelisse.

Abigail obediently followed Daisy, and at the other girl's polite gesture made to enter the cloakroom.

Pushing the door open was a little hard, and then something landed on her head, and Abigail was choking in a thick dust of some white powder.

A voice said, through her temporary blindness,

"Oh, by Jove, that's torn it, that isn't Hannah."

"You *twins*," said Daisy, awfully.

"Oh please!" said Felicity, "we are sorry, it wasn't for the new girl, it was for Hannah!"

Abigail had recovered enough by this time to see the funny side, and she started to laugh. She could now also make out two identical and anxious faces.

"You little horrors!" she said. "I trust you'll help me get cleaned up?"

"Oh *yes!*" said Philippa.

"Not only will you help Abigail to clean up, by

beating her clothes and reflecting that some governesses would think you well served if you were beaten," said Libby's crisp and cold voice, "you will please also write out one hundred times, 'I must not be disobedient', for I told you to leave Hannah alone, and you said you had understood. I am most disgusted."

"Oh, please, Miss Freemantle," said Philippa, "we did say we understood, but we did not promise to obey."

Libby, robbed briefly of words, looked helplessly at Elinor.

"You have broken an implied promise," said Elinor, her voice under very strict control. "Though I teach you in my literature class that language should be used precisely, there are, nonetheless, certain conventions of speech. And the convention that understanding an injunction also means obeying it is one of those. Dear me, is that flour?"

"Yes, Miss Fairbrother," said Felicity, whose face, like her twin's, was flaming red at the rebuke.

"How very wasteful," said Elinor. "You shall sweep it up and mix a dough with it to feed to the estate chickens, and then for... dear me, there is quite half a pound there... for two weeks when the others have cakes, you will have none, as you have used your share of flour for that time."

The twins were well and truly deflated.

"Why had you set a trap for this Hannah?" asked Abigail, in curiosity.

"Because without Phoebe here to gripe at, she was saying that Daisy's club foot was a punishment from God for her parents' sins," said Philippa.

"I don't think they had much opportunity for that much creative sinning," said Daisy. "I do dislike that child, Miss Fairbrother, and the twins were kind to take up cudgels on my behalf."

Elinor sighed and looked to Libby for support.

"I will reduce the sentence of no cakes to a week,"

she said, "but the lines and the clearing up stand."

"Hannah is, as you all are, bereaved, and upset, and angry," said Libby. "I fear she takes out her frustration in being unpleasant to others. Give her time."

Daisy flushed.

"I was determined to do everything wrong, as I had been told too often that I could do nothing right," she said, in a small voice.

"But you, my dear, are older and wiser, and realised that was foolish," said Elinor. "Twins, why are you still here and not fetching brushes to clear up? Abigail, my dear, leave your pelisse for them to deal with, and your bonnet, and Daisy will show you up to the room you will share with her."

"And if we are quick, it might be done before Hannah comes in and asks questions," Philippa was muttering to Felicity as they made a sharp exit.

"I have never shared a room with other girls before; is it jolly?" Abigail asked Daisy.

"I don't know; I have never done so either," said Daisy. "You are the first older one, and we have privileges of having a kettle in the room, and permission to make up our own fire. You're a year older than me, Miss Fairbrother said, and you've run your own house. I ran my grandmother's, in a manner of speaking, so perhaps we'll both understand each other."

"So long as you don't mind me being a bit of a bluestocking," said Abigail.

Daisy brightened.

"Why, so am I!" she said. "I am learning Latin and Greek and Mathematics."

Abigail's eyes lit up.

"We are permitted to learn so much? Then I pray you, help me to catch up! I read a bit, but only in English and some French."

"We'll be bottom together in Italian, then," laughed

Daisy. "Though Latin does help! I expect you know more about literature than I do, the vicar who was teaching me only had the Bible and Shakespeare – he had a copy of the old version of King Lear too, before it was made jolly by a Mr. Tate. The vicar had a 1623 folio version, so not long after Shakespeare wrote it. Most of the rest of his books were in Latin or Greek."

"I love Shakespeare," said Abigail, "though I do not know this King Lear. The grandeur of the way he uses language thrills me!"

"Oh, the vicar said the King does not care for Lear, because it is about a king going mad; and the poor king is so often ill himself," said Daisy.

"Why, if that is the subject of the play, I can quite understand it," said Abigail. "I have heard that it might be necessary for the Prince of Wales to be declared Regent at some point, though I am not sure if that would make much difference to political decisions, even if he does favour the Whigs."

"Oh we're going to get on just splendidly with serious discussion!" declared Daisy. "I was so dreading having someone who hated learning and made fun of my club foot."

"And there was I, wishing I had your looks, even if it came with two club feet," laughed Abigail. "Do you realise, I've said more to you, in coming upstairs, than I've said to anyone else inside a week?"

"Well, we're plainly made to be friends," said Daisy. "But seriously, you don't want even one club foot. It hurts too much. Anyway, you have lovely eyes and a beautiful smile. And I don't normally talk this much either, by the way!"

"What are you doing?" asked Hannah.

"We made a mess," said Philippa, shortly.

"That looks like flour. What were you doing in the cloakroom with flour?" demanded Hannah.

Philippa and Felicity shared a look. Being twins, they had one of those flashes of insight that meant they knew each of them wanted to tell Hannah that they planned to trace magical symbols in it to do witchcraft on her, but Hannah was such a little fool she might actually believe it. They sighed.

"We planned to have it fall on your head, but we caught the new girl instead," said Felicity, with devastating honesty.

Hannah goggled at her in incomprehension.

"But why would you do that?" she asked.

"Because you're unchristian enough to say nasty things about Daisy," said Philippa.

"I am not unchristian! The Bible says 'the sins of the fathers shall be visited unto his children even unto the third and fourth generation," said Hannah.

"Oh what a little fool you are!" said Felicity. "That means real sins, like gambling debts, because it takes generations to get over them. Or, if it comes to that, vicars interfering in politics when they have no right to be involved."

"She didn't mean that," said Philippa, hastily.

"I'm sorry," said Felicity, instantly, going white as she recalled Libby's words about speaking hastily. Apologies came naturally to her now!

"I suppose your father is the hardened gamester that you mentioned," sneered Hannah.

"He gambled on the 'Change," said Philippa, "not cards, but we do have to pay for his foolishness. But that was foolishness, not a sin, because that's not like playing cards or dice for money."

"Well, my Papa was trying to help *stop* people getting hurt," said Hannah, furiously.

"Then I'm sorry twice, and I expect you're sorry for assuming about our Papa," said Felicity, "because that makes him a hero."

"But you're angry with him, aren't you?" said

Philippa. "You're angry because he chose to do something brave and dangerous, and he chose trying to help *them* over choosing *you*, and living for you. That's why you're so cross all the time, isn't it?"

"It isn't! you don't know *anything!*" cried Hannah, running upstairs.

The twins exchanged a look, and shrugged. After a bad start there, they had actually tried to be nice, and it had not worked.

Hannah was odd.

"I feel sorry for Hannah, but she does not make herself likeable," sighed Elinor.

"She is so angry," said Libby.

Dr. Macfarlane cleared his throat delicately.

"Bearing in mind her obsession with sin," he said, "Has it no' occurred to you ladies that she might be suffering from being too much sinned against?"

"The twins aren't that bad," said Libby, "You can't call them sinners!"

"Little hoydens, maybe, but generally not bad girls," added Elinor.

He looked at them in exasperation.

"I wasnae meaning yon wee hellions," he said, his accent thickening. "I meant that she might have been taking the place of her mother, since her mother died...."

Elinor looked at him as if he were insane.

"Well, of course she has!" she said. "When my mother died, I, too, took on the role of ordering the household, deciding the meals and checking the accounts. That, Dr. Macfarlane, is perfectly normal."

"Are ye really baith sich a pair of innocents?" he snapped. "Dear God, I believe you are! Have ye never heard of men who take their daughters to bed?"

Elinor and Libby stared in horrified consternation.

"Surely not!" cried Elinor. "Why, that's horrible! I

– surely no man could be so wicked?"

"It happens," said Dr. Macfarlane, grimly.

Libby was white.

"But… but Hannah's father was a vicar, and accounted quite saintly!" she said.

"And you don't think that the words 'whited sepulchre' might refer to a sanctimonious sinner?"

"Oh dear!" said Elinor. "The good Doctor is evidently wiser to the world than we, Libby! And how very difficult. If one asks her outright, and she has no knowledge of this, it could shock her unbearably, and yet we must ascertain if such a suspicion may be so."

"I have an idea," said Libby, "but not one I like to discuss in front of a man."

"I'm a doctor, Miss Freemantle. And as I appear to have more knowledge about this situation than either of you, my opinion might be valid."

Libby flushed.

"Well," she began, "I wondered if I might ask her if she yet suffers from the monthlies. She is very young, but it has been known…. And it is something all parents should prepare their daughters to face."

"In which case," said Elinor, "it might be better if we talk to all of them, and mention that there are some things that girls their age are too young for, and invite confidences is any want to speak to us."

"That sounds very practical," approved Dr. Macfarlane.

Chapter 9

The girls received the lesson on the transition to womanhood with more or less shock and horror, save Abigail, who had already discovered the trials of being a woman. Hannah displayed no more repugnance to dealing with matters regarding the unmentionable parts than any of the others, and merely looked faintly outraged when Philippa mentioned that it happened to bitches too, and that was when the dogs wanted to cover them.

"Male animals have different parts," said Philippa, wisely, "and they…"

"Thank you, Philippa, we do not need a lesson in animal husbandry," said Elinor, hastily. "Animals act on instinct, so it is not a true parallel at all."

Felicity also poked her twin, and Philippa subsided. Elinor concluded that the girl's interest was not one of indelicate prurience, but true interest in how animals acted, and how such mechanisms worked. Least said, soonest mended.

"And humans are modest and speak not of such things, and wear clothes to cover themselves and prevent thoughts of sin," said Hannah, "which was why Noah was so shameful," she shot a poisonous look at the twins who had been wont to bathe happily in front of her.

"Well, one would hardly expect to walk in on one's parent in a state of déshabille," said Felicity, with a giggle. "Too outrageous!"

"I'd not care, if I had my parents back to walk in on," said Abigail. "Besides, a polite child knocks before walking in on their parents, though I suppose one would be puzzled how to knock on a tent. It's not nice to interrupt grown-ups without permission to enter."

Daisy squeezed her hand.

Elinor watched narrowly. The twins were not grieving deeply for their parents, more for the lost lifestyle. Elinor concluded that perhaps they had not been close either to their mother, who had died some months previously, nor to their father. Daisy had not known her parents, though she grieved for her grandfather; Abigail's words had struck a chord with Hannah, though, for the child had nodded briefly, before trying to look scandalised. She showed no signs of having uncovered her father's nakedness, like Noah, despite bringing the subject up, so it appeared that Dr. Macfarlane was, fortunately, wrong about that.

However, assuming him to be correct about the existence of the aberrant phenomenon, it was something to watch out for in the future.

Hannah was just generally angry.

Elinor was surprised when Philippa slipped a hand into hers when the lesson ended and they broke for a drink and cakes.

"Miss Fairbrother, was that more pointed than just telling us that people have seasons too?" she asked.

Elinor looked at her thoughtfully.

"We wanted to check that none of you had any inappropriate knowledge," she said.

Philippa flushed.

"Is it inappropriate, Miss Fairbrother? Only I can't help noticing the animals, you know."

"Oh, your knowledge is not inappropriate, my dear," said Elinor. "Though speaking about it is not such a good idea. It was to get an inkling of whether any of you had gained such knowledge from a man taking advantage of a motherless child, in which case that would have been inappropriate."

"Oh, I see," said Philippa, her face clearing. "I say, may I change the subject and tell you what I think about Hannah?"

"So long as there are no tales," said Elinor.

"Oh no, Miss Fairbrother! I just thought, maybe she's so cross all the time because she's angry with her father for getting himself killed for other people, and leaving her. Fee and I were awfully angry at Papa, but we talked about it, and we decided there was no point, as he's always been feckless, and we ought to know that by now, so it wasn't really a big surprise, you know."

"And you were not, I think, very close to him?" asked Elinor.

Philippa shook her head.

"We didn't know our parents very well," she said. "Mama was always sick, and Papa was mostly out hunting, or in London. We cried more for our dear Fippy, Miss Philpot, our governess, when she died."

"When was that?" asked Elinor.

"A bit before Mama," said Philippa. "Mama said we should have another governess, but she was too sick to see to it, because of keeping trying to give Papa a son, you know. And when she died, Papa forgot, so we had to bring ourselves up."

"Under the circumstances, you haven't made a bad job of it," said Elinor, wishing she could bring Mr. Goyder magically back to life, solely for the purpose of shaking the irresponsible man quite thoroughly.

"Your suspicions appear, fortunately, to be unfounded," said Elinor to Dr. Macfarlane.

"Well, better to fear the worst, and have pleasant surprises," he replied.

"Do you have an answer to everything?" asked Elinor. The Scots Doctor managed to irritate her sometimes just by doing so.

He considered.

"A wise man knows when to stay silent, but I saw no justification in this circumstance," he said, "or you might conclude that I am disappointed when my guess falls awry. Which I am not; I am quite delighted."

"We have been much exercised in our minds over nothing," Elinor accused.

"Hardly nothing," said Dr. Macfarlane. "If I had not spoken, I should be failing in my duty of care towards the girls, as you plainly knew nothing of this kind of sin. And now you are forewarned in case it happens to another, and ready to see it."

"It is so disgusting! I …. I have thought about this, and I cannot readily believe that men of our class would act as animals like that," said Elinor.

The doctor frowned.

"If you think that aberrant behaviour is confined to the lower orders, Miss Fairbrother, you are a fool; and that is not something I ever thought you to be," he said.

"I am not a fool! But surely the training given to men of our estate, in self-control, and discipline, and with an education grounded in the classics…"

"You have not, then, read those classics which deal with the vices quite fully, it appears," said Dr. Macfarlane, dryly. "As for the training, why, there are plenty of men of our estate who feel that their very class gives them the right to do anything they wish, and that their rank in society permits them to get away with any vice or crime; and often this is true, because their social inferiors will not lodge a complaint against them. It is only the traditions of containment of emotion that has prevented British aristocrats from behaving as badly as the French aristocrats, which precipitated that unfortunate country into revolution."

"Surely not!" gasped Elinor.

"Aye, and the fact that we do have rule of law in Britain, so that if any will bring complaint, even a peer of the Realm must be punished if found guilty," said Dr. Macfarlane. "The French aristos cared nothing for the people. Here, there is at least some sense of duty to one's dependants." He laughed, ironically. "Strange, is it not, that the country which coined the phrase '*noblesse oblige*' failed to observe it."

"I have never met any émigrés," said Elinor. "But it is hard to imagine that sophisticated men should be so crude."

"Sophisticated men consider their views to be sophisticated, which means they dress up bad behaviour in classical allegory, and wear silks and velvets, not linen and cotton," said the doctor. "The French aristocracy had the power of life and death over their peasantry, and be pleased we have not such powers here. I have every sympathy for those who fermented the initial revolution, though it was usurped by men of ambition who were no better than those they replaced."

"Why, Dr. Macfarlane, I believe you are a radical!" said Elinor.

"If it is radical to believe in a fair deal for all, equality before the law, and equal respect for all God's children, then I'm a radical," said Dr. Macfarlane. "I believe that children should not work in mines or up chimneys or in factories either."

"We are certainly agreed on that point," said Elinor.

"Amazing," said Dr. Macfarlane. "You seem determined to pick a quarrel with me. One might almost think you to be eleven-year-old Hannah Loring picking an argument to release your own exercised feeling."

"You are insufferable!" cried Elinor, flushing, as she realised his words were true.

He bowed.

"It goes with the job," he said.

Elinor stared at him, then began laughing, weakly.

"Oh, you *are* indeed insufferable, Dr. Macfarlane, but I cannot remain angry with you for long, even when I have worked myself up to it," she said.

"Oho, I was right, was I?" he asked.

"You were. You are…safe… to take issue with, to relieve the feelings."

"Well, now, it's the first time I've been likened to a

safety valve on a steam engine," said Dr. Macfarlane, continuing as she looked at him in incomprehension. "If the pressure in the boiler builds up too much, it may explode," he explained, "so every engine has a special valve, and if the pressure is too high, it can open and steam be released. I must take you to a pumping station some day," he added.

"Oh what fun! And the girls would find it very educational," said Elinor, looking pleased. He gave her a quizzical look.

"I had been thinking of just taking you," he said, "but I make no doubt you'll not be happy unless our brats come along too."

"Stop right now, or I shall be out of charity with you again," said Elinor, with mock severity to cover her suddenly rather rapid heartbeat. "Brats, indeed!"

He laughed.

"Brats!" he reiterated.

"And as for referring to them as *our* brats...." said Elinor, "has it not occurred to you how that might sound to any outsider?"

She had not realised that his eyes could twinkle so mischievously.

"Why, it had not," he said. "I must try mentioning it, and see how many people misread the situation."

"Why, you...." Elinor was briefly outraged, and then joined in as he laughed.

"I believe I bammed you quite nicely there," said he.

"I believe you did," agreed Elinor.

The twins were on their honour to eat no cakes at tea, which Hannah noticed.

"What's wrong with you two?" she asked.

"Nothing," said Felicity.

"What should be wrong?" demanded Philippa.

"You are not eating any cake; are you ill?" asked Hannah.

"No," said Philippa. "We used our share of the flour while trying to shower you with it. It would have been well worth it if we had succeeded, but as it is, we accept that punishment follows mischief."

"You should not have even considered doing such a thing, and to catch some other person is too bad," said Hannah, giving a prim and patronising smile to Abigail.

"I thought it was funny," said Abigail. "I could wish to have a twin to share jokes with, though now I have a friend in Daisy, that's almost as good."

"You must not condone their bad behaviour!" said Hannah. "It will only encourage them to wickedness!"

"Who died and made you Archbishop of Canterbury, small fry?" said Felicity, indignantly. "We had the jaw from Miss Fairbrother and Miss Freemantle, and accepted our several punishments, and it's their business to reprove us, not yours."

"And if you think I'm going to be told what to condone by a babe like you, young Hannah, you are sadly mistaken," said Abigail, in an amused tone. "Of course it was naughty. They have been punished. I did not take offence at being in the wrong place at the wrong time. That is an end to the matter."

"Oh, but you do not have to share a room with these awful girls," began Hannah.

"Nor do you; Miss Freemantle found you one of your own so as not to freeze the rest of us with your uncharitable coldness," said Philippa.

"You are unkind and insensitive," said Hannah.

"Not as unkind and insensitive as you were to poor little Phoebe," retorted Philippa. "The sooner you realise that you are angry at your Papa for dying, and learn to forgive yourself for that, the happier you'll be."

"Why should I be angry with Papa? He did nothing wrong, nothing, not like your wastrel of a father!" shouted Hannah.

"Try to moderate your voice, Hannah," said Daisy.

"Remember, you are a lady."

"I don't take orders from a cripple," said Hannah.

"Yes, you do," said Daisy. "By virtue of me being older than you by some considerable margin, and placed as a responsible person to coach you younger ones in those subjects where you are behind. And you are behind even the twins, who have had no lessons in two years," she added. "And if you do not behave in a way that is suitable for a young lady, I will ask that you be permitted to take your meals alone, so the rest of us need not be disturbed by your impertinent questions and comments, and your intemperate and ill-bred outbursts."

Hannah went white; Abigail was nodding approval, as was Felicity, though only Abigail was old enough to be considered a responsible older girl. Only Philippa looked sympathetic, and Hannah wanted none of Philippa's sympathy.

"I hate you all!" she said in a low, furious voice.

"You are quite entitled to do so, if it makes you happy," said Daisy, with heavy irony, "providing you can behave like a civilised young lady who has sufficient breeding to conceal most of the outer display of hatred. I suggest that you confine yourself to cutting sarcasm and witty ripostes at our expense. If you can manage it. And would you please be good enough to pass the bread and butter?"

Hannah would have liked to have thrown the bread and butter at Daisy, but she did not dare.

She wanted to cry, which if she had only permitted herself to do, would have gone a long way to both helping her and evoking the compassion of her fellows. As it was she was proud of herself for containing the tears that threatened.

Chapter 10

Phoebe returned to the school in good spirits, with the pretty, but quiet, Rachel Cohen. Rachel had dark curls and a piquant, if solemn, face, and she and Phoebe were plainly already fast friends.

Philippa heaved a hidden sigh of relief as she and Felicity helped the two girls to unpack; Felicity had warmed to Phoebe somewhat, especially in the face of opposition from first Mrs. Rawson and then Hannah, but Felicity was inclined to jealousy over her twin's attention. If Phoebe and Rachel were essentially a second pair in this bedroom, they would be able to be friends with them, not come between the twins if Felicity took to sulking.

Philippa sometimes had rather deep insights for her age.

Hannah pointedly ignored both Phoebe and Rachel, giving them the cut direct when Rachel tentatively said, "hello", when the two came face to face with Hannah.

Rachel looked upset.

"Don't worry, Rachel," said Phoebe, earnestly. "She's just afraid of catching Jewishness. We're better off with her not speaking to us, because she's not nice."

Hannah could not, of course, dignify this with a reply, even though she fulminated over the idea of being afraid of catching Jewishness! And she told herself that it was no moment to her if a stupid little brat like Phoebe called her 'not nice'.

Rachel frowned in thought.

"You have to be born a Jew; you cannot *catch* Judaism, it is not a disease," she said.

Phoebe giggled.

"Oh, I know, but she seems to be afraid of being near a Jew as she would near a leper, so I think she thinks it's catching," she said. "She isn't very clever."

"You horrid ridiculous brat!" cried Hannah, exercised beyond bearing.

"Terribly bad form to give the cut direct and then to comment to the one you've cut," said Daisy, sardonically. "Surely you can manage at least to stick to your decision to cut someone?"

"You stay out of this!" hissed Hannah, furiously.

"I'm not sure that I shall," said Daisy. "Phoebe seems to have hit the nail on the head. Are you afraid of catching being crippled, too? You cringe back from me as if I had some loathsome disease."

"Oh, you go away and….and I hope you get smallpox and get pock marks on your stupid face!" said Hannah.

"Not me; I've been inoculated," said Daisy. "You're quite a loathsome child, you know, bullying little kids like Phoebe, and ill-wishing me as though you wanted to be a witch. I do wish you'd do as Philippa suggested and learn to live with yourself. It's decidedly uncomfortable for the rest of us living with you until you do so."

"*Good!*" said Hannah, and flung off.

Elinor was looking out of the window when she saw the small figure of Hannah Loring come almost at a run out of the house, and head down towards the river. Elinor's heart lurched, and she quickly wrapped her shawl about her shoulders, and hastened out of the French windows in pursuit of the little girl. Exercise had strengthened Elinor, but she was breathing hard by the time she caught up with Hannah, standing on the ornamental bridge and staring at the fast-flowing water below.

Elinor was there in two rapid steps.

"My dear, that is never a solution, you know," she said, wrapping her arms around Hannah.

Sudden kindness on top of the child's black

contemplations finally broke Hannah's iron control of her emotions, and she began to cry. Elinor held her, soothing her, stroking her hair, then drew her over the bridge and away from the river, to the Greek temple on the other side, to sit on the marble bench, there to sob her fill in relative comfort.

"Oh Miss Fairbrother, it isn't fair!" cried Hannah.

"No, my child, it is not," said Elinor. "Tell me all about it."

"I *hate* Philippa Goyder, how dare she know that I am so angry with Papa for dying?" flared Hannah.

"Oh, my dear Hannah, why should you hate her for knowing how she has felt, herself? Felicity and Philippa have been angry too, but they are fortunate – or unfortunate – enough not to be so close to their Papa as you were to yours, and have managed to put the past, and their anger, behind them," said Elinor.

"They don't feel anything about their wastrel of a father!" said Hannah.

"No, poor children. They grieve mostly for their governess, who died a couple of years ago, who was more a mother to them than their own. And their father took little notice of them. Truly, Hannah, would you really envy them their ability to get over so small a grief, since it would mean that your father had not been close to you?"

Hannah's eyes widened in horror.

"I should just hate it!" she said.

"Then you should have the Christian charity to pity the twins, for never having proper, loving parents," said Elinor. "You are angry because it all happened so suddenly, and you had not been able to say goodbye properly, and your life was then turned upside-down. Is that not it?"

Hannah nodded.

"It's worse than that," she whispered. "Papa said he was going to try to stop that riot, and I told him it was a waste of time, and he said he had to try. And so we parted with a quarrel between us!"

Elinor cradled Hannah to her.

"You poor little mite," she said. "But surely you realise that your Papa knows that you love him, and that the words between you were not a contradiction to that? And he can surely see you from Heaven, to know that you grieve."

Hannah looked guilty.

"He will not like how I have behaved," she whispered.

"No, my dear, he will not, any more than God, who sees all, likes it," said Elinor. "But both the Good Lord and your earthly father understand that it is hard for a little girl. Now, do you know what I suggest?" Hannah shook her head, and Elinor went on, "I suggest that when we go back to the school, and you have washed your face, I introduce you to the others as though you were a new girl, and tell them that Cross Hannah has gone, and ask them to help Sad Hannah instead."

It was a way out for Hannah; Elinor suspected that the child was continuing to take her obstinate stance purely out of an inability to know how to back down and learn how to be friends. It was so hard to break out of taking a perverse pleasure in being contrary when one was hurting!

"Oooh…" said Hannah. She had come to hate being ostracised, but did not know what to do about it. "Do you think they will? Oh please, can we do that now?" and she jumped up.

"I fear not," said Elinor, quietly. "For I ran after you, and I am recovering from… well, it is a long illness. And I do not think that I can readily walk back to the house at the moment."

Hannah looked at her in alarm; Elinor was very white.

"I'll run and get Dr. Macfarlane," she said, and

galloped off coltishly.

Hannah ran into Dr. Macfarlane's office, panting.

"Oh please, Dr. Macfarlane, Miss Fairbrother is ill and it's all my fault!" she cried.

Graeme Macfarlane was on his feet in a trice.

"Where?" he demanded.

"In the folly," said Hannah.

He was striding off there immediately, Hannah following as best she could.

Elinor had a little more colour in her cheeks by the time Dr. Macfarlane reached her, and managed to smile tentatively at him.

"And what were you thinking of?" he demanded, roughly possessing himself of her wrist to read her pulse.

"I saw Hannah running off towards the river. I had a terrible premonition of danger," said Elinor. "So I went through the French windows to follow. And I was glad I did, she was on the bridge, contemplating…."

Dr. Macfarlane turned to glare at Hannah, who quailed.

"Did you dare even think for one minute of throwing away the gift of life the Good Lord has given you?" he demanded.

"I wanted to be with Papa again," sobbed Hannah.

"Leave the child," snapped Elinor. "We have had a good, productive talk, and she is ready to make a new beginning. Do not go upsetting her now she is feeling more like herself!"

"No, it's you, I should be angry with, Miss Fairbrother, I apologise, Hannah, I should not take it out on you! Honestly, you silly widgeon, Elinor! Did it never occur to you to ring for a servant to go after her?"

"Not at all," said Elinor, tartly. "*Just* the thing to drive a grieving child into jumping, to be pursued by servants like a common felon! The children are my responsibility, and Libby's; it is not down to a servant to have to help them when they are upset. And as for sending someone for you or Libby, I did not think there was time. And you have told me that my heart is healthy, so what else was I to do but trust your word to me, and run as fast as I could?"

Dr. Macfarlane grunted.

"Your heart is healthy, but it still is not ready for so strenuous an exercise all in one go! A run, even downhill, of close to a mile is more than it is ready for," he said, "I am not surprised you feel faint and ill! What a fright you have given me!"

"I am sorry, Miss Fairbrother," Hannah chipped in. "And thank you, sir, for saying you did not mean to shout at me."

"You have no need to be sorry, my child," said Elinor. "I chose to run. And you were a good girl and fetched Dr. Macfarlane most promptly. Now run inside and wash your face, so he can shout at me more expeditiously, without watching his words for the ears of a child."

Hannah hesitated, then ran off.

"Oh Elinor Fairbrother!" said Graeme Macfarlane, in exasperation. "How can I look after you if you will not look after yourself?"

"You have to admit that there was nothing else I could do that would answer as well," said Elinor.

"I do not *have* to admit it, and I am not sure that I do," said the doctor. "But I do admit that you did what you felt was the only thing to do."

"Sophistry," said Elinor. "If you will but lend me your arm, I may now, I think, walk back to the house."

"Oh, no!" said Graeme Macfarlane. "You will not walk!" and so saying, he swept her up into his arms.

Elinor was torn between outrage at being so babied, comfort against his broad chest that made her want to snuggle, and a desire to burst into tears from an excess of emotion.

She decided to forestall tears by protesting.

"I'm not a baby to need carrying," she said.

"You're a bairn that needs looking after," said Dr. Macfarlane.

Elinor gave up and leaned against him.

"I must go to tea with the girls, Libby, and explain all about Hannah!" Elinor expostulated with her one-time governess, as that worthy firmly put her to bed with a hot water bottle and hot chocolate.

"No, Elinor, dear, I will tell them," said Libby, firmly. "Just tell me all about it, and leave it in my hands."

Elinor knew when arguing would get her nowhere, and open defiance needed one to feel less limp and drained than she did. Meekly, she explained the whole to Libby.

Consequently it was Libby who tapped on Hannah's door, telling her that she would take Miss Fairbrother's place in supporting and introducing her.

"Oh Miss Freemantle! Is she very ill?" asked Hannah, apprehension in her eyes.

"No, no, she is unwell, and I want her to rest, but she will be quite well after a good sleep," said Libby. "Come, my dear."

The girls listened warily as Libby explained to them that Cross Hannah had gone, and asked them to welcome Sad Hannah into their number.

"Does Sad Hannah hate Jews too?" asked Phoebe, pointedly.

"I don't know anything about Jews, but everyone says they are greedy and they killed Jesus," said Hannah.

"Well, be fair, Hannah, you might just as well hate

Dr. Macfarlane because the Scots killed lots of people with the Jacobite rebellions," said Abigail. "And you can't blame all the Jews for what a few nasty people did. Why don't you get to know Rachel and Phoebe rather than listening to 'everybody'? Because 'everybody' here would have reported that Cross Hannah was a horrid girl. Rumour almost always lies."

Hannah flushed.

"Nicely put," murmured Daisy.

"All right, I will try," said Hannah, a little ungraciously. "I ... I want to blame people for my Papa being dead, because I didn't want him to go help at that riot, and I was cross at him, and then he was dead!"

Even Felicity managed a murmur of sympathy over that.

"Oh, that's even worse than being angry at him for being dead," said Philippa, with ready compassion. "I'm not surprised you felt so bad, Hannah, but I wish you'd only said so we could help earlier."

Hannah shrugged her shoulders up and she looked mutinous.

"I didn't want to," she muttered.

"It's hard to share how one feels with total strangers," said Libby. "Now, I shall leave you girls to enjoy your tea in peace."

Hannah almost panicked, and considered fleeing; but Abigail handed her some bread-and-butter, and if the others were a little wary at first, they were not hostile.

"And I hope," said Libby to Elinor and Dr. Macfarlane, "that this will solve that particular problem!"

"At least she may be a happier little girl, even if it seems unlikely that any deep friendships are about to be formed," said Elinor.

"With luck, another child of the same age may

arrive; and that will give someone for Hannah to be friendly with," said Dr. Macfarlane.

Elinor giggled.

"As long as she's nothing outlandish like a Presbyterian," she said.

"It's my opinion, woman, that you are as much of a minx as those twins!" said the doctor.

Chapter 11

The self-invited visiting cleric, who introduced himself as the Reverend Matthew Endicote, rubbed his hands unctuously. The small child with him stood behind him, scowling at his back.

"Ah, what a saintly woman you are, Miss Fairbrother, to extend Christian Charity to these poor little foundlings," he said.

Libby looked at him rather askance.

"I am Miss Freemantle, the headmistress of the school. The child you have here is rather younger than any we had considered taking. I wish you had written first to ask if there was a place available, and giving details of your charge."

The vicar looked nonplussed.

"But Miss, er, Freemantle, there is nowhere else for her! Obviously I cannot take her into my own home as I am unmarried!"

"How did she come to be in your care?" asked Libby.

"A sad story of human frailty! Lucy here is a bastard, I fear. I beg your pardon?" as Libby made a ladylike cough of expostulation.

"We do not think it nice to label children quite so baldly with words that might make any lady shocked to the point of swooning," said Libby, sternly. "You were explaining how Lucy is a love-child?"

"Er, quite, born in sin…" he moved hastily on as Libby glared at him. "Her mother was the daughter of the Manse, and should perhaps have known better, and her father was some soldier," he added dismissively. "The wages of sin, alas, are death, and Amabel Lamming, Lucy's mother, died bringing her, er, love-child, into the world. The vicar who preceded me and his wife took the noble, if perhaps unwise, step of rearing their granddaughter, and now that both have passed on, it seemed a little improper to put the child on the parish. Her family, on her mother's side at least, is of gentle stock."

"No, indeed, it would be monstrous to put her on the parish. But I cannot see a bar to you raising the child in a familiar milieu for her, as she is scarcely old enough to be compromised," said Libby. "But I have no doubt that you would find yourself insufficiently charitable to manage the wages of a nursemaid for her."

"Oh there can be no question of the poor child remaining where she is filled with sad reminders of her dead grandparents," cried the Reverend Endicote, who had missed the insult to his Christian charity. "It is for her own good that she should make a clean break!"

"Poor little lamb," said Libby, who thought the Reverend Endicote to have as much Christian charity as the codfish he so nearly resembled, with his pasty skin and loose, weak mouth. "Come here, Lucy."

The child trotted obediently over to Libby, and looked up at her anxiously.

"Please can I live with you, not with him?" she whispered.

Libby smiled down at her.

"Well, Lucy, you will be the school baby, and perhaps one of the big girls will help to care for you," she said. "Ah, here is Miss Fairbrother," as Elinor joined her friend.

"Miss Fairbrother! Delighted to meet such a saintly woman!" cried the Reverend Endicote, appreciating Elinor's trim figure and ethereal beauty. "Such a tragedy that such kindness, such charm, such beauty may be expected to be cut short before you have yourself had a chance to experience much life and love!"

Elinor later described the reverend gentleman to Dr. Macfarlane as someone who recalled to her the sort of clever, but tediously interminable music that some young ladies played at musicales. He had evidently heard that she was considered likely to die young, and though Dr. Macfarlane believed this to be untrue, Elinor considered it bad taste in the extreme to bring the subject up.

"The Reverend Endicote has brought us Lucy, as he is unable to care for her properly himself," said Libby, neutrally. She would share Lucy's story and her own thoughts on the subject later.

Elinor managed a smile.

"How kind of you to bring her to where she will be cared for," she said. "Have you far to go to return to your parish?"

He smiled.

"Oh, not too far," he said. "Why, I am close enough to make regular visits to obtain progress reports on little Lucy from you, Miss Fairbrother."

Lucy shuddered.

"I hardly think that such a suggestion constitutes what you spoke of as a 'clean break'," said Libby, tartly.

"Oh, I shall not disturb the child of course; but perhaps if Miss Fairbrother could spare the time to let me know how she does, perhaps by coming out for a drive with me, so Lucy need not be reminded, by seeing me..." he smiled ingratiatingly at Elinor, virtually ignoring Libby.

"Miss Freemantle can prepare a monthly progress report to send to you, so you are not thus inconvenienced, if you are interested," said Elinor. "You will not be wanting to put yourself out."

"Why, for the pleasure of hearing the news from your beautiful lips of how she does, it will be no trouble!" said the Reverend Endicote. "I shall return on the first of the month to take you driving, Miss Fairbrother," and he made a bow to her.

Elinor was far too taken aback to make any coherent

retort until he had gone.

"Make sure all the servants know that I will not be at home if he calls," said Elinor, firmly.

"Oh, *you* do not like him either?" cried Lucy.

Elinor regarded the little girl. One did not tell children the shortcomings of other adults, especially men of the cloth, but nor should one lie.

"I don't like him, Lucy," she said, "but that does not mean he is not a worthy man as he may very well be."

"He does not want to be bothered with me; he did not like grandmamma still being in the manse, but she was too ill to move," said Lucy, "and Mrs. Cummins told him she'd see that nobody came to church if he put us both on the parish as he said he would do."

"Dear me!" said Libby. "I like the sound of Mrs. Cummins. We must pray that God enlightens the Reverend Endicote's soul and grants him a little more Christian charity. Now, I need to find you somewhere to sleep, dear me, how very difficult, you will not like to be alone in a strange place, I am sure. Perhaps Hannah will be kind enough to look after you; she is a bigger girl."

"I can dress myself, Miss Freemantle, and fold my clothes, but I cannot reach to make my bed alone," said Lucy.

"How old are you?" asked Elinor.

"I am six, Miss Fairbrother. Grandmama said that my Papa meant to marry my mama but that his regiment recalled him when the…the Peace of Ammy-ons ended."

"I see," said Elinor. "Many people were taken by surprise by the ending of the Peace of Amiens, I fear. My poor child, it seems likely that he died fighting, but perhaps we can find out. Come and sit with me in my sitting-room while Miss Freemantle makes arrangements for your sleeping accommodation."

Hannah did not feel gracious about sharing her room with a very little girl, but she was ready to do so to please Miss Freemantle and especially Miss Fairbrother. When she found out that Lucy was by way of being akin to the daughter of the manse it disposed her more kindly to the little girl. Hannah was shocked that Lucy was illegitimate, but faithfully promised Libby to say nothing about it to the little girl. Libby had hesitated before telling her, but had decided it came better explained properly than from either Lucy's lips, or worse, rumour. As it happened, Lucy was a sufficiently self-sufficient child that Hannah found her no trouble at all, bar needing to help her make her bed; and as Lucy cheerfully helped Hannah with her bed, and with her middle button on her gown, Hannah accepted the charge with better grace as she got used to the little girl.

"Why, the shilpit wee gomerall!" exclaimed Dr. Macfarlane, when Libby and Elinor recounted the events of the day to him. "and to threaten to come on Easter Saturday of all days, forebye!"

"I do not understand the Scots language, I fear, Doctor," said Elinor.

"Och, it's no' swearing," said Dr. Macfarlane. "I called him an insignificant little idiot, or at least that's close enough. I find my own idiom satisfying when I am irritated."

"Oh, quite unexceptionable," said Elinor. "I did not like his dubious gallantry."

"And well you might not, my dear Miss Fairbrother," said Dr. Macfarlane. "It's my thought that the wretched creature is muckle fu' of unvicarlike lusts for your fortune, as well as an unwholesome longing for your beauty. Ugh!"

"I did cringe, rather, myself," said Elinor, "but I wondered if it were merely an excess of sensibility for not having gone much into society, that I be not used to obtaining the sort of Spanish coin one is warned that young men tend to pay."

"Oh, any compliment to your looks can be no Spanish coin," said Dr. Macfarlane.

"'Item: two lips, indifferent red'..." quoted Elinor.

"Havers! You are a beautiful woman. And to deny it is a false modesty, and a form of vanity which I despise," said Dr. Macfarlane. "You are like a pale flame, for ye're no one o' these ethereal women who cannot stir from a couch, even when you thought you were dying, the life and vibrrrrancy shone frrrom you!" he rolled his r's in emphasis.

"Why, Doctor Macfarlane, you are quite a poet!" said Elinor. "Oh, I pray you, try not to blush, it clashes so horribly with your hair!"

"I cannot help it when you must tease me so, when I am quite serious," said Dr. Macfarlane.

"I teased you not, I thought it very poetical, and as I know you are more likely to tell me off for something than compliment me, why then, I know it to be genuine!" said Elinor.

"I admit, you're more of a beauty now you've got a touch of colour to your cheeks, spring in your step, and even more of a sparkle to your eye," said Dr. Macfarlane, examining her judiciously, "though you've a way to go before you look fully healthy."

Elinor laughed.

"Ah, the compliment tempered with criticism; that is more what I expect from you!" she said.

"I am sorry; I do not mean to nag you, Miss Fairbrother," said the doctor.

"Oh, I appreciate that you have my best interests in mind," said Elinor.

Dr. Macfarlane grunted.

"Well, as I do have your interests at heart, I have to warn you that a disturbing thought has occurred to me," he said.

"How ominous that sounds!" said Elinor.

"Not perhaps *ominous,* Miss Fairbrother, but perhaps you should be aware that it is my opinion that this vicar may only be the first of a series of potential fortune hunters."

"Fortune hunters?" said Elinor, puzzled. "But my fortune is to be dedicated to the children!"

"Don't forget that marriage invalidates any previous will, and your fortune passes to your husband on marriage, unless a marriage settlement is written to the contrary," said Dr. Macfarlane.

Elinor looked aghast.

"I had not thought of that," she said. "I confess, I had never thought about love and marriage, when I thought I was not going to live long, and I have not sufficiently come to terms with the idea of living a normal lifespan to really contemplate the things young women generally take for granted. I suppose I had also half thought that I am old enough to be almost on the shelf."

"Balderdash!" said Dr. Macfarlane. "Besides, if I may be cynical, it would not matter if you were an ape-leader with buck teeth, a squint, warts and losing your hair on your head only to grow it on your upper lip, because you have that beautifying effect of a fortune. That you are beautiful is an advantage to any young or not so young fortune hunters who are likely, I fear, to seek you out."

"Dear me!" said Elinor. "How very vexatious! But the solution is simple; I will not go into society so I shall not meet any!"

Dr. Macfarlane laughed, cynically.

"I wager there will be excuse made to call on you," he said.

"But I cannot permit strange men to turn up here!" said Elinor, aghast. "It is most ineligible!"

Graeme Macfarlane shrugged.

"I am afraid they may neither consider that, nor care," he said. "I fear that you are a matrimonial prize, and I should be failing you if I did not mention it."

"Oh, quite, I do appreciate your warning," said Elinor. "But how will they know?"

"Rumour always flies fast," said the doctor. "Your father's death was announced, he is known to leave a daughter, and to have been a warm man when he died. Your endowment of a school will not have gone unnoticed, on the heels of that news. This Reverend Endicote appears to have heard about it. He will not be the only one."

"Oh dear!" said Elinor, crossly. "What a nuisance! Perhaps I should invent a spurious fiancé who is overseas, or something."

"Not such a bad idea at that," said Dr. Macfarlane. "But bear in mind, you may wish to consider courtship and marriage and any decent man will be happy to draw up a marriage settlement giving you absolute control of your own fortune to use and dispose as you so wish." He chuckled suddenly. "Many a solicitor might be scandalised at a woman being so little protected from being parted from her fortune in being permitted her own use of it."

"Protected, fiddlesticks!" said Elinor with asperity. "Most of my fortune is down to the speculation I suggested, that my father made; and indeed, I am quietly amassing more, by like efforts. It's fun," she admitted.

"That should scare most men into running, however beautiful and wealthy you may be," said Dr. Macfarlane. "If there's anything that scares a man even more than a bluestocking, it's a woman who understands finance."

"Dr. Macfarlane, I am also a bluestocking," said Elinor.

"Well, there you have it; quote Plato at any suitors and discuss his ideas of governance, and watch them run," said the doctor. "And any who don't run might even make suitable suitors."

"You held your own admirably when we were discussing 'The Republic' the other evening," said Elinor.

He shrugged.

"And I put my support behind educating girls, because it seems to me only fair that education should be equal for all. And an educated man needs, in my opinion, an educated companion in his wife, or it would be a tedious sort of marriage, I think. I beg pardon; I am haranguing you like a street-preacher."

"Your enthusiasm echoes mine," said Elinor.

Chapter 12

Edward Atherton, St. Clair Wincanton, the Honourable Julian Nettleby and Abernethy Rivers were not entirely sober.

They were also four young men of impeccable *ton*, excellent education, and fashionable mien, who had known each other since their schooldays. They had burst upon the town more or less together, got drunk together, had been arrested together and been rescued by irate fathers together. Those wilder days were largely behind them; but they did have one other point in common.

They were all, for one reason or another, drowning, as one says, in the River Tick.

Mr. Atherton had dropped a packet on the horses, and was unfortunately not expecting his allowance to be paid in full for about five years, as it was mortgaged that far ahead. Mr. Wincanton was in danger of failing to be a Pink of the *Ton* as his tailor had treacherously threatened to make no more coats for him until he paid a few of his bills for the last five years. Mr. Nettleby, who was a poet, was disgusted to find that the expensive Paphian he was keeping expected presents of a more material kind than poems to her exquisite eyebrows. Finally, Mr. Rivers was a gamester who always expected the next card to make his fortune. His skill and luck never quite measured up to his aspirations.

It was Mr. Rivers who came up with the Idea.

"It's a sort of bet," he said, "except that everyone wins."

"Doesn't sound like any sort of bet I've ever come across, Abby," said Mr. Atherton.

"Well, it's more by nature of a challenge," said Mr. Rivers.

"Oh, just tell us what it is without trying to justify it with anything sporting," said Mr. Nettlebey.

"Well, I heard about it from Milverton – you know Milverton," said Mr. Rivers.

"Sneering fellow, gulls young idiots like you into gaming houses?" Mr. Atherton asked.

"You can't talk," said Mr. Rivers resentfully. "Yes, that's the fellow. Seems there's an heiress who's going to die."

"My deah fellah!" said Mr. Wincanton, pausing in the act of taking snuff from a silver filigree shovel. "If you think anyone wants to court some old dame who's more corpse than courtable, you have another think coming!"

"Who said anything about an old dame?" said Mr. Rivers. "Milverton overheard his broker talking about her. He, that's the broker, that is, has an uncle who's her accountant, and her father made a packet in speculation. He's dead, the father that is, and she's young, pretty, and she has a diseased heart and is likely to stick her spoon in the wall at any time. And if someone doesn't marry her, she's going to leave all the dibs to a pack of orphans!"

There were cries of outrage at this sacrilegious use of money that could be spent better on clothes, fine wine, wenches and horses, though not necessarily in that order for all of them.

"So, how much is she worth?" asked Mr. Wincanton.

"Not a penny under eight thou, Milverton reckoned," said Mr. Rivers.

"I could get through that in a couple of years," said Mr. Atherton.

"That's per year," said Mr. Rivers.

He had their full attention.

"Of course," said Mr. Wincanton, "we have to hope she ain't like that wench, what's her name, Frances Kendrick, in the Ballad of the Berkshire Lady who turned down all her suitors and insisted on fighting a duel with the one she married."

"Oh don't be an idiot," said Mr. Rivers. "How is she going to be fighting a duel when she's dying? Besides which, that's a ballad, and this is a real female."

"So was the Kendric female, I think," said Mr. Wincanton.

"It don't signify; the rustics who write ballads take a lot of liberties with the story," said Mr. Nettleby loftily. "And it don't matter a damn if an accomplished seducer like Milverton is in the game. Is Milverton making a push for her?" He asked, warily.

"Of course he is! But I figure that if we could get in front, any one of us being more personable and younger, however accomplished the old fox is, we might have a pact that half of her fortune goes to the one who wins her, and the rest shared between the rest of us," said Mr. Rivers. "Providing, of course, that we hang together on this, and none of us tries to sabotage the suit of any of the others."

"We can't exactly hunt as a pack, as one does with lightskirts," said Mr. Atherton.

"No, of course not," said Mr. Rivers, irritably, "but we don't hinder each other. No warm stories about each other, no cutting in on a conversation, you know the sort of thing."

They nodded. They had each used various such tactics without giving or taking offense over the attempts to win the favours of some opera dancer or other, but when it came to marriage, that was different.

"I haven't seen her on the town," said Mr. Wincanton, after sneezing violently. "Demme, I don't like this new snuff of Avery's."

"Why use it then?" demanded Mr. Atherton.

"Because he's all the crack," said Mr. Wincanton.

"Only if you want to look like a wasp with shoulders about to burst with fake wings of buckram," said Mr.

Atherton. "I haven't seen her on the town, either, Abby.

Mr. Wincanton had heard worse from his friend and took it in good part, wanting to hear what Mr. Rivers had to say.

"That could be because she ain't on the town," said Mr. Rivers. "Do be sensible, Ed, the girl is dying. She ain't hardly likely to be racketing about town, is she? Even the fit ones declare themselves burned to the socket by halfway through the season. But she lives out in Richmond, and that's where Julian comes in."

"Me?" said Mr. Nettleby. "I ain't parodying 'Sweet Lass of Richmond Hill for her."

"Wrong Richmond," said Mr. Rivers, impatiently. "That one's about the Richmond in Yorkshire, not the one just out of the city. And I ain't asking you to do anything of the sort. But you have a mad great aunt who also lives in Richmond. You need to persuade her to invite the girl to some quiet soirée or something. She's sweet on you for some reason, ain't she, this aunt of yours?"

"Aunt Augusta likes my poetry," said Mr. Nettleby, with hauteur.

"I said she was bats," said Mr. Rivers, cheerfully. He had to retreat rapidly behind Mr. Atherton as Mr. Nettleby put up his fists and advanced. For a poet, Mr. Nettleby had a rather good physique.

"Here, you wouldn't hit a fellow smaller than you, would you, Julie?" cried Mr. Rivers, plaintively.

"I certainly shall if you call me Julie," said Mr. Nettleby. "It's never stopped me before. Anyway, you always say that short men have an aura of greatness, like Nelson and Napoleon. Say 'pax' and apologise for insulting my aunt!"

Mr. Rivers knew when to throw in a bad hand.

"Pax," he said, sulkily, "and I'm sorry I said your aunt was bats."

Mr. Nettleby resumed his seat, and took a swig from

his tankard.

"Reckon I might visit my Aunt Augusta and see whether she knows the female," he said. "Did you have a name for her, Abby?"

"Fairweather, or some such," said Mr. Rivers.

"Five will get you ten that the little rat has got it wrong," said Mr. Atherton. "Only thing he can remember is the fall of cards."

"My Pater knows a broker or two; I'll ask him," volunteered Mr. Wincanton. "He'll be so pleased I'm taking an interest he'll provide me with names. One of them is bound to know. Come to think of it, the Pater might have known her father," he added.

As Mr. Wincanton senior was well known to do very well from buying and selling shares, this was accounted a good idea. Mr. Wincanton was assured an excellent fortune on the death of his father, and it was in his favour that he would never have wished for his father to die, especially if his own financial difficulties could be solved by some faceless lady, whose death was already inevitable.

The courting club, as it had become, broke up with avowals to meet again and pool information as soon as they had any to pool.

Unaware of being the subject of discussion of some of the town's gazetted fortune hunters, Elinor was more interested in the newest and youngest of her charges, younger than she had intended to take in at first.

Lucy was settling in very well. She was fortunately a child who had been gently trained to obedience, and to not expect much in the way of material goods, whilst cheerfully accepting embraces and kisses as her due. The older girls, even Phoebe, would have treated Lucy as a little living doll had not Libby and Elinor been quite firm in preventing this. As it was, Lucy was made much of, but seemed not to use her position as school baby to try to get her own way.

It would not have got her very far even if she had tried.

Although Hannah helped Lucy in her daily ablutions and dressing, it was Philippa to whom the little girl gravitated more. Philippa was a child to whom animals and smaller children responded well. There was, however, a shell of reserve about Lucy that Elinor and Libby hoped would break down with time. Whilst accepting embraces, Lucy was also happy to run off and play on her own, and did not seem ready to permit anyone deeply into her confidence.

Hannah, meanwhile, was being coolly polite to Rachel and Phoebe; and Philippa and Felicity put their heads together with their Jewish friends to come up with a way of teasing any nonsense out of her, once and for all.

They came down to breakfast with their faces covered with red spots; and Rachel, trying not to giggle, announced,

"The twins have caught Judaism!"

Abigail looked at them dubiously, as Hannah yelped, "Smallpox!"

Daisy said,

"So which of you sneaked your paintbox upstairs?"

The entire complement of that bedroom started giggling, and Hannah went red, then white, then peered more closely.

She burst into peals of laughter that had some relief in it.

"They aren't spots, they're that Jewish symbol!" she said.

"The Star of David," said Rachel, "and it was most awfully difficult painting them on!"

"They kept giggling, 'cos it tickled," said Phoebe.

"Go and wash, you horrid pair," said Abigail.

"Hannah, how pretty you are when you are happy!"

"Am I?" said Hannah.

"Indeed; with laughter in your eyes and a nice smile, you look very attractive. Don't get vain about it," she added.

Hannah smiled at her.

"Thank you," she said, shyly.

"What a pair those twins are, eh?" said Abigail. "Now you understand why I laughed over being covered in flour."

"Yes, I do," said Hannah, in some surprise. "They don't really mean to hurt anyone."

"No, but it's Daisy's and my responsibility to check they don't go too far," said Abigail. "It was clever of them to paint little Stars of David, not spots, though, because spots for real might have frightened the two little ones, and that would have been wrong."

Hannah nodded. She was beginning to understand.

"You handled that very well," said Daisy. "I haven't the patience."

"Oh, I feel sorry for the poor brat," said Abigail. "She reminds me of Kate in 'Taming of the Shrew', who couldn't do anything right in her father's eyes, compared to Bianca, so she delighted in doing everything wrong. Having been given a bit of attention for the right things, she can realise that she need not bite to have people notice her."

"Do you think of everyone in terms of Shakespearian characters?" asked Daisy.

"Oh, pretty much so," said Abigail. "He was such a good observer."

The twins, having made their point, went out of their way to draw Hannah in to a game of battledore and shuttlecock. They and Rachel could truthfully say that they needed a fourth to play, as Phoebe had been taken with Lucy for a nice walk by Elinor, who proposed to improve the shining hour with an impromptu botany lesson on the way.

Hannah enjoyed herself, but caught herself up as she shouted with pleasure at a good shot, and turned anxiously to her partner, who happened at the time to be Rachel, to say,

"Am I betraying Papa's memory to laugh and have fun?"

Rachel lowered her racquet, and put her head on one side in thought.

"Do you believe in Heaven?" she asked.

"Yes, of course!" said Hannah.

"Do you have any doubts that your Papa is there?" asked Rachel.

Hannah frowned,

"Of course not!" she said.

"Then you surely cannot want him to see you be miserable, can you?" asked Rachel. "I think you would only betray his memory if you stopped remembering the good times you spent with him. But I don't know if my thoughts are the same as yours. We Jews hold a vigil when one of our loved ones dies; and we share all the good memories and thoughts about them, as well as mourning their loss to us."

"That sounds lovely," said Hannah, wistfully.

"If you would like," said Rachel, tentatively, "I will ask Miss Fairbrother and Miss Freemantle if you may come home for the weekend, and I know my parents would gladly sit Shiva with you, so you can celebrate your father's life as well as mourn his death. It's usually done before the burial, but we also remember our dead at other times, on the anniversary of their death, and at Yom Kippur, but if you have not had the chance to mourn him properly, perhaps it is better to do it sooner, rather than wait."

Hannah gave her a puzzled look.

"You would do that, even though I am not of your people?" she asked.

"God has put us on the earth to be good to each other," said Rachel, "and I know that I would miss my Abba – Papa – very much indeed."

"I … thank you!" said Hannah. "I am sorry I was rude to you."

"Oh, it was only Cross Hannah who was rude," laughed Rachel. "And she has gone. I would like Sad Hannah to be Happy Hannah, because Phoebe *is* only a very little girl, and the twins have each other, and it would be nice if I had a friend my own age!"

"Then … yes, I would like to come with you," said Hannah.

Mr. and Mrs. Cohen may have been a little taken aback to be asked if they would sit Shiva with a gentile child, but when Rachel explained how upset Hannah had been, they agreed that although they could not say the Kaddesh for someone else, they might sit with the little girl and help her through the mourning process and comfort her. After all, a child was a child, and religion did not have to be a bar in helping her!

Chapter 13

It was quiet in the school with three of its members away for the weekend; Hannah with Rachel and Phoebe had been collected on Friday afternoon, after lessons finished. The twins were busy, entertaining Lucy by helping Mrs. Ashley to dye Lucy's white dresses black, using boughten dyes, as the Reverend Endicote had neglected to see to this duty. Elinor had decreed that it might wait until Lucy was settled in, and besides, someone had to have the time to go to town to purchase dyes. Black was never easy to produce evenly, and the country method of using oak galls was not entirely satisfactory. The twins had been in mourning for long enough that their gowns were purchased especially, but as Lucy would fast grow out of her clothes, it was profligate to buy new ones.

Abigail and Daisy made the most of a fine day to walk in the grounds, while the twins were otherwise occupied and needed no amusing. Daisy was out of mourning for her grandfather, and Abigail was in half-mourning, and Elinor decreed that this should be indigo or white muslin with black or lavender trim, since lavender and grey were disastrous for Abigail's complexion, Anyone seeing through the gate the charming picture of two young girls together, one fair and one dark, talking earnestly, must have assumed that they were talking about the time they might dance the night away at balls; it is doubtful that anyone might guess that Daisy was helping her friend by hearing her Latin declensions!

The figure who came through the gate certainly had no idea that young girls might hold such conversations; for it was the Honourable Mr. Julian Nettleby, who had engineered a reason to call after the Courting Club had pooled their knowledge, and learned the direction of

Miss Elinor Fairbrother, heiress.

Mr. Nettleby came up the drive, glancing curiously at the two girls, and pausing as they altered direction to intercept him. The blonde was extremely pretty, and Mr. Nettleby fumbled for his quizzing glass. He was amazed to see her go white, and take half a step back, a look of dismay on her face as he ogled her. He hastily put the glass back in his pocket.

"'Pologies if I disturbed you, miss, I was overwhelmed by such charm and pulchritude," said Mr. Nettleby, sweeping off his hat and bowing.

The girls looked at each other.

"I don't think you should say things like that to schoolroom misses like us," said Abigail, severely.

"You're schoolroom misses? Hard to tell these days," said Nettleby, abashed. "You ain't, either of you, the lady of the house then?"

"No, sir," said Daisy. "And you don't look like a lawyer, nor someone come to consult either Miss Freemantle or Miss Fairbrother about an orphan for our school."

"Demme, you're part of a school? Already?" Nettleby said, startled.

"Already, sir?" queried Daisy.

"Don't know what I'm talking about. Never mind," said Mr. Nettleby. "Miss Fairbrother, eh? Would that be Miss Elinor Fairbrother?"

"Yes," said Abigail. "Why, sir, do you know her?"

"Well, no, not exactly, but I've heard my Great Aunt mention her," said Mr. Nettleby, who had almost said 'yes' and then realised he would be in the suds as a liar when he persuaded these girls to take him to her. "A school, by Jove! Many of you?"

"Only eight of us as yet," said Abigail. "You ask a lot of questions, sir. And I do not think you are expected."

"Well of course I ain't expected," said Nettleby.

"Thing is, my curricle met with an accident. Axle broke. I was coming to ask for aid."

"Are your horses hurt?" demanded Daisy.

He smiled.

"What a nice girl you are to think of them! No, they are unhurt, and I have hobbled them to eat grass while I seek aid," he said. He was genuinely touched that a schoolroom chit should ask after his prads. "I need to ask if I might bring them in, and see about arranging to have my curricle fixed."

Mr. Nettleby hoped that Miss Fairbrother would extend hospitality to him whilst her own man fixed his curricle; such generosity from one member of the aristocracy to another was often extended. And then he might get to know her quite well enough to steal something of a march on his three friends. Mr. Nettleby did not see this as cheating in any respect, as any of the others might have done the same thing if only they had been clever enough to think of it. Mr. Nettleby was very pleased with himself, and set out to chat to, and charm, these schoolgirls, and find out how come orphans were already at school here when Miss Fairbrother was not yet dead.

His air of address was sufficient to overcome the initial suspicions of the girls, and soon Mr. Nettley learned that Miss Fairbrother had already set aside a sum for the school, and was clever with stocks and shares and was busy making more money. Mr. Nettleby was more impressed than scared off. To him, money was a sordid sort of thing to do with housekeeping, and housekeeping was what women were supposed to do. If Miss Fairbrother was able to make more while she was still alive, then he could afford to be generous to his friends when he married her. Visions of a life of idle luxury, and his poems bound in calf-skin with gilt letters started to fill Mr. Nettleby's dreams.

He was brought somewhat down to earth to find that

he was being taken to a study and introduced to a stern looking lady of uncertain years, and as well to an absolute diamond of the first water. There was also a tall gangling fellow with red hair.

Mr. Nettleby gaped at Elinor, who was particularly in looks for the soft glow to her cheeks from the walk with the little girls. He managed to stammer his way through greetings as Daisy introduced him.

Libby frowned.

"You girls should never have spoken to a strange man at all!" she scolded. "You should have come straight to the house, to apprise us of his arrival!"

"Sorry, Miss Freemantle," said Daisy. "It seemed rude not to greet him."

"And a gentleman on foot might have had a distressing accident, which he had, but fortunately no-one hurt," said Abigail.

"Very well; run along," said Libby, confident that she could put it in such terms now, since Daisy could, after a fashion, run in her heavy boot.

Daisy was gratified by this, and also that Mr. Nettleby had not seemed to have noticed her heavy boot or slightly dragging foot.

Mr. Nettleby had noticed; but was far too much a gentleman to remark upon it, thinking only a vague passing pity for the child.

Once the girls had left, Elinor asked,

"And what can we do for you, Mr., er, Nettleby? Abigail mentioned an accident?"

"Yes, Ma'am. My curricle axle broke. My horses are none the worse, I left them cropping grass, but seeing this fine house I walked back to request assistance," said Mr. Nettleby. "And when the girls mentioned that the owner was a Miss Elinor Fairbrother, I recalled my Great Aunt Augusta, that's Augusta, Lady Herongate, having mentioned you," he bowed to Elinor, "though she had not mentioned your exquisite beauty."

"I have not spoken to Lady Herongate since Papa took me to pay respects after Lord Herongate died," said Elinor. "As I recall I was about Daisy's age with bad skin and plaits. A pale, skinny and unremarkable child. I believe I was also sick on her."

"The number of sweetmeats she fed you, that was hardly surprising," said Libby, dryly. "I know she meant to be kind, but it was misplaced."

"Great Aunt Augusta is kind," said Mr. Nettleby, "and her cook makes the most delightful sweetmeats, so I understand the temptation! Why, I am sure she would like to see you again for she was speaking to me only last week about how sad it was that you have lost all your family, and do not enjoy good health! I can quite see why you might want to surround yourself with other young girls," he added, with a moment's insight.

"Well, you must stay here for tea, of course," said Elinor, "and then I will have John Coachman take you to the coaching inn. They will be able to send someone to collect your curricle and take it along for repair. John can also collect your horses and tie them to the back of the carriage, so you need be under no apprehension of any horse thief making off with them." She rang the bell, and when a footman answered gave orders for both tea, and for John to put the carriage up ready to take Mr. Nettleby to the coaching inn.

It may be said that Mr. Nettleby was somewhat disappointed. Apparently it showed, because Elinor gave him an austere smile.

"You understand, of course, that I cannot offer you hospitality when I have young girls in my care; most ineligible," she said.

Mr. Nettleby's eyes strayed to Dr. Macfarlane, who smiled cynically.

"I'm the school doctor," said he. "Would you be the Julian Nettleby who had a poem accepted by the '*Mirror of Fashion*'?"

"I am," said Mr. Nettleby, much gratified. "Did you like it?"

"I thought it had promise," said Dr. Macfarlane, who felt he had to give credit when it was due. "It's a shame you overworked it; I could see where you polished it too much and it made it the most awfu' drivel in places. Where you left it alone, I liked it fine well. You should trust your first feelings and not try to be too high-sounding, for it does not suit you."

"Oh, the piece *'To a Shell'*," said Elinor. "Libby and I thought it excellent in parts, but I fear I must agree with Dr. Macfarlane; I cannot like poetry with too many classical references in it, for it always sounds as if the writer is merely showing off his education. I suppose the editor made you put in all the references to Amphitrite?"

"He did," said Mr. Nettleby, who had been torn between gratification and chagrin. "And I was not that happy with those two verses. I must say, it's very nice to be able to converse about poetry with knowledgeable people; my usual friends just scoff. I've known them since we were at school together," he added by way of explanation.

He included Dr. Macfarlane in that warm encomium, pleasure in discussing his poetry briefly overcoming the object of his visit. Still, it might be turned to advantage!

After tea, Mr. Nettleby made his farewells, thanking Elinor for her kindness, and being equally assiduous in his thanks to Libby and Graeme Macfarlane. They would not be surprised now to receive invitations from Aunt Augusta. And at a soirée he might read some of his better poems to impress Miss Fairbrother, and gain some knowledgeable criticism too.

"A personable young man, I suppose," said Libby, when Mr. Nettleby had gone.

"For a rogue," said Graeme Macfarlane.

"Do you think it was all a ruse?" asked Elinor. "If his axle was not really broken, would he not wish John not to see it?"

"Oh, I'm sure he managed to break the axle, or brought a broken one along and hid or threw away the good one," said Dr. Macfarlane. "I suspect he quizzed those little girls quite well too. But at least he's not an idiot like the Codfish in a dog-collar."

"It would be hard to be less personable, and more foolish," said Elinor, who had no difficulty in recognising the Reverend Endicote in that description. "Libby, prepare a written report on Lucy's progress, I pray you, before the first of next month, that the Reverend Endicote may be given by a servant when he turns up. I shall be diplomatically indisposed or busy," she added. "Surely, Dr. Macfarlane, you are being a trifle over-anxious in your anticipation of fortune hunters? It is not unreasonable to suppose that Mr. Nettleby should be in this vicinity if he has been visiting Lady Herongate. A broken axel might happen to anyone, especially a young man in a curricle taking corners too fast without regard to the condition of the road."

Dr. Macfarlane shrugged.

"You may believe what you like, Miss Fairbrother, but I find a distinct smell of fish in a fortuitous accident almost right outside your gates. Just because he is personable and pleasantly spoken does not preclude him from being a fortune hunter. I am just suggesting caution. Now, if you will excuse me?"

"I pray you, do not take umbrage just because I am concerned lest your cautiousness be misplaced," said Elinor.

"I am not taking umbrage. But I have work to do," said Dr. Macfarlane, stiffly, bowing before he left.

"Impossible man!" said Elinor. "Also stiff-necked, and suspicious of anyone who might happen along."

"I would take his advice to be cautious, nevertheless, if I were you, my dear," said Libby. "The young man may have been plainly quite smitten by your beauty, and even if he is a fortune hunter, it does not follow that he is not a pleasant fellow. If he courts you, then you should be business-like from the very first, because an honest suitor will be honest about his situation."

Elinor nodded.

"Very true, Libby. And any man who comes to care for me at all will also care for my desire to help girls who are less fortunate. I could wish that Dr. Macfarlane was less suspicious, though. He is kind to be looking out for me, in such respect, but I have to say that I have never had the opportunity to be treated as a beautiful woman, and I should very much like to enjoy the sensation without him glowering."

"He does not wish you to be hurt, my love," said Libby.

"Well, I suppose that is true, and is kindly of him," said Elinor. "He is a fine man, and so clever, but then he manages to do or say something that irritates me, and all the camaraderie that has built up between us dissolves into argument! I like Mr. Nettleby," she added defiantly.

It may be said that Elinor was not the only young woman to find Mr. Nettleby quite personable, and despite the bad start over his quizzing glass, Daisy found her dreams disturbingly invaded by Julian Nettleby.

Naturally, she dismissed such foolish thought from her mind!

Chapter 14

It may be said that though Philippa was entirely indifferent to Geography with Globes, Felicity fairly hated it. Neither of the twins was looking forward to Monday morning, on Friday. Each girl had been assigned a country, which they were to have researched, with regards to its produce, and to have a good idea of the borders of the country. This border outline was to be drawn on the chalk-board, with major geographical features added, and the girls were to speak about the major exports of their assigned country.

Since Rachel and Phoebe were absent for the weekend, and not in their normal beds, and therefore unable to notice any nocturnal activities, the naughty twins slid out of bed when the rest of the house was asleep. There was much subdued giggling, and certain preparations were employed in the schoolroom – as yet there was only one – before they returned to bed to sleep far better than their consciences deserved.

The twins were, of course, heavy-eyed and sleepy at breakfast, and Mrs. Ashley, presiding, asked sharply if they felt unwell.

"Oh no," said Felicity.

"We didn't sleep well," said Philippa with daring honesty. "My feet were cold," she added with inspiration. Her feet had been cold. She had forgotten to put on slippers.

"So were mine," said Felicity, who had remembered and had still got cold.

"I will ask for a hot brick to be placed in your beds tonight," said Mrs. Ashley. "We don't want to risk chilblains or chills!"

They murmured guilty thanks!

The arrival back in school of Rachel, Phoebe and Hannah distracted official notice from the twins' heavy eyes, fortunately for them, for Hannah was quite a different child, pale but animated and full of how kind Mr. and Mrs. Cohen had been.

Rachel, her arm through Hannah's, and with Phoebe along, begged that Phoebe and Hannah might exchange sleeping arrangements, for Phoebe rather fancied the idea of being the older one with Lucy, rather than being the baby with the three older girls.

Libby was glad to agree to this, and was pleased that Hannah had been so well helped. If exchanging ideas worked so well, then having a wing solely for Jewish orphans would be quite beneficial!

In the schoolroom, it was the youngest girls who must say their piece first, though it was deemed beyond Lucy's abilities at her age. She was still working on reading, writing and figuring with Elinor. Hence, first to go was Phoebe.

Phoebe had been given the United Kingdom, as the easiest country, since she was so much younger than the group of eleven and twelve year olds who were the next youngest. Phoebe took up her piece of chalk with some trepidation.

"England is an Island," she began, and placed chalk to board.

It gave a horrible squeal, and Libby winced, as did the other girls.

"Do be careful, Phoebe," said Libby.

"Yes, ma'am," said Phoebe, glaring at the chalk, and trying again.

Another squeal.

"Whatever is wrong?" demanded Libby, exasperated.

"Please, Miss Freemantle, I can't help it!" said Phoebe, close to tears. "And it isn't leaving a mark! There's something wrong with the chalk!"

Libby frowned slightly, and took another piece of white chalk from her desk, and attempted to draw a line across the board.

It squealed horribly and left no mark.

Libby lightly touched the board with one finger.

"I see," she said. "Who has soaped the chalk board?"

The twins rose.

"We did, ma'am," said Felicity.

"We didn't mean to upset Phoebe," said Philippa.

"I see," said Libby. "And when did you perform this, er, treatment?"

"After everyone had gone to bed," said Philippa.

Libby's brows rose as she regarded the pair.

"Very well," she said. "You will wash off the soap thoroughly while the rest of the class get on with their mending or embroidery; and we shall have geography after the mid-morning break. During the break you may each write an apology to Phoebe; to me; and collectively to your fellows for this disruption. I hope you will prove well-prepared for your lesson afterwards, or you will have to repeat it. After luncheon, you will go to bed whilst the rest of the class have their dancing lesson, by way of making up for your lost sleep."

The twins were aghast. Not only had they failed to prevent the hated lesson, and miss dancing, but they must apologise too, something Felicity in particular hated. This Libby knew full well, of course, and as she suspected Felicity of having talked Philippa into the scheme, the extra punishment for Felicity seemed meet.

It did not occur to the twins that going to bed rather than taking strenuous exercise was more for the good of their health than being intended as a punishment. They struggled through their apologies, having washed off the board, and fervently hoped that they would not still be smelling soap when eating their luncheons!

Once the apologies had been read out loud to the class, Phoebe made her map and produced a clear account of Britain's cotton and wool trade, and how other countries learned from the steam power that drove the looms; Rachel tackled India, with its cotton and spices, tea, silk and ivory; and Hannah declared that Denmark exported actors, having become rather confused with 'Hamlet'.

"Well, Hannah, you have had a difficult time," said Libby, "but I think you might have managed a little better than that. You need not repeat the lesson in front of the class, but I will expect you to present me with a more coherent list of Denmark's produce than princes from Elsinore."

Hannah went red, and returned to her seat.

And then it was the turn of the twins.

Somehow Philippa managed a not too inaccurate outline of Spain, and managed to say something of its exports, even if she became sufficiently muddled with history to claim both Francis Drake and the Duke of Palma as principal exports alongside merino wool, horses and Xeres or sherry wine.

Felicity made a dismal showing with Italy. She managed the outline of the boot-shaped country without too much difficulty, but having no idea what Italy might export, she claimed that it exported nothing, being under the joint heels of the Pope and Joseph Bonaparte and the Romans.

"Oh Felicity!" said Libby, "you have relied too heavily on avoiding this lesson. I fear you must lose your leisure time after tea, to study this lesson again, and you may repeat it to me before you go to bed. And Philippa, you managed Spain's exports, but Francis Drake was more by way of a temporary and unwelcome import, and belongs, like the Duke of Palma, in your history book. It might have slipped the notice of you both, but Joseph Bonaparte is no longer King of Naples and Sicily, but is now King of Spain. I am sure, however, that Daisy and Abigail will be able to tell us a lot about Canada and America."

There were no dramatics nor startling revelations from the older girls, who had taken their studies seriously, and it gave Libby a chance to calm down before going to the staff sitting room to bury her head in a cushion to give vent to whoops of laughter.

It may be said that the new principal exports of Denmark, Spain and Italy afforded much amusement to both Elinor and Graeme Macfarlane!

The twins were much refreshed for sleeping during the afternoon, and Felicity was later able to speak with what passed for confident knowledge about Leghorn straw hats, wine, fruit and pumice stone, as well as marble and culture. She had been helped by her twin to come up with this list.

Libby accepted that Felicity had done her best, and sent her to join her fellows.

Elinor received an invitation for herself, her companion and the resident doctor, to visit Lady Herongate, who would be at home the following Saturday.

"It's April the first; I hope it's not an April fool's joke," giggled Elinor.

"The April Gowk will be yon stuffed cod of a clergyman who threatened to call on you on the firrrst," said Graeme, cheerfully.

"Why, how fortuitous!" said Elinor. "I had been half inclined to decline, since it is also Easter Saturday, but to avoid Mr. Endicote, I shall accept. Libby, if you have completed that progress report, let us place it in a wrapper and send it to his address, for Lucy knows his direction, and a little note that one could not expect him to call in person, especially on the Easter weekend, so we thought to arrange to have the budget to be delivered. He will have to pay for it too," she added, cheerfully. "Of course, his threat to visit might have been hollow."

Graeme Macfarlane sniffed.

"He'd call, drawn as is a needle to north pole in a compass, to the lodestone of your wealth," he said.

"You are a cynic, Dr. Mac," said Elinor affectionately.

"Aye," he agreed. "Dr. Mac? Wheel, I fancy it's quicker to say, especially when you're shouting at me for ma caution."

"Oh, I'd want to shout at you in full," said Elinor. "You don't wholly like this invitation, do you? Even if it does get us out of having to greet the Reverend Endicote?"

"I don't trust young Nettleby's motives, but if he's a scoundrel, at least he's an amiable scoundrel, unlike yon nasty critter that has had wee Lucy screaming in nightmares. Mrs. Ashley roused me to give her something to help the puir bairn sleep. Seemingly she's afraid God is like the Reverend Endicote, and her poor Mama and grandparents in his clutches. I told her that he was no more like God than a cod, and that cheered her up."

"Better medium than a sleeping draught, I'd say," said Elinor. "Why did you not tell me?"

"Weel, Hannah had raised Mrs. Ashley, rather than disturb you, and after three nights running, Mrs. Ashley fetched me, and as the nightmares then seemed to stop, I did not think you need be disturbed," said the doctor.

Elinor frowned.

"Libby and I always need to know, even if it is now sorted out," she said.

"To be honest, I forgot, with yon young fellow turning up," said Graeme, apologetically.

"Ah, the human reason of forgetting, I am happier about," said Elinor. "Rather than think you were keeping anything from me."

"I raise my hands to the omission, ma'am," he said.

Elinor chuckled.

"Well, I wish to go to Lady Herongate's little gathering, even if only avoid the piece of cod that passeth understanding," she said.

"Och, you are a naughty piece," said Doctor Macfarlane. He did not seem to mind her facetious mangling of the prayer book.

Hannah and Rachel were quickly firm friends, and as Elinor said to Libby, a nice quiet antidote to the terrible twins.

"There's no vice in the twins, they just don't think," said Libby.

"Oh, I know, but they have the other two now to think for them, now Hannah has decided to be a nice little girl, and not so noxiously pious," said Elinor. "I wager they'd not have been out of their beds at all hours if Hannah had been in the room, and she won't be going to the Cohens as a regular matter, even if they are kind enough to invite her again."

"I agree," said Libby. "Well, they now have learned that creative shirking doesn't work, so that is a lesson which will stand them in good stead, if it goes in."

"Yes, I learned the same object lesson, trying to get out of embroidery, and encouraging cook's kitten to play with my threads," said Elinor, with a wry smile. "You made me untangle them all without cutting them, and I still had to embroider that wretched cushion cover. No-one can avoid a duty, and attempting to do so only costs time and effort."

"I think it was your one real rebellion, my love," said Libby, "and I concealed from you that I was so delighted that you had found the spirit to rebel, invalid though you were. Once we began debating, which I felt readily able to do after that, as you had shown yourself ready to display your own mind, I was quickly able to see that you have plenty of spirit."

Elinor chuckled.

"Some might say too much spirit," she said. "I confess, you channelled it very effectively in teaching me how to understand percentages, profit and loss, so I could help Papa."

"In my opinion, you were always the more astute financial mind of the two of you," said Libby. "I could not do it for myself, but I could understand your choices, and marvel at the acuity of your transactions."

"Perhaps we should teach the girls," said Elinor. "It may be considered unwomanly, but if they understand finance, they are less likely to be swindled out of any small sum they accrue."

"Indeed," said Libby. "My dear, would you think it forward or pushing of me to suggest loaning the older girls a small sum to try speculating for themselves with Mr. Everard's help, to make it more real for them?"

Elinor looked thoughtful.

"Why not?" she said. "They might then keep any profit they make, placed into a bank account for them, which would give them a cushion of some financial security. A nominal sum to loan them, perhaps, say an hundred pounds, and if they lose it, then they may do work to cover the loss, to discourage reckless gambling."

Libby nodded.

"Very wise, my dear, to permit them to pay back any loss with work. Though of course an hundred pounds is not a nominal sum to most people."

"It is hard to speculate properly with much less, though, not and expect a good profit," said Elinor. "They have a better chance of making some real money that way. Or if speculating frightens them, they may choose their speculation to be merely to put it in government funds for a year, and take but a return of four pounds. And that is commendable caution at that."

A letter penned to Mr. Everard brought that worthy

to visit the school, and the girls thus received their first visit by a trustee. Mr. Everard did his duty in hearing lessons to encourage the girls. Unfortunately Felicity dreamed enough during her lessons to inform him that a giraffe had a long neck and was like an ostrich with spots, meaning [as Philippa explained] that both came from Africa and had long necks even though one was an animal, and the other a bird. Mr. Everard laughed, and said he had never had any interest in zoology in any case, and his one interest in ostriches was that their feathers might be bought abroad for four shillings a pound, selling wholesale at a pound a pound, and selling retail for anything from six shillings to a whole pound each, depending on how expensive a dye had been used if any, and that since there were a lot of feathers to the pound, it was a deucedly profitable trade.

"My goodness!" said Felicity, shocked. "That is quite a lot to pay extra for vanity!"

"And I wager the poor natives who gather the feathers get a pittance," said Hannah, who had been reared by her father to think of things like that.

"Poor ostriches," said Philippa, predictably.

This led neatly into discussing markets, and the profit to be made by selling something that cost relatively little in one place for a profit in a place where it had scarcity value, and Felicity cried out,

"Why, now I understand about wine being exported, and why it is imported here, because of grapes growing far better in warmer countries!"

Finally! Thought Libby. Finally, Felicity grasps the point of Geography!

It may be said that both Abigail and Daisy were quite excited at the idea of being permitted loans to speculate, once they had learned enough of the theory. They listened avidly to the explanation that high profits on such goods as ostrich feathers might be affected by the next season's fashion decreeing that feathers were *passé*, so that the goods became valueless, and that such high profit speculations carried a concomitant high risk! Mr. Everard took them to one side to discuss such things, and have their first lesson in economics.

Chapter 15

"My father was in the East India Company, Mr. Everard," said Daisy, thoughtfully. "I know he was only a clerk, but they were allowed to speculate, and at first there were gifts sent home, that Grandmama had to sell after Grandfather died. I think it might be in my blood, because I find the idea of speculating very exciting, especially since Miss Fairbrother has done so well from it, so nobody can say that a lady cannot."

"Miss Fairbrother is very talented," said Mr. Everard. "Your father did not manage to speculate later?"

"All I know is that he wrote to Grandmama saying that he had the chance to buy some shares that were a bit risky, but which could make the family's fortune," said Daisy. "it was not long after that when he and my mother died in some epidemic ailment, I presume, without realising any profit, or possibly without even having bought the shares."

"Dear me!" said Mr. Everard. "Well, well! I will make some enquiries. Though it may be some considerable time before I hear anything, of course!"

"Oh that is quite in order, sir; indeed I was not asking for any such favour," said Daisy, quickly. "I am resigned to being poor, though I am not so resigned to being parted from Grandmama."

"I am happy to make enquiries; more than I should have been had I thought you were fishing for me to do so," said Mr. Everard. "It is no trouble, I assure you! And if your father was defrauded in any way, then there might be some recourse through the John Company, that a man of affairs might get set in train where a little girl would be ignored. Besides, I confess myself intrigued," he added, honestly. "Now, what sort of goods or shares would you consider speculating in?"

"Fashion accessories," said Daisy, without hesitation.

"They seem to be cheap items that are marked up considerably, because the *haut ton*, and indeed the burgeoning middle classes, do not care what they pay for the correct accessories. And I should, if Miss Fairbrother is serious about making us a loan, like to purchase silk and muslin and fabric dyes, and such irons as are used for shaping, gophering irons, I think they are called, and set up one or two poor girls in business, paying them a wage with some share in the profits as a bonus, to make flowers for hats and gowns, only I do not know how to administer that."

"Well now!" said Mr. Everard, beaming approval. "I suggest I might negotiate a percentage of the profits if I act as your agent in this, and see to the details for you, if that is acceptable?"

"If that is the proper practice, then I should be very happy, sir," said Daisy, earnestly. "I have fashioned silk flowers from scraps myself, but the milliners have special small irons that they use to shape them, on starched and painted muslin as well as silk."

"Very enterprising," said Mr. Everard. "Have you ambitions to be a modiste or milliner rather than a governess?"

"No, sir, but if I may make a little money by sponsoring other girls, and do good for them too, then it seems a good idea," said Daisy. "It is a long time before I leave school, and by then, many things, may have changed, so I would be foolish to think too far ahead."

He nodded.

"Long term planning is often wise, but at your tender age, a year or even two ahead is quite enough for you to consider," he said.

Abigail was less ambitious than her friend, beyond being set in her ideas that she would not purchase shares in goods like coffee or sugar that rested on the slave trade. She preferred to wait and learn more, and then to stick to the trade of shares, not actually set up a business as Daisy wanted to do!

Meanwhile, Philippa's propensity to collect needy animals had led to Elinor suggesting a menagerie, where Philippa might house the half-fledged birds fallen from nests, which were her main focus for the moment. Most died, leaving the little girl quite woebegone, but a robin with more will to live than most had survived, and delighted the school with his liquid song. Libby was tolerant of the little bird insisting on riding around on Philippa's shoulder, but she drew the line at a three-legged frog in the pocket of Philippa's pinafore. Libby firmly informed Philippa that this was causing the frog to suffer, since he needed a damp place, and resignedly permitted the child to use a chipped hand-basin as a makeshift pond in her menagerie.

Arbuthnot the rat could not be banned by so cogent an argument, after Philippa rescued him from a trap in which he had received a broken leg and tail, and as the creature came to a rapid accommodation with Allan-a-Dale the robin, Libby merely adjured Philippa not to permit her rodent to disrupt lessons.

Mrs. Ashley, however, banned all animals from the table, which decision Libby and Elinor upheld.

Philippa had an ally in the cook over kittens, as that worthy was an ailurophile, and merely warned Philippa to keep Arbuthnot out of the clutches of Corinthian Tom, the kitchen's resident ratter and rake. Until cook had had him gelded, Tom had provided most of the kittens in the vicinity, and still mounted any queen in heat, though, as Elinor said, fortunately without resultant progeny. As Tom did not permit any other males on his range, including his own offspring, this did reduce the number of spring kittens rather, only those enterprising travelling queens producing litters.

It may be said that Dr. Macfarlane became Philippa's hero over one such kitten, whom Philippa, sobbing in earnest, brought to his office. The kitten, a tabby and white little girl, had had her eye pecked out by a jackdaw and was screaming piteously.

"Please can kitty have laudanum, Doctor?" asked Philippa.

"No, my dear girl, Laudanum has the opposite effect on cats and would make…her…feel worse," said Dr. Macfarlane, having quickly checked under the triangular tail. "I will give her valerian."

Dosed up with valerian, the kitten was moderately quiescent, and Philippa staunchly held her still, ignoring bites and scratches, as Dr. Macfarlane deftly removed the ruins of the eye, cleaned the socket, and stitched it up.

The kitten thenceforth rejoiced under the name Columbine, and even Mrs. Ashley tolerated her sleeping in Philippa's bed. Mrs. Ashley would have been less happy had she known that Arbuthnot was wont to curl up there with Columbine as well; but even Hannah, who disliked rats, did not let on. Nor did Cleo Ashley, who was in on the secret, and who admired Philippa greatly!

Philippa's pets were tolerated by the other girls, even Hannah finding compassion for Arbuthnot, even if she, and some of the others, privately referred to him as 'that wretched rat'.

Elinor was very dubious.

"If that child has a mania for keeping unusual pets, she'd never be acceptable as a governess," she worried.

"Nonsense," said Graeme Macfarlane. "The child would be perfect as a governess to small boys. Besides, I was thinking, you might prefer to permit her to work in the stables, and employ her yourself to teach younger girls to ride and drive. She's quite as horse mad as she is crazy for any other animal."

Elinor was much struck by this idea.

"Dr. Mac, there are times when I could quite hug you for your practical good sense," she said.

He laughed, blushing.

"I'll not object," he said. "It seems to suit being given a nickname"

"Now don't spoil a good friendship by flirting," said Elinor.

"Well, I like that!" said Graeme, in mock indignation. "When it was you who started it by threatening to hug me!"

Elinor laughed.

"Well, I don't deny it's a good idea to offer Philippa the choice to work in the stables. It does relieve my mind!"

"With small numbers, you can afford to keep the girls until a perfect situation arises, too," said Libby, "although that will not be practical if the school grows."

"I feel a responsibility towards them, to find somewhere suitable," said Elinor. "But as always, you are correct, dear Libby. We cannot keep all of them forever."

"You might consider keeping the bluestockings, however, and make this school a haven of academe," said Dr. Macfarlane. "Offer paying places to young women who have the means not to need to marry, and who would have been more suited to a university education. You may have to extend the library, of course."

"That is something I would scarcely be likely to object to!" said Elinor. "And as well to have as broad and deep a library as we might. Perhaps you will keep an eye out for library contents for sale in families that have fallen on hard times, Doctor Mac! And I, for one, will enjoy a life of quiet contemplation and study, myself."

"Quiet? With nine children?" said Doctor Macfarlane, with heavy irony."

Elinor shrugged.

"I suppose it is a matter of what you call quiet," she

said. "I find the voices of children, however loud, quite soothing if they are not vexed in tone. It would be the bustle of town and the mayhem of the social whirl I would find disturbing."

"Why, woman, do you want your cake and eat it too?" demanded Dr. Macfarlane. "You said you would have liked to be courted by the likes of young Nettleby!"

Elinor chuckled at his outraged look.

"Well, yes, and in my salad days, I might have liked the social whirl, at least for a while. Now, however, I find I am satisfied with the occasional social event like Lady Herongate's 'at home'," she said.

"Salad days, forbye, as though you were past your last prayer," said Dr. Macfarlane.

"Indeed, you are still young, my love," said Libby.

"But past the first blush of youth," said Elinor, "and beyond the foolishness of secretly longing to dance until dawn. Though how much of that was the natural desire of a young girl, and how much was a longing for the forbidden and impractical things I was not supposed to be healthy enough to do, I could not truly say."

"Oh it is the desire of almost all young girls to want to dance to dawn," said Libby. "I had the same urges, I assure you, but as the daughter of an impoverished clergyman, I had, like you, to put aside such thoughts as impractical, even if for different reasons."

Elinor embraced Libby.

"Should we give our girls each one season?" she asked.

Libby considered.

"The expense of a season is considerable," she said. "Perhaps... perhaps it might be something you might offer as a special prize to the girl who is voted by the others to be the most amiable and pleasant? It is, at least, not something you need think about for several years, as none of them are old enough."

"What a good idea!" said Elinor. "And if a Season goes to the one felt most deserving by the others, it cannot be thought to be unfair. When we have more pupils, after all, we cannot expect to provide for all of them in like fashion."

"It won't do any harm that the chances of a season rest on their own behaviour," said Dr. Macfarlane, "and might prevent any difficult ones from putting on their parts quite so thoroughly."

"Cynic," said Elinor.

"Yes. I'm Scots," said Dr. Macfarlane. "Seriously, though, girls of a certain age tend to be somewhat emotional, and jealousies and cliques can form in ladies' academies. Incentives for good behaviour have always seemed to me to be better than punishment for bad behaviour."

"I heartily agree. I am sure Libby and I both feel as you do on the subject," said Elinor, cocking an interrogative eyebrow at her one-time preceptress, who nodded.

"Ah, I'm back in favour, am I?" asked the doctor.

"You usually are in favour," said Elinor. "We've had arguments through misunderstandings, but I hope we are now all friends and able to disagree and quarrel amicably."

"For a governess," said Dr. Macfarlane severely, "such a paradox in your language as 'quarrelling amicably' is distressing."

"Does he look distressed, Libby?" asked Elinor.

"Not in the least, my love," said Libby.

"What, you're ganging up on me, are you?" ginger eyebrows rose.

Elinor giggled.

"Oh, we must make game of you when you are so horribly pedantic at us," she said. "I have just had a thought! Do you think that Lady Herongate might consider inviting our older ones to small gatherings, to give them some social experience?"

"Not knowing the lady, I cannot comment," said Dr. Macfarlane.

"Dear me, I am not sure," said Libby. "She is, as I recall, a trifle eccentric, my dear, and indeed, I believe, given to quixotic gestures. I suspect much will depend on whether she decides to like you, for she will not even notice me, and whether she considers your desire to educate girls left destitute to be a noble gesture. I fear she might equally consider it a futile gesture, and refuse to have anything to do with the girls. She will," she added, "approve of Dr. Macfarlane, whose views tally with her own. I recall her telling your father that he did you no favour in encouraging invalidish habits, but suggested that he should let you play like other girls your age. He was outraged at what he saw as callousness, which, I fancy, is why you never visited again. She said that fresh air and exercise might do you the world of good, and if it killed you at least you would die happier for it."

"Dear me, I wish I had known" said Elinor. "I believe I find myself quite in charity with her, and so I shall say!"

"Your father forbade me to mention it, for fear of losing you, too," said Libby. "He meant well."

"An epitaph that can be ascribed to only too many," said the doctor.

Chapter 16

"Lady Herongate!" Elinor smiled as she greeted the old woman, clad regally in the brocades of her own time.

"Hmmph, you look healthier than the last time I saw you!" said Lady Herongate.

"Well, you see, I have just learned from Libby that you suggested sensible measures to my father, that so horrified him, which Dr. Macfarlane also recommended to me more recently. He was of the same mind as you, and has been making me run about and play in the fresh air. Or rather, take vigorous walks, which have been most beneficial!"

Lady Herongate regarded Dr. Macfarlane through a pair of ornate lorgnettes, with the most modern oval eyepieces. Apparently her nod to the fashions of the past did not extend to the wellbeing of her eyes!

"A fine figure of a man. Pity he's red," she said, regardless of the doctor's feelings. "Well, young man, I just dismissed my physician for his inability to cure my tiredness. What would you suggest?"

"A course of chalybeate waters, cabbage soup once a week and an egg every day, go to bed before midnight at least five nights a week, and buy shoes that are comfortable and not in the fashion of the last century," said Dr. Macfarlane, promptly.

"You subscribe to the belief that Chalybeate waters are of assistance, then?" demanded Lady Herongate.

"You are pale, which suggests your blood needs building up. Ale will help too. But Chalybeate waters have been shown to have an excellent effect on a flagging constitution," said Dr. Macfarlane. "Country folk drop a nail in water until it rusts and drink that instead, it's the same thing. You pay your money and you take your choice, expensive waters and the social life in a spa town, or a bag of nails for a penny and your own company."

She laughed.

"I like you, doctor, you do not seek to flatter me. I may just try a rusty nail in water; I dislike spa towns. Full of old people, invalids and people of flagging constitutions. They remind me of what I am and it depresses me."

"Then avoid them; depression of the spirits can never be recommended," said Dr. Macfarlane.

"May I steal him?" said Lady Herongate to Elinor.

"No," said Elinor, "I like his progressive ideas in my school. If he cares to come to a private arrangement with you to visit as your physician when I don't need him, that would be between him and you."

"Well?" demanded Lady Herongate of Dr. Macfarlane.

He bowed.

"If my duties permit, I should be delighted. A patient who is open and honest and does not want to be flattered is a patient any sensible doctor should be delighted to have."

"Humph, operative word there being 'sensible'," said Lady Herongate. "Well, well! I'll introduce you about, don't suppose you'll remember all the names, there are some I wish I didn't remember, but one is obliged, with neighbours, you know... and my great nephew's idiot friends that he would have me invite. He's up to something, but I'm fond of him, so I indulge his little plots. Probably fishing for an heiress," she added, then asked, "*Are* you still dying?"

"Not according to Dr. Macfarlane, and I have come to mostly trust his judgement," said Elinor.

"Well, I shall put Julian right about that, then, before he reads his idiot poem about beauty nipped by frost. Not that it ain't a good poem, because it is, at least, I think so but it ain't appropriate. Thought it was tactless enough before, but still!"

"I would like to hear it, nevertheless," said Elinor, "as I might not have done if I had been dying! It may not be appropriate, but if it was well-written, it cannot displease!"

Only Libby heard Graeme Macfarlane mutter something about how much it might displease him.

Mr. Nettleby quickly moved forward to extract the object of his interest from his aunt, who could be, as he said to his fellows, a bit too much of a good thing.

"Miss Fairbrother!   And umm... Permit me to introduce you about, I will happily make introductions for you, Aunt Augusta! Come and meet my particular friends first!"

"Don't forget that I have other guests here too," said Lady Herongate, tartly, "and that she ought to greet the Dowager Countess Heatherston first as a matter of precedence."

Mr. Nettleby had forgotten, but he flashed his ready smile at his aunt, saying,

"Of course!" as he propelled Elinor to meet a beturbanned dowager, who looked as though her heavily leaded face might crack if she smiled.

"What's this I hear about you starting a charity school, and letting girls in to enjoy your legacy before you're even well buried?" she snapped.

Elinor subdued the rebellious urge to snap that it was more likely to be someone who looked like an Egyptian mummy who was likely to be buried first, and smiled. If her smile was a trifle brittle, the dowager did not seem to notice.

"Why, indeed, I have started a charity school, for just the female orphans of gentlefolk for the time being, but it has given to me such a lease of life that I have decided not to die after all," she said.

"Hmmph," said the Dowager. "Of course, I subscribe to a charity school in my parish, but naturally they are taught according to their station in life."

"Naturally," said Elinor, dryly, picturing depressed peasant children learning enough to read the Scriptures, plain sewing for the girls and perhaps enough botany to make simple herbal remedies if they were lucky. She might have to visit this school, and if its preceptress was amenable, offer scholarships to any children clever enough to crave more. In which course, it would be as well not to antagonise this acidulated old woman, who was doubtless one that Lady Herongate wished she could forget.

"I presume you are fitting your orphans to be governesses or other such genteel employment?" demanded Lady Heatherston.

"Oh, yes according to their natural bent," said Elinor, resisting the temptation to say 'no, we are training them to be acrobats for Astley's Amphitheatre' since Philippa would probably consider that a fine idea. She went on, "All children are different, of course, and all have different talents to explore. These first ones, as may be assumed, I may train up to teach specific subjects at my own school, so that future orphans have a rounded education to offer. One would wish them to give the best possible service as governesses, of course, and there are, too, genteel jobs for lady illustrators and colourists, modistes, music teachers, librarians; and for those with no skills but sweet nature, companions to lonely ladies, or even as chaperones for hire!" and she smiled brightly.

"Hmph!" said Lady Heatherstone, unable to find any fault.

Mr. Nettleby tactfully extracted Elinor.

"Frightful old bore," he said. "Scares me silly."

"Yes, but she may be useful to my orphans, so I did not say what I was thinking," said Elinor serenely.

139

"Here, I say, you ain't looking on me as useful to your blast- to your orphans?" demanded Mr. Nettleby.

"You mean as a poetry teacher? Or to teach them how not to descend to blushing confusion with the opposite sex?" she asked.

He stared.

"Miss Fairbrother!" he expostulated in a hurt tone.

Elinor relented, and laughed.

"Oh, I will be pleased enough if you take an interest in my blasted orphans," she said, "but I do not demand it. Now Dr. Macfarlane has assured me that the diagnosis of heart disease was entirely incorrect, I may enjoy the children at my leisure, and need not throw myself into their wellbeing with the frenetic fervour I had intended when I thought I was dying."

He stared at her.

"You are not then living on borrowed time?" he asked.

"No, indeed; and I am already healthier for the good doctor's regime," she said gaily.

Warring emotions stirred in Mr. Nettleby's breast; but the finer ones won. He seized her hand and shook it vigorously.

"Congratulations!" he cried, and beckoning for his friends, declared, "Miss Fairbrother ain't going to stick her spoon in the wall after all, that red doctor of hers has cured her!"

"Strictly speaking, there was nothing to cure," murmured Elinor, amused and also hurt at the looks of shock and chagrin that warred with the admiration of her beauty on the faces of Mr. Nettleby's friends. His own pleasure in her health was gratifying, but alas, Dr. Macfarlane had been correct, irritating of him that it was, about Mr. Nettleby being a fortune hunter, and his friends too. However, there was no reason not to enjoy their company, if admiration of her looks overcame a desire to have the advantages of a rich wife's legacy without the disadvantages of having her growing old first. It was unpleasant to think that she was more use to any one of them dying than living, but Mr. Nettleby's congratulations had, she felt sure, been quite sincere. Maybe his friends might get to know her for herself too.

The others were assessing the fact that Elinor was very beautiful and was still worth eight thousand pounds a year, and that one might take mistresses when she lost her figure in bearing children.

Abernethy Rivers recovered first, though he was disconcerted that Miss Fairbrother was several inches taller than he.

"How delightful for you to have a permanent reprieve, Miss Fairbrother," he said.

"Indeed," said Elinor, "though I confess that I am taken aback to discern that my supposed heart disease is common knowledge, and even a matter of gossip. Since I have always lived quietly and never came to town, this is a shock."

They exchanged guilty glances.

"Word of a diamond of the first water soon spreads, ma'am," said St. Clair Wincanton, earning him a look of approval from his friends.

"Very pretty," said Elinor, brightly. "One might almost suppose you were thinking purely of my looks, and know nothing of my fortune at all."

"One cannot but be aware of your fortune," said Edward Atherton. "After all, there are many diamonds of the first water every season; and also many heiresses. The scarcity value in having both in one person is remarkable enough to fuel gossip."

"Your friends do think very well on their feet, don't they?" said Elinor to Mr. Nettleby.

"What have you said, Julie?" demanded Mr. Atherton, being the only one of the other three sufficiently sportingly inclined to take the risk of using Mr. Nettleby's hated nickname.

"Nothing," said Mr. Nettleby, indignantly.

Elinor nodded.

"But you just have, Mr. Atherton," she said. "Well, it is interesting to be prized for my fortune, not my conversation, my intellect, or even my looks." The scorn in her voice made Mr. Nettleby wince.

"It's not like you think," said Mr. Nettleby, unhappily.

"Tell you what," said Mr. Atherton, "Why don't you and your companion come for a trip down the river? We could row down to Eel-pie Island and eat eel pie?"

"What a splendid idea!" said Elinor. "Two boats, each with two gentlemen rowers, Libby and me as chaperones, one in each boat, and let me see, the twins, Harriet and Rachel in one boat, the two older ones, Phoebe and Lucy in the other, and no reason little Cleo should miss out on a treat too. I will make arrangements to have the boats reserved. Next Friday, and we meet at Richmond Bridge at ten in the morning?" she suggested.

Mr. Nettleby gave a crack of laughter.

"Miss Fairbrother, you are the most complete hand!" he said. "Da...dashed if I've ever seen Neddy Atherton so thoroughly silenced before!"

"Been years since I rowed," said St. Clair Wincanton, mournfully, looking at his beautiful white hands and assessing the effect rowing would have upon them.

"Oh, if you aren't capable, Mr. Wincanton, I am sure Dr. Macfarlane can take your place," said Elinor. "He's an Oxford man, so of course he can row."

"I didn't say I was crying off, Miss Fairbrother," said Mr. Wincanton, indignantly.

"Well said, Sin," said Mr. Nettleby.

"Sin?" asked Elinor.

"Short for St. Clair," said Mr. Nettleby.

"Of course," said Elinor. "Silly me. Is that agreed, then, gentlemen?"

There were rather shifty murmurs of assent, and Elinor smiled serenely, and moved on to speak to other guests.

"Piqued, repiqued and capotted," said Abernethy Rivers, gloomily. "You sure you didn't tell her anything, Julie-an?" he hastily added the name's ending as Mr. Nettleby frowned.

"I didn't," said Julian Nettleby, "but by Jove! A girl who can work it out, who's that pretty *and* rich is a girl worth courting. Dammit, it would be worth courting her even if she weren't as rich as a Nabob!"

"I'm beginning to wonder if it's worth it at all," said Mr. Atherton, gloomily. "Nice compliant cit who wants the entrée to the *ton* would be much less trouble."

"You ain't crying off, either," said Mr. Nettleby, firmly.

"I am going to regret this," said Mr. Atherton.

"This is harder work than you made it sound at first," said Mr. Wincanton, accusingly.

"I had no idea she had a brain as well as looks and a fortune," Mr. Rivers excused himself. "It's Nettleby's fault for putting the wind up her somehow."

"I did not," said Mr. Nettleby. "If I had, she wouldn't have come, would she?"

There was no argument to that.

Mr. Nettleby reflected that he had discovered something about Elinor's abilities when he had found out that she had made her own fortune. He wondered if he should feel guilty about not having shared that with the others, and decided that they would not have appreciated the significance of this, and therefore he had been under no obligation to do so.

"I reckon Neddy's right that we are going to regret this," said Mr. Wincanton.

"Crying off?" said Mr. Nettleby, hopefully, suddenly realising that if his friends backed out, it left the way clear for him. He had a feeling Miss Fairbrother liked him despite her insights.

"I say it's harder than we thought, and winner take all," said Mr. Rivers.

"Taken," said Mr. Nettleby, quickly.

"No. We have a pact," said Mr. Atherton.

Mr. Nettleby mentally shrugged. Neddy and Sin would drop by the wayside, and it would only be between him and Abby. And Abby was shorter than Miss Fairbrother.

Chapter 17

"You were right," said Elinor, on the way home.

"About him being a fortune hunter?" said Dr. Macfarlane. "Believe me, my dear lady, it gives me no joy."

"I prefer to know," said Elinor. "I do not know exactly what is going on, but he and his three friends somehow have some kind of agreement. I do not know what, but I suspect that these wretched young men plan to share my fortune if any should win me."

"Impudent puppies!" growled Dr. Macfarlane.

"Are they not, indeed!" said Elinor. "However, they may as well be useful until they have realised that it is a bad idea to try to fool me, so we are taking a trip downriver with them next Friday."

"We?" said Dr. Macfarlane, with deep suspicion.

"Libby, me, and the girls," said Elinor. "You shall please yourself whether you come or not, since the one decrying the damage to his hands did not wish to cede his place as a rower to you."

"I'll come," growled Graeme Macfarlane.

"Excellent," said Elinor. "It will be good to have a reliable man along in case any of them manages to hurt his silly self. Perhaps you will organise the hire of two boats large enough for the trip?"

"I will, and I shall enjoy watching those precious young men trying to row," said Graeme, trying not to snigger.

"I fancy they are skilled enough," said Elinor. "Or else I should not trust the girls to their rowing. I fancy that Mr. Nettleby at least will urge them on, for I believe his pleasure in my good health was quite genuine."

Graeme scowled.

"I have to admit that I believe you are correct," he

said, reluctantly.

"Is it very missish of me to have wanted to cry because they wanted to be rich widowers?" burst out Elinor.

Graeme ground his teeth.

"I'll knock all the young puppies out!" he declared.

"That might be satisfying, but making use of them to give the girls a treat is more so," said Elinor, "and they cannot row if knocked out."

"Forgive me; any decent man would want to set about those wee naifs for behaving so," said Graeme.

"I find it rather nice to know that my anger and hurt is not unreasonable," said Elinor. "I feared I was being altogether too full of sensibility."

"Oh my love!" said Libby, "how very lowering it has been for you, I cannot begin to imagine how you must feel!"

A small sob burst from Elinor's lips, and Libby put her arm around her.

Graeme Macfarlane produced a large handkerchief.

"The world is a wicked place," he said.

"It has cured me of wanting to be courted and flirted with," said Elinor. "I am glad, though, that I did not go into society when I was a callow child of seventeen or eighteen; I might not have seen through their scheme. And then I might have ended up marrying one of them, or another like them."

"But you have not, and you see clearly now," said Libby. "And you will doubtless make a good choice when you want to marry."

"If I ever meet many men who are not elderly because they are my trustees," said Elinor. "Mr. Nettleby is amusing, and I had hoped…."

"My dear, if he is honest to you after this, you need not give up hope of him," said Libby. "So long as he is aware that you have already tied up half of your fortune in trust for the orphanage."

Elinor brightened.

"And I shall see then if it is me that he is interested in, or only the money," she said.

"Huh," said Graeme Macfarlane.

Elinor's butler was waiting, portentuously.

"Why, what is the problem, Baxter?" asked Elinor, anxiously.

"I'm waiting here in case that wretched clergyman comes back, Miss Elinor," said Baxter, grimly.

"Oh, he did turn up, then?" said Elinor.

"Yes, Miss Elinor. And he said he'd wait, even though I gave him the package that there wasn't time to send by post, and I commented how fortuitous that he was passing by. A hint," said Baxter, heavily, "that passed through one ear and out the other, Miss."

"Nothing in between to impede its progress," said Dr. Macfarlane.

"No, sir," agreed Baxter. "He said he might wait for you to return, for he was sure you would want to offer him dinner if it was late before you returned."

"*Did* he now!" said Elinor, eyes sparkling angrily.

"Yes, Miss Elinor; but Mrs. Ashley routed him, if I may say so, horse and foot. She stood there and harangued him about how the girls should not have strange men in the house with only herself as chaperone, and before he knew where he was, he was out on his ear," he added with glee.

"Mrs. Ashley is quite invaluable," said Elinor. "The man is insufferable! If he calls again, you may tell him that my orders are that he is not to be permitted in the house at all. And if he forces his way in, you may call the stable boys to eject him with force."

"Very good, Miss," said Baxter, with a satisfied bow.

It was, after all, of some moment to the servants too, who was courting Miss Elinor!

It may be said to have proved a quiet Easter Sunday, providing one did not count the necessity to retrieve Philippa and Cleo from the stable roof, after the rooster chased Columbine up there in the afternoon.

Columbine wailed piteously, and Felicity ran for adult aid. Philippa climbed up the decorative brick work, followed by Cleo.

Dr. Macfarlane brought a ladder, which he told the girls severely might have been better to have been used in the first place, rather than the projections and niches at the corners.

"There wasn't time! I was afraid she would fall!" cried Philippa, peering anxiously at her pet, perched, washing unconcernedly, on John Coachman's windowsill, overlooking the ridge of the stable.

"Felicity," said Dr. Macfarlane, "Ask John Coachman to go to his room and open the window carefully. If he can grab that dratted animal, so much the better. The girls will be safer climbing in the window than having me carry them down the ladder. Stay with him to encourage your sister and Cleo."

"Yes, doctor," said Felicity, impressed by this show of common sense.

Finding Felicity in John Coachman's room, Elinor swiftly opened the wardrobe door to hide the rather salacious print on the wall beside it, and shutting it hastily on finding that John had pasted the even more salacious French lithograph on the inside of the door. Hopefully the girls would be too preoccupied to notice the naked ladies. John gave a sickly smile, and firmly stood in front of the print. Elinor gave him a nod of approval.

"Sorry to invade your privacy, John," she said.

"You're welcome, Miss," said John in resignation.

Libby waited at the bottom of the ladder to back up Graeme's commands from the top of the ladder if necessary.

148

It was Felicity who managed to scruff an indignant Columbine just before the kitten shot off back down the ridge. Felicity called to Philippa and Cleo,

"I've got her safe, come along the ridge and in here!"

Philippa nodded, and shakily rose to her feet. Libby gasped.

"Oh no...." she whispered. "She cannot *walk* the ridge, surely!"

Philippa, however, could and did walk the ridge, and reached the window safely.

"I... I *can't*!" cried Cleo.

Philippa promptly turned round and walked back. Elinor and Libby both stifled cries of consternation.

"You don't have to walk, Cleo," Philipa said. "Of course, your Papa was a gunner, and didn't go aloft, so nobody could expect it. If you get your knees each side of the ridge, you can crawl along."

Cleo nodded trustfully, and did as she was bid. Philippa never knew how many bad moments she cost her preceptresses as she strolled backwards along the ridge, encouraging the little girl. Dr. Macfarlane stood ready on his ladder to catch her if, as one might hope, she fell on the side he was; which was at least the dangerous side, being the side of the cobbled yard.

Elinor watched, heart in mouth, as Philippa sat down on the windowsill and held out her hands to Cleo.

"You have to credit the little miss with being pluck to the backbone," declared John Coachman.

"And a very naughty child," said Elinor, crisply as Philippa put one of her legs inside, lest she get any ideas from John that she was a heroine.

"But Miss Fairbrother, I had to go after Columbine," said Philippa.

"It was not that which angered me," said Elinor, helping Cleo over Philippa's lap. "It was over endangering another child. You should never have persuaded Cleo to come with you!"

Philippa looked aghast.

"Felicity and Hannah would not," she whispered. "Cleo volunteered…"

"Better a volunteer than three pres'd men," said Cleo, with a lopsided and shaky smile.

"Cleo, you should, instead, have asked one of the men for a ladder to assist Philippa," said Elinor. "The pair of you will go straight to bed, and you will have only bread and milk for supper. I don't want you having nightmares on anything richer. Cleo, you are very fortunate that your mother is out, and has not yet heard about your escapade. If you promise me that you will try to think before pursuing some mad cause, I will try to make sure that she does not find out."

"Oh, Miss Fairbrother, thank you!" said Cleo, dropping a curtsey.

Elinor gave an exclamation.

"That gown will never be the same again! Philippa, you will give Cleo one of your gowns to compensate. *Why* were you girls not wearing pinnies?"

"Because it's Sunday, Miss Fairbrother," said Philippa, "and Easter Sunday at that. We're in our best."

Elinor sighed.

"Of course," she said.

Trust that dratted cat not to take any account of the day!

"And if I had had a weak heart, I swear that watching that wretched girl walk back and forth along the ridgepole would have carried me off with a heart attack if nothing else would," said Elinor, wrathfully, to Libby and Graeme.

"At least it proves your heart is as strong as anyone's," said Graeme. "The child has no nerves at all!"

"And I have aged a dozen years, I swear," said

Libby. "I can only comfort myself that those twins must surely learn some sense and discretion as they grow older."

"I shouldn't lay a wager on it, with Philippa, if any animal is at risk," said Graeme, cheerfully.

"No, nor should I!" agreed Elinor. "But at least it was an act of compassion, not of deliberate naughtiness, though I had to punish her for risking a child of lower estate, and younger than she is. At least Mrs. Ashley was away for a pleasant afternoon's walk away from children, and need not be troubled. I did not have to tell Cleo how frightened her mother would have been had she seen her; I think she will be more sensible in future."

"There's that in Philippa that attracts animals and other children to her," said Libby. "Fortunately, she is utterly unconscious of it, and it would never occur to her to use it to lead other children. But sick animals trust her, and other children follow her."

"Keeping her on, to teach riding and carriage driving really is the safest option," said Elinor. "I dread to think of the reaction of any employer if their governess strolled about on the ridge of their stable block."

"At least she had the sense of responsibility to go back for Cleo, and use her influence to the good," said Graeme.

"Oh, my dear Doctor, yes, indeed!" agreed Libby.

"Apart from that walking backwards, which had me terrified, I should have punished her more severely had she not gone back for Cleo; and I see why she went backwards too," said Elinor. "You are right, Libby, the hearts of the terrible twins are in the right place, even if their intellect sometimes seems to be..." she struggled for a word.

"Awa' with the fairies," supplied Dr. Macfarlane.

"An excellent and apposite phrase," said Elinor.

It was Libby who came upon a woebegone Felicity, sitting in the dark in the library; for Libby had overheard a stifled sob.

She went directly to the window-seat where Felicity was lurking behind curtains, and sat down and put an arm around her.

"Your sister is quite safe, my dear," she said.

"Oh, I know, and it isn't that," said Felicity. "Not that I don't care, because I do, because I'd hate anything to happen to Philippa, but you see..." she hiccupped. "... Oh, Miss Freemantle, have you ever wished to be as brave as someone?"

"Yes, my love," said Libby. "I could have wished to have been as brave as dear Miss Fairbrother, who has lived believing she was dying; and yet speculating as hard as she could, and taking financial risks to make sure that girls like you would be taken care of, even if she might not be here to see it. She is not as ill as was believed, but believing erroneously that you are going to die is no easier than if your belief is correct. I admire her tremendously, but I know that I am different, and I have other skills and talents. As you are different to Philippa, and have other skills and talents. *You* were the one who had the good sense to fetch adults other than those daft stablehands who did nothing but gawp. You have grown up such a lot in the few weeks you have been here, and I am so proud of you!"

Felicity cast herself on Libby and wept. Why she was weeping she would have been hard pressed to explain; but Libby suspected it was mostly in relief at her twin's safety, and partly because Libby was proud of her as she was, and did not expect her to be 'pluck to the backbone' as those idiot stable-hands had called Philippa.

Chapter 18

Monday brought a letter from Mr. Nettleby, and Elinor raised an eyebrow, wondering if it was a polite recollection of another engagement on Friday.

Far from it, Mr. Nettleby declared that he had persuaded his friends to meet with the orphans on Wednesday, for a picnic tea, in the school's own grounds. He wrote that this would mean that the girls had a chance to meet four strange men, and overcome their shyness, before being plunged into a river trip, and would hopefully thereby avoid being plunged into the river in an excess of sensibility. If, he added, such an arrangement should prove acceptable to Miss Fairbrother.

She read the letter out to her confederates.

"You have to hand it to the wee tyke, he is determined," said Graeme, when she had finished reading it out.

"Dear me, and quite sensible, too," said Libby. "Getting all the giggling out of the way on our own home territory, so to speak, is preferable to having silly little girls indulging in silly behaviour on Richmond Bridge."

"Aye, it's a clever suggestion," said Graeme. "And can do no harm that I can see; if the wee lasses are acquainted with men who are fortune hunters, it'll be no harm to their education, forebye."

Elinor duly wrote back, a cheery letter of acceptance, and thanked Mr. Nettleby for his suggestion. She asked him to pass on her thanks too, to his friends, for their indulgence of the little girls involved.

She had no doubt that Mr. Nettleby's friends were firmly damning him for having landed them with this extra duty. Elinor wondered if they were murmuring the extent of her fortune to themselves like a litany, as a means of bolstering their courage for the ordeal of nursery tea with nine schoolroom misses. Well, the schoolroom misses would not learn any younger how to prepare a picnic tea to entertain gentlemen.

The girls were quite excited about the idea of preparing a picnic for gentlemen, and, as Elinor pointed out, a governess might have to entertain the father or brothers of her charges, so it was a skill that might prove useful.

Abigail and Daisy declared that it would be a simple meal of sliced ham, sliced beef, mustard, pickles and salamagundy in bowls, and bread-and-butter.

This was a meal that was simple enough to be a suitable nursery meal, and yet not looked down upon by gentlemen, who would be assuaged by copious quantities of ham and beef. They might feel a lack of pies and pasties, but bread-and-butter would make up for pastry. Rachel and Phoebe declared themselves happy to eat just hard-boiled eggs with their salamagundy, and might have more of that, as it was hard to arrange a picnic in which some food was Kosher and some was not. The Cohens kindly supplied the little girls with food suitable for their beliefs for normal meals, for which Elinor was grateful.

When Wednesday arrived, and Abigail and Daisy were packing the hamper, Daisy suddenly cried,

"We have forgotten to ask Mrs. Baxter to get us any salad stuffs, and I declare, nothing here is yet grown enough!"

"What are we going to do?" asked Abigail, in consternation. "We must have salad for the Salamagundy!"

"Country salad," said Daisy, pulling herself together. "The twins do well at botany; let's tell them to get some edible greens."

Felicity and Philippa thought it hugely exciting to gather country salad, and Daisy sent them to check in Culpepper's illustrated herbal to seek out comfrey in the herb garden, and smallage, and chives, and watercress in the stream if they could manage to gather it without falling in.

"I don't trust them to tell wild parsley from hemlock," said Daisy, "and we shouldn't want to poison anyone!"

"I don't think I could tell wild parsley from hemlock," said Abigail, candidly. "Where did you learn so much?"

"Galen and Pliny, mostly," said Daisy. "And I also helped the vicar, who taught me by making simples for his poorer parishioners. I can't cook or sew to save my life, and I have no accomplishments like piano or harp, but I can tell one herb from another. Hannah and Rachel and Cleo can wash and chop the greens whilst you and I gather parsley, dandelions, young nettle tops and anything else I notice that is edible."

"Goodness, there is a lot to eat in the country!" said Abigail. "But won't nettles sting our mouths?"

"Silly, we shall pour boiling water on them to remove the sting!" laughed Daisy. "Nettles are good eating, and you can also make soup from them, or cook them in butter with onions and a little garlic."

Abigail was amazed!

All was prepared, and the children were setting off as Mr. Nettleby arrived, and offered to help by carrying the basket.

His friends were not far behind, and if Elinor thought it profligate of the efforts of their horses not to share a carriage, she did not say so. They were scarce more than boys, after all, and proud of the toys they drove.

A fifth carriage was seen coming up the drive, and it stopped half-way to permit a figure to alight, as the groom took the carriage the rest of the way.

Lucy gave a little cry of consternation, and hid behind Phoebe.

"Drat the man, it's that Endicote fellow," muttered Elinor.

"Is he a problem, Miss Fairbrother? Can I rout him and lay his scaly tail at your feet?" asked Mr. Nettleby.

"Oh dear, I should not have spoken so, and out loud," said Elinor, in a low voice. "He brought Lucy without a by-your-leave, and he basically informed me how grateful I should be to receive his suit. Or that was the impression I gained. I escaped him by being at your Aunt's 'at home' on Saturday, when he called, but I fear I have no pressing engagement elsewhere. I pray you distract him while I slip away; I fear losing my temper and saying things that should not be uttered in front of the girls."

"Willingly will I distract the slimy wyrm!" said Mr. Nettleby, gaily. "Why, hello, sir! Can I help?" he hailed the vicar.

"A picnic? How splendid! I shall join you!" said Mr. Endicote, rubbing his chubby white hands together. "Dear me! Have we brothers of the orphans, or can it be that I have rivals in the suit of Miss Fairbrother?"

"What sir, surely you are not considering courting so young a lady as Miss Fairbrother, are you?" said Mr. Nettleby, with well-feigned surprise, and longing to plant a fist in the man's fatuous face.

"Indeed, and why not?" huffed Mr. Endicote. "The spiritual guidance of a man of the cloth is so important for a young thing so soon to meet her maker!"

"I think you will find reports regarding Miss Fairbrother's impending demise may have been premature," said Mr. Nettleby.

"Aye, they are," Graeme stood up. "I'm the lady's doctor, and the only thing likely to make her unwell is you, you canting hypocrite."

"Dear me! *Red* of course," said Mr. Endicote, sitting

himself down calmly on the rug. "Salamagundy? Splendid!" and he began to help himself.

The girls, used to waiting to be told they might eat, stared in horrified fascination.

"Well, if he can, I can," muttered Edward Atherton. "I'm famished."

"I'd wait for our hostess if I were you," muttered Sin Wincanton; but Mr. Atherton winked, filled a piece of folded bread-and-butter with salad and ham, and disposed of it in two bites.

"We'd be in awful trouble if we were greedy pigs like that," muttered Felicity, resentfully.

"Gentlemen are supposed to eat like pigs," said Philippa.

It may be said that her voice was more carrying, and Mr. Atherton flushed, and refrained from any further forays into the food.

"Children should be seen and not heard," said the Reverend Endicote, with his mouth full.

Most of the little girls turned away in disgust.

"*Who* is this, exactly?" demanded Mr. Rivers.

"Och, he's but some opportunist who believes Miss Fairbrother to be dying, who wants his ring on her finger to inherit the wee bitty amount of her fortune that is not entailed," said Graeme Macfarlane, loudly.

"I beg your pardon? Entailed?" said Mr. Rivers.

Graeme smiled, beatifically.

"Miss Fairbrother has entailed her fortune to be used for the orphanage. She has left only a nominal sum for herself," he said.

Endicote actually stopped eating.

"You jest, surely!" he cried.

"Not at all," said Graeme, who was enjoying himself at the looks of outrage and consternation. It might not be strictly true, but as Elinor had sent for Mr. Embury to see about making some provision of the kind, and was therefore in the spirit of truth.

"She's a fine woman, and any man she chose would be fortunate indeed, with or without money," said Mr. Nettleby.

Graeme gave him a searching look.

"I respect you for that," he said.

Mr. Nettleby regarded him with as much thought.

"May the best man win," he said.

"*Julie!*" said Mr. Atherton, awfully.

Mr. Nettleby shrugged.

"I didn't know," he said. "Don't make any difference to me. Not like gundiguts over there." He nodded at Endicote.

"*Well!*" said the Reverend Endicote, "I won't stay here to be insulted.... And I feel damned ill!"

"Don't swear in front of the children," said Libby, who scarcely knew how to deal with so much bad mannered behaviour.

"I'm not surprised, the way you were stuffing your face, without so much as Grace being spoken," said Graeme. "Man, you look ill!"

"I... I feel giddy.... My heart! I have palpitations!" cried Mr. Endicote.

Daisy quickly poured water from a carafe into a glass, and stirred in a generous amount of mustard.

"Drink this," she said.

"I can't...."

"*DRINK THIS!!*" cried Daisy. "Twins, show me your comfrey leaves." She emptied the rest of the salamagundy into the picnic basket and thrust the bowl at Endicote.

"Dear Lord," said Graeme, "Miss Freemantle, have you smelling salts? Sal ammoniac and emetics are an antidote to digitalis, quick work, Daisy."

"I have smelling salts," said Elinor, who had just returned, having noted the men helping themselves and deciding that Libby might need support rather than maintaining a cowardly distance.

"I say, we had better purge Mr. Atherton, too," said Daisy.

"I'll see to that, Miss Daisy," said Mr. Nettleby. "C'mon, Ned, mustard in water, and retire behind a bush to throw up; you're more civilised than that cleric."

"Did we really *poison* him a little bit?" asked Philippa, in hushed tones.

"You tried to kill me!" yelped the reverend, between heaves.

"It was an *accident*!" sobbed Felicity.

"I will have the *law* on you for this and you will be hied off to gaol, and the school will fail," said Endicote, viciously.

"You will not," said Graeme. "How childish of you to scare children with lies like that!"

"It was an *accident!*" reiterated Philipa.

"To be sure it was," said Libby. "Dear me. And if the gentlemen had only waited for Grace to be said and permission to eat, I am sure I would have noticed, as would Daisy, that the leaves were quite wrong, and they would not have been ill; a lesson upon greed, my dears. At least Daisy has aimed Mr. Endicote and the bowl away from the food, which you had better pack away, and we shall have ham, beef, pickled and boiled eggs, and such salad as may be safely extracted, and we shall eat indoors."

"I hope the lot of you die of it," said the Reverend Endicote.

"I do wish the doctor hadn't been here, then *he* might have died," muttered Lucy to Phoebe.

"Hush! That isn't a nice thing to wish!" said Phoebe. She spoiled this excellent sentiment by giggling.

"How thankful I am that I did not get ahead of myself like Ned!" said Mr. Wincanton.

"Gluttony is one of the deadly sins," said Elinor. "My dear Dr. Mac, do you think that you will pull him through?"

"Thanks to Daisy, yes," said Graeme. "And thanks to her, and to your ammonium, we should be able to send him home to sweat and vomit to his heart's content before nightfall, so you won't be troubled by him."

"I'll drive along with him, if you like," said Mr. Nettleby.

"Thank you," Elinor smiled warmly at him. "We cannot have him die because of our silly girls, who cannot tell the vein pattern on comfrey from that of foxglove! I believe our next botany lesson must be to draw both, side by side."

"A useful lesson," said Graeme. "As well for them to only poison parsons on purpose."

"You are too full of levity to set a good example," said Elinor, reprovingly.

He merely beamed at her. Apparently he was well aware of this fault and indifferent to it. Elinor shook her head, laughing. What could one do with a doctor who chose alliterative word play over good taste?

Mr. Endicote, ministered to by Daisy, Elinor and Dr. Macfarlane, whilst Libby saw the girls inside, was a moaning, shivering mound. Daisy later described him to Abigail as looking like the ghost of a blancmanger.

"I'm going to the nearest inn for a proper meal," said the thoroughly purged Mr. Atherton.

"Me too," said Mr. Rivers. "Still, the look on that fellow's face…"

"I think we've had a lucky escape," said Mr. Wincanton. "Just imagine; if the mort ain't about to turn up her toes, we'd be saddled with pestilential brats for the rest of our lives."

Mr. Nettleby's friends retired, vowing never to return.

"So much for the river trip," said Elinor, who had overheard more than the young men had intended.

"Oh, I'll see if I can hire a couple of sturdy sailors, if

the doctor will row with me," said Mr. Nettleby.

"Oh, would you? I'll give you the wherewithal to pay them, of course," said Elinor.

"It would be a pleasure," said Mr. Nettleby. "I haven't laughed so much in an age. I like the brats. Here, load that quivering thing into its carriage; he's an offence to the landscape."

"I almost like you," said Dr. Macfarlane.

"Are we in awful trouble again?" Philippa asked Libby, later.

"No, my dear, because you are both fully repentant of your foolish mistake, which was in no wise a deliberate act. And as Miss Fairbrother says, we shall diligently study the differences between comfrey and foxglove. Perhaps Daisy gave you too much credit for recognising one from the other, and I am sure she feels guilty for not overseeing what you gathered. No real harm has been done! I think, however, it is about time that all you girls who have not already got a commonplace book should start one, to keep. It will be something you will have all your lives, as future reference, and to inscribe interesting knowledge and sketches."

"We were given them by our governess before she died," volunteered Felicity, "But we had not put much in them, beyond the poem she wrote for each of us, on...." She flushed.

"On stopping to think before we did or said anything we might regret," finished Philippa. "What should we be putting in them?"

"Oh, all kinds of things!" said Libby. "It depends much on your interests. Some girls and women sketch scenes in them; others collect recipes, for culinary dishes or for medicines, or both. Miss Fairbrother has some fine botanical paintings in hers, and also calculations of the stock market."

"I have written wise sayings that I have heard in mine," volunteered Rachel, "And recipes that I can adapt to being Kosher."

"Daisy has caricatures of Cicero in hers, with some of his quotes," said Abigail.

"Also recipes for a variety of simple and cures," said Daisy. "And yes, I am kicking myself that I did not check your leaves, twins! But because we all collect different things, it is why it is called a commonplace book. One places in it the commonplace thoughts one wishes to remember. And I am going to draw a series of sketches of the Reverend Endicote, just because it will make Lucy giggle, so she won't have nightmares again. And then I can look back in later years, and enjoy the irony of saving the life of someone that I think we had all half hoped would choke to death on his own gluttony."

"Oh, Daisy, it is quite true, but I wish you will learn not to say what everyone is thinking," sighed Libby.

Daisy shrugged.

"I was taught not to be a hypocrite," she said.

"Well, my dear, in time you will learn that there is a fine line between hypocrisy and tact," said Libby. "Dear me, *what* an eventful day!"

Chapter 19

Rabbi Cohen turned up early on Friday, and asked Elinor if she would be kind enough to give a situation to a widowed Jewish woman of his acquaintance, who could cook for the two Jewish girls, and would be willing to visit the Israelite Markets in Duke's Place, Houndsditch, whilst Mrs. Baxter was shopping in whichever markets she favoured.

Mrs. Baxter favoured Leadenhall Market, famed for its excellent quality, which was also convenient to East India House. Here one might purchase tea and muslin, such supplies being needed regularly, if less frequently than comestibles. Leadenhall St was not very far from Houndsditch, so a joint shopping venture was quite practical. Besides, said Mrs. Baxter, when the matter was broached to her, she was not averse to visiting the Duke's Place Market herself, preferring it for the purchase of its excellent fish to the sometimes rough and unsavoury Billingsgate Market.

Elinor was happy to employ this Mrs. Isaacs, as a favour to the Rabbi, since Mrs. Baxter was more than happy to have someone to prepare kosher food. Elinor duly invited the Rabbi to bring Mrs. Isaacs at his convenience, and invited him to join the boating trip.

Simon Cohen declined gracefully, as time would be, he said, a trifle tight, if he wanted to see Mrs. Isaacs installed safely, and he would not wish to delay the excursion.

Elinor suspected that he preferred to avoid the unseemly scene of being taunted by gentile sailors in front of the children, and could have wished to have unsaid the invitation lest it caused him distress; but decided that least said was soonest mended. He had, after all, managed a perfectly reasonable excuse. As for Rabbi Cohen, he was actually more pleased than embarrassed that the gentile lady had issued the invitation quite as naturally as if it had been to the relative of any Christian child. He felt a little mean to have refused, but it would do the children no good to be subjected to a potentially ugly scene.

The little girls were excited at the outing, and Libby and Elinor found it necessary to hush them more than once, and threaten to leave behind anyone who behaved like a hoyden!

Needless to say, this resulted in much improved behaviour.

Nine nice young ladies walked sedately from the carriages to the landing place. The two sailors and Mr. Nettleby were already there.

"A word with you, Miss Fairbrother, if I may, while the girls climb into the boats," said Mr. Nettleby.

"Oh dear me, I fancy it might be better to have a word with me before they attempt to get into the boats," said Elinor. "I should like to have Miss Freemantle and myself in the boats first, to encourage the children."

"Ah, of course," said Mr. Nettleby. "Beg pardon, Miss Fairbrother. I'll be brief, if you will walk with me for a moment…"

Elinor stepped to one side, wondering greatly.

"What is it, Mr. Nettleby?" she asked.

"You already guessed that my friends and I were fortune hunters and had a pact to help each other to win an heiress," he began, "Which, I confess, I now feel ashamed of, since I know you as a person, not a name."

"I am glad of that, Mr. Nettleby," said Elinor. "I suspected that to be so, or I should not have encouraged your continued association with myself and with the school."

"I admire you tremendously," said Mr. Nettleby, abruptly. "However, that is by the way, but it may explain why my fellows have… have…."

"Fallen by the wayside in seeing that I am not an easy ripe fruit for plucking?" said Elinor.

He winced.

"Er, quite," he said. "But you see, though I've known those three since we were children, and never stopped to consider much about them, I have always known that Ned Atherton can be... mean. He...he is vindictive. And he blames you for being humiliated in having to be purged at the picnic. Even though it was his own stupid fault for eating before anyone else did."

"Dear me," said Elinor. "I trust that he is not aware of the names of the children accidentally responsible?"

"He ain't interested in children, and I'll make sure he never finds out," said Mr. Nettleby. "But he does hold you responsible, and I heard him swearing vengeance."

"What could he do to gain revenge, and dear me, how very melodramatic and childish that sounds, for his unfortunate experience?" wondered Elinor.

"I'm not sure, but I fancy he'd like to see you humiliated and he don't care if you and any of the children get hurt," said Mr. Nettleby. "I'll try to find out."

"Thank you, Mr. Nettleby, I appreciate that," said Elinor.

"What makes me truly sore at Ned is that the whole scheme was thought out by Abby Rivers, but Ned blames me, because I got Aunt Augusta involved," said Mr. Nettleby, grimly. "He's not entirely rational about it. But just a word to the wise to look out."

Elinor nodded.

"I will. I dislike intensely that you lent yourself to this scheme, but you have behaved with perfect propriety since seeing its impropriety. I am only sorry that it has led to one of your friends acting so badly, and losing your friendship; though the loss is much more his than yours."

"True," said Mr. Nettleby. "I can do without friends

who would be willing to cause trouble for a splendid lady and innocent children."

The girls embarked upon the boats, with more or less difficulty, a few shrieks and a lot of giggles, interrupted only by Cleo saying sharply to the two sailors,

"Belay that, you lubbers!" as they murmured something.

The two men looked sheepish.

"We didn't know Miss was the daughter of one of our own," said one.

"Who I am doesn't matter, you shall not speak so of our kind governesses!" said Cleo.

"Cleo," sighed Elinor, "Your partisan and staunch loyalty is appreciated, but that is quite enough. What the sailors think is of no moment, though, I am tempted to dock some of their pay for commenting inappropriately within the hearing of children. They are paid to utilise their skill rowing, and their strong arms for the same. What they do with any stray thoughts that they may muster, providing kept behind their teeth in front of children, is between them and God."

She pretended not to hear when Cleo muttered to the sailors,

"And any stray thoughts are so few that roundshot could pass through your ears without disturbing them!"

The chastened sailors rowed without comment, and if Mr. Nettleby and Graeme Macfarlane could not match their strength and skill, they did not make a bad showing. Libby had encouraged the girls to bring their commonplace books, having supplied some for those girls who did not have them. She made suggestion that they make sketches or write word pictures of anything that caught their attention, and fervently hoped that this would not include any salty language.

There was a sufficiency of visitors to Eel-Pie Island

to make the girls quite shy, which Elinor was thankful for. The island was inhabited by an elderly couple. The husband set his traps for eels, and cut osiers with which to weave his traps, selling excess to others for basketry. His wife, meanwhile, made the eels into pies that were sold to food sellers throughout the metropolis. The old man explained to the party of children that he was also responsible for the care of the swans, and his good lady sold bags of crumbs and pastry for the delighted little girls to feed to these magnificent creatures.

Lucy was somewhat nervous of the big birds, for when one stood tall, flapping its wings in stately, circular fashion, it towered over her. Phoebe who was no less nervous, staunchly held her hand.

The swans were plainly used to being indulged by the visitors to the island, and only became aggressive if it appeared that any visitors did not plan to pay out a ha'penny for some food for them, that was a treat beyond their usual diet of water plants. The girls could not refrain from laughing when one of the majestic white birds advanced, hissing, on a coster who declared that he was not going to waste his ready on feeding a bunch of fat birds nobody but the king ever got to eat. He fled in short order from the wrath of the bird as it pursued him in search of titbits.

"I am not sure that bread and pastry can be entirely good for them," murmured Libby.

"I should not like to explain that to any of them, however," said Elinor, dryly.

Most of the little girls were able to make attempts at drawing the swans in their commonplace books, and Lucy managed a poem, which read:

"O swan you are verry wite
You shyn with worter lyk lite,
You gave me such an orful frite,
I hope you are not going to bite."

For a little girl of six years old, Elinor thought this

quite a thoughtful effort, and resolved to work on spelling with the little girl.

"It is a good job we came this week," said Graeme. "After Easter, the Season begins in earnest, and rowing down to Eel-Pie Island after a drive out to Richmond, is, I believe, a popular outing for groups of young people with an eye to courting."

"Fortunate indeed, if it is even busier than it is now!" said Elinor.

"At least it is one of those venues which is typically British, and which the French could never understand," said Graeme, "for it is a trip that is quite egalitarian, and one is as likely to find the coster from Billingsgate and his best girl as Lord Blank of Noseintheairshire, and Miss Nabobsgirl, his intended. The French Revolution happened because the French mindset did not consider such things possible."

"Truly?" asked Elinor.

Graeme nodded.

"In France, before the revolution, if any aristocrat wished to be rowed down to the island – I doubt any of the effete fools could manage the rowing for themselves – it would be first cleared of anyone he would consider as peasantry, regardless of whether it was the only day off for Mr. Coster of Billingsgate, or perhaps I should say M. Poissonier of Meung-sur-Loire, on which he might go out with his best girl."

"You sound quite Revolutionary yourself, Dr. Mac," said Elinor.

"I am in sympathy with the original revolution. Even, maybe, the trials and execution of the worst oppressors. But I draw the line with how far they went, and with Regicide," said Graeme. "It stopped being about escaping tyranny, and became political. And rogues as tyrannical as any before them took power," he added.

"And it lasted less than a decade as a Republic before

they replaced a king with an emperor," said Elinor. "At least the Americans have been constant in their republicanism."

"Oh, you can always tell an American, but you cannot tell him much," joked Graeme.

"Now I thought that was what they said about Scotsmen," Elinor teased.

"Well, as many English still distrust we Scots, even half a century or more after the Forty-Five rising, we have only Americans and the Welsh to look down on," he laughed.

"It is a shame that there are arguments about who may be pressed into the Navy that makes for some disagreement with America," said Elinor. "Not that I think that press-gangs are at all proper ways to recruit, in any case."

"I suppose with Bonaparte wishful to rule the world, they feel they must use any and all means," said Graeme, "though I make no doubt I'd be less sanguine if I were on the wrong end of the press-gang. Now, I fancy the girls have finished feeding the swans and sketching, don't you?"

"I was just thinking it was time to recover our charges and row back," said Elinor. "I trust your hands are not too sore from rowing?"

He laughed.

"Oh, it will be a case of 'physician, heal thyself'," he said. "I brought a salve for Nettleby too."

"That was kind of you," said Elinor.

"I like him fine well, and more than I should have thought," said Graeme. "He told me about that fellow Atherton making threats, so I'll be looking out, too."

"I fancy I am too well protected for his threats to amount to anything," said Elinor.

"I hope so," said Graeme. "I do not want you to worry."

"It is hard not to be a little concerned, lest his puerile

efforts should cause fear or distress to any of the children," said Elinor. "But I have a suggestion to make to you, regarding an equitable division of labour, since I am not yet fit enough to pace and worry."

"And what is that?" asked Graeme.

"You pace, and I shall worry," said Elinor.

Graeme laughed.

Elinor gave her attention to Mr. Nettleby on the journey home.

"Did you do much rowing at University?" she asked him.

"Oh, by Jove, yes," said Mr. Nettleby. "The four of us were a team, we used to race, before Sin got so nice about his hands. Of course, in pairs, Ned and I were the champions; he fancies himself as a Corinthian, and I keep myself trim."

"It is not what one considers to be the stereotypical view of a poet," said Elinor.

"Oh, I learned young that a lad who dreams, and writes poetry, is always going to be picked on by the bullies," said Mr. Nettleby. "It was why I teamed up with Ned; asked him to teach me to box and so forth, so I could hold my own, and I helped him with his Latin. We took Sin and Abby under our wing, and hunted as a pack, as you might say. Well, not strictly hunting, as it was defensive, but nobody was about to take on all four of us, even bigger boys. It weren't worth the candle to them."

"An excellent reason for forming a friendship," approved Elinor.

"You're wondering what went wrong?" asked Mr. Nettleby.

"I'm not sure the little pitchers here need to listen," said Elinor.

"Well, I disagree," said Mr. Nettleby. "And I'll tell you why; we all admired Ned for being such a sportsman, and it all went to his head, and he got arrogant, and standoffish, and wanted adulation. And that ain't a healthy friendship, and the young ladies need to be aware not to change like that, if they be one who is admired, nor to give too much admiration to someone as will make them change."

"Well said, Mr. Nettleby," said Elinor. "You were right; the girls take nothing but a salutary lesson from the experiences you have learned painfully. And Mr. Atherton's assumptions that he had the right to start eating before anyone else but that dratted parson is a sign of his arrogance and assumption of a false superiority."

"And his temper after being a little bit poisoned opened my eyes, and I wish I'd laughed at his arrogance many years since," said Mr. Nettleby.

Chapter 20

"Abigail," said Daisy, "Do you think that Mr. Nettleby is a fortune hunter?"

"A fortune hunter? What's he doing visiting us if he is?" asked Abigail. "We don't know anyone with a fortune. Oh, you mean Miss Fairbrother? But her fortune is tied up, isn't it? I thought she was going to marry Dr. Macfarlane."

"Oh, do you think so?" asked Daisy, diverted.

"Well, he's quite spoony about her, as anyone can see, and they bicker constantly but without meaning it, as though they were already married," said Abigail. "Why do you think Mr. Nettleby is a fortune hunter?"

"It's the way he and his friends turned up, and Dr. Macfarlane said so firmly that all of Miss Fairbrother's fortune is entailed, which it wasn't, because I eavesdropped on her talking to her solicitor yesterday to see if it could be...."

"*Daisy!*" Abigail was shocked.

Daisy shrugged.

"I'm nosy," she said. "Anyway, when the doctor said that, Mr. Nettleby's friends turned all huffy, and it sort of precipitated The Cod being ill as he was put out too."

"Daisy, should you call a clergyman 'The Cod'?" asked Abigail.

"Dr. Macfarlane calls him 'The Piece of Cod that Passeth Understanding', and you can't say the doctor isn't devout enough," said Daisy, unrepentantly. "But what do you think?"

Abigail considered.

"Well, I was rather coming to the conclusion that the Reverend Endicote was after Miss Fairbrother's fortune, but I didn't know the doctor was making May game of him, by speaking only of her intent, not fact. It was not a lie in spirit though," she added, judiciously. "The reverend struck me as making Malvolio look wholesome, the greedy pig. It hadn't occurred to me that others might have ulterior motives too. Dear me! But if Mr. Nettleby believes her fortune tied up, he would not have taken us boating, if he were a fortune hunter."

"Yes, that's what I've been trying to work out," said Daisy. "Either he knew it was all a hum, and that Dr. Macfarlane was bamming, or he's in love with her anyway, or he only needs to marry someone who isn't poor. Or he's not a fortune hunter at all."

"What does it matter to us?" asked Abigail. "It's none of our business, and I'm sure Miss Fairbrother knows her own business well enough."

"I like Mr. Nettleby and I should dislike it to turn out that he is not very nice," said Daisy.

"Oh," said Abigail. "I don't think Dr. Macfarlane or Miss Freemantle or Miss Fairbrother would permit him to have anything to do with us if he were not an honourable man."

"'As are they all, all honourable men,'" quoted Daisy, ironically. Abigail flushed.

"Well, he doesn't have a 'lean and hungry look' like the other one that the twins poisoned," she said.

"True," said Daisy. "And of course, Miss Fairbrother would not permit him to court her if he were not all that a gentleman should be."

Elinor had been a little taken aback when Graeme Macfarlane explained the subterfuge he had undertaken, but after a moment's irritation that he should see fit to discuss her fortune, and speak of as fact an idea she had considered only, she calmed down. In truth, she realised that he had acted with the best of motives, and, indeed, to good effect. It was the high-handedness that had irritated her.

Mr. Embury, summoned, had been adamant, however, that if Miss Fairbrother was not about to die in short order that she should be ready to make provision for any future family that she might have. He had drawn up a document naming Swanley Court as the property of Swanley Court School, but that the grounds, the Dower House, the home farm and any outbuildings were to remain the property of Miss Elinor Fairbrother, her heirs and successors, reverting to the ownership of the school only if she died without issue or other visible heirs. Elinor did not rule out the possibility that she might adopt any orphan who touched her heart more nearly than most; and was thinking about Daisy in this capacity. As to Elinor's fortune, Mr. Embury permitted her to entail one hundred thousand pounds, leaving her with the income of all to spend as she chose in her lifetime, and one hundred thousand pounds to be left in the funds for her own fortune, as he said. Elinor smiled austerely and murmured that her speculations since they had last discussed her fortunes, that had increased to one hundred and twenty thousand pounds in the funds. Mr. Embury, who knew when he was beaten, had laughed, and said that he doubted if any of Elinor's heirs and successors would starve whilst she was still dealing with stocks and shares.

Elinor thought Mr. Embury had made some sensible suggestions, on the whole; because she might yet marry. She said so to Libby and Graeme.

"To be sure, my love, there is no reason why you should not," said Libby.

"I suppose Mr. Nettleby is the man who has put you in mind of marriage," said Graeme, frowning.

"I suppose, actually, in a way, it was you," said Elinor, "for you warned me of fortune hunters, which made me actually consider that marriage was a possibility."

"To be sure; for after all, I'm not a man to make you

think of marriage for myself, being only the doctor, and Scots into the bargain," said Graeme, with a touch of asperity.

Elinor looked surprised.

"Why, Dr. Mac, being Scots, has nothing to do with it," she said, "but I rather despise those women who at least half-flirt with their doctor, just because they have a privilege of intimacy. It seems to me to be most unfair and embarrassing to any doctor to be mooned over by their languishing female patients."

Graeme looked at her thoughtfully.

"I see," he said. "I had not thought of that at all, which shows how little I have been in general practice. I have not suffered that particular problem, though of course I am red-haired, which may have something to do with it."

"Nonsense," said Elinor, "you are a very handsome man, Dr. Macfarlane."

"Well, it's nice of you to say so," said Graeme.

"It's no Spanish Coin, it's true," said Elinor. "But you need not worry that, other than reassuring you on that misapprehension; I will not make you uncomfortable with any kind of flirtatious comment. Besides, we are good friends, are we not? How foolish it would be to spoil a good friendship with romance!"

"Oh, indeed," said Graeme, dryly.

"Oh, Dr. Macfarlane is a good enough friend that he will not mind teasing, or friendly flirting, I am sure, my love," said Libby, "For the women that you mean are doubtless those who also use illness to get attention, and gushing unbecomingly at their doctor is but another way of attention seeking!"

"How true!" said Graeme. "And nobody, my dear Miss Fairbrother, could ever accuse you of gushing, or undue flattery!"

Elinor laughed.

"Now that's a two-edged compliment, my dear

doctor!" she said.

"If we are such good friends as you say, Miss Fairbrother, perhaps you will recall that my first name is not 'doctor' but 'Graeme'," said Graeme.

"Then you must be as free with our names, too, and call us Libby and Elinor," said Elinor, after a glance at Libby for a nod of approval permitted her to accept the intimacy of the use of a first name.

Graeme bowed.

"I should be delighted," he said.

Abigail awoke in the night and went to adjust the window curtain. Her sleep had been disturbed as the curtains had a gap to them, permitting the rising gibbous moon to shine brightly enough in to wake her. She paused as she saw the figure of a man walking in the grounds. She eased open the casement, in time to recognise Dr. Macfarlane's voice addressing the waning moon.

"Friendship. *Havers!*" he said.

Abigail eased the window shut again silently, and twitched the offending curtain properly closed.

"Oh dear," she murmured to herself. "Miss Fairbrother either doesn't return his regard, or she has not noticed his partiality. *What* are we to do?"

"If you're up, what one might do is to remove that dratted kitten of Philippa's; she's got in here and is biting my toes," said Daisy, plaintively.

Abigail giggled, and evicted Columbine. With due consideration for the feelings of others if the little creature should cry for her little mistress, Abigail placed Columbine in the room that the four girls of the middle age group shared before she went off to bed.

"Miss Fairbrother only wants to be friends with Dr. Macfarlane," she told Daisy.

"How do you know?" asked Daisy.

"He was complaining to the moon about friendship,"

said Abigail, "and I wondered how to further his suit."

"Leave well alone," advised Daisy. "Grown-ups don't much like having their love affairs interfered in, I shouldn't think. They can sort themselves out. She might just not want anything but friendship from any man, you know; she's a true bluestocking, and needs no man to satisfy her."

"But a clever man like the doctor is a far better husband for a bluestocking than any fribbles like Mr. Nettleby, however nice he may seem," said Abigail.

"Mr. Nettleby is very well educated, and he's a poet, remember?" said Daisy. "Marriage isn't everything, especially when you're well off. And even if Miss Fairbrother *has* made over all her money to the school, I wager she'd soon make more on the 'Change, because she can't resist playing the numbers. So she don't have to marry. Go to sleep and let them worry about their own problems!"

Abigail sighed, and did her best to heed this very sound advice.

If Abigail had known that Mr. Edward Atherton had plans to interfere with Elinor's love-life, with malice aforethought, she might have slept less easily. However, fortunately for her peace of mind, she had no idea.

It was the middle of the night for the little girls of Swanley Court, but it was still early for the members of the *ton* who were enjoying the first part of the Season. Mr. Atherton was on the prowl, looking for a particular person.

Arthur Renfrew, Lord Milverton, no longer easily attracted the very young heiresses with his good looks and charisma; age and dissipation had robbed him of the first, and increasingly sour temper had left a dent in the second. He had been foiled in one abduction attempt that had been well enough hushed up so his reputation was, in theory, as untarnished as that of the young lady involved; and foiled in more seduction attempts than he cared to remember. His reputation might not be officially tarnished, but Lord Milverton was a known rake, and guardians of nubile and susceptible daughters had been sure to keep a watch on them, and remove them from his influence one way, or another.

It spoke much of Milverton's unsavoury reputation that the high sticklers of the *ton* had even unbent to warn a cit with a handsome and well-dowered daughter against aspiring to that particular title. Fortunately for the girl, and unfortunately for Milverton, the manufacturer of brass buttons had cared enough for his daughter to avoid her becoming prey to a man said, in whispers, to enjoy hurting women.

Lord Milverton, it may be said, enjoyed causing distress in anyone, regardless of their sex; and he received a good commission for introducing green young cubs to gaming houses, which monies kept him in town where he enjoyed watching the descent into despair, the humiliation, and even suicide of the youths he arranged to have ruined. It was whispered that his ways with women were more basic, but there were brothels which catered to such tastes, where they might be hidden, and where society could happily ignore the distress of girls of low birth.

Even a cit girl was, however, on the fringes of society, and so words had been dropped in the ear of the button manufacturer who could not be expected to know what everyone else knew without acknowledging. As a result, a golden prize had passed Milverton by, and he was feeling sore.

Edward Atherton ran into Lord Milverton, playing a hand of whist with several dowagers. Milverton enjoyed play for the sake of it, and for himself was as happy playing whist for chicken stakes, or silver loo, as he was playing faro or piquet for enormous odds in a gaming house. Indulging the dowagers also earned him free meals through invitations he might not otherwise have had. As to the higher staked games, he tended on the whole to win enough to keep his head above the water, because he was good at calculating the odds. For Milverton the joy was in the skill, not the betting, and half his pleasure in ruining young sprigs was because he despised gambling for its own sake, perceiving an enjoyment of the same as a weakness. Milverton despised weakness.

Milverton, seeing that someone wanted to talk to him, nodded to Atherton, and calmly finished his rubber.

Mr. Atherton wandered off to observe the rest of the people at a ball sufficiently large that it had been no hardship for him to gatecrash it. Presently, Milverton strolled up, and offered him a pinch of snuff.

Mr. Atherton nodded thanks, and took snuff. It was an unspoken message of a kind of fellowship, that there was no enmity. Lord Milverton was careful these days. A man did not take another's snuff if he intended him ill-will.

"What can I do for you?" he asked, neutrally. Milverton knew Atherton by sight; he knew him as an associate of the young fool, Rivers, who was not so foolish a young fool, however, to permit an introduction to a gaming house. This made Mr. Rivers more memorable than many young fools.

"It's about something you said to Abby Rivers," said Mr. Atherton, having recalled whose fault it was that the four friends had pursued Elinor Fairbrother, Abby Rivers would regret it in due course, but for now, revenge on Miss Fairbrother was his main desire.

"And what was that?" asked Milverton, cautiously.

"You mentioned an heiress; a Miss Fairbrother, who was worth eight thousand pounds a year," said Mr.

Atherton.

Milverton shrugged.

"And isolated. If you want the girl, you make your own play. I have no desire to try to scrape an acquaintance with some invalid I can't impress with my dancing. I don't see how anyone can court a whining mound in the dark on a couch whilst nurses and so forth are hovering about."

"Well she wasn't on a couch in the dark when I went to a picnic and got poisoned by her blasted orphans," said Mr. Atherton. "She's a diamond of the first water, too."

"So what do you want with me?" asked Milverton.

"You have an old and respected name, and if you married her out of hand and immured her in your country house, nobody would make a murmur," said Mr. Atherton. "I live with my parents still, except my apartments in town, so I'd be constrained to live in her house."

"I heard Swanley Court was a gracious residence," said Milverton.

"The house? It's beautiful," said Atherton. "The blasted orphans she's installed there aren't so attractive. And the wretched woman is devoted to them. I don't have the resources to find a way to carry her off. You do."

"And what do you get out of it if I did?" Milveron was sceptical.

"Revenge. One of the brats picked the wrong leaf for the salamagundy. I was as sick as a dog."

Milverton laughed, and Mr. Atherton winced.

"So you don't much care if her orphans might get hurt as well?" Milverton asked.

"I … no," said Mr. Atherton, who was too squeamish to even ask what Milverton might have in mind.

"Well, I'll put my mind to it," said Milverton. "I won't make any promises but I'll think about it. If I succeed, don't expect to touch me for a loan though."

"That's good enough for me," said Mr. Atherton, who was well aware that Lord Milverton was completely out of pocket in his gaming, having met a man whose play was as scientific as Milverton's own. Milverton scraped by, on the whole, and received credit on the strength of that, but he had borrowed heavily on the certainty of marrying the button-maker's daughter, and the reverse of some fifteen thousand guineas was enough to make his creditors nervous. It would take a lot, or an heiress, to recoup that.

The die was cast.

Chapter 21

Lord Milverton's need for a bride was, it may be said, as much dependent on his need to get an heir, as on his need for ready money. A nobleman who did his duty might be given some leeway. If it had been purely money at stake, Lord Milverton might just have taken himself to a town which abounded with manufactories, where he might be expected to cut an unwontedly fashionable dash in the provinces, and expect to become the son-in-law of a man of more social ambition than sense. The button manufacturer's main attraction was that his wife had been of the gentry, giving their daughter some pretensions of being of the right class, and Milverton had been in two minds over whether he would have gone through with marriage, if he could instead have persuaded the man to pay him to leave his daughter alone.

Milverton accounted arrogance amongst his manifold faults, but considered it a virtue; and he definitely would not like the child of a cit as his heir. It was bad enough that his current heir, a scrubby schoolboy at Eton, was the son of a mere Major of Artillery. Lord Milverton's sister had married late, and had managed to provide a son before her brother, sick of her attempts to reform him, had sent her a quantity of 'very special chocolate' which he had painstakingly melted and re-formed with the addition of generous quantities of ground yew seeds. The Major of Artillery had also succumbed to a wound in battle, and died. In this he was somewhat aided by the introduction of more yew into his dressings, by an orderly bribed by Milverton. Hence the boy was Milverton's only living relative since Milverton had discovered the wonderful properties of taxine when ensuring his own succession. Lord Milverton had no plans to kill his nephew yet, since he needed someone to carry on the name; however his own son would be preferable.

It might easily kill a woman with heart disease to have a child, but that consideration did not bother Lord Milverton. For entertainment there were always more women for sale.

Lord Milverton duly made plans, and removed to a hostelry near Richmond where he might observe the comings and goings of Swanley Court. Lord Milverton believed in finding the easy way to any goal, and there was usually an easy way to any goal, if one was not troubled by moral scruples. He set himself out to be thoroughly charming to the Innkeeper and his bevy of daughters, especially the oldest. Being charming was a skill he had practised and he could still achieve, so long as he had rested well to hide some of the lines of dissipation. His title was, of course, an added charm so far as simple country folk were concerned.

Milverton was good at making himself likeable without being touched by any inconvenient feelings such as a returned liking towards those he charmed.

Unaware of the misanthropic attentions of Lord Milverton, and half-dismissing the idea that Mr. Atherton might prove childish enough to want to exact revenge for a foolish accident that caused no serious harm, Elinor continued her teaching duties assiduously and in happy oblivion. She took her exercise with Graeme Macfarlane in attendance, and spoke of her ambitions for the school.

"If we achieve a good reputation for turning out governesses, I hope that those persons who are in need of the same might approach the school directly with their needs, and have a choice of girls in the upper forms to interview," she said.

"That is ambitious, indeed!" said Graeme. "Though why not? Governesses are sent for on no more recommendation than a notice in the paper, as often as not. Of course, you will have a large upper form in some six or seven years time, or so, when that large group of young ladies is old enough to consider leaving school; but is that usual?"

"Graeme, I know most academies for young ladies only have two dozen girls at most, but often they are in town houses, where a dozen girls may be as many as can be readily accommodated," said Elinor. "Look at Swanley Court! It is a massive building, and so long as the girls are encouraged to make their own beds, and tidy their own rooms, it will not take an extra army of servants to care for them, even if we have as many as fifty girls, with five mistresses for as many forms, and such specialist masters and mistresses as seem appropriate. To run any ordinary academy costs as little as four hundred guineas a year, leaving aside extras, and the income from what I have entailed is ten times that amount. Even taking into account that some must be set aside for necessary repairs to the structure of the building, I cannot see that it would in any way be unfeasible. To feed and clothe a girl in the station of a gentlewoman is no more than twenty guineas a year, and we should employ a seamstress who may also teach good, plain sewing. The more girls there are, the more the salaries of specialist masters and mistresses are spread amongst them, even if we pay them a really good salary to be resident preceptors and preceptresses, not visiting as many dancing masters, say, do."

Graeme nodded. By visiting two or three schools, a dancing master might take as much as one hundred and fifty guineas a year, but from that must also be found the cost of his lodgings and food for himself, and a servant to cook for him and see to his clothes, that he would not have time to do for himself. Provided with accommodation, board, and a shared valet with other masters and the school doctor, then one hundred pounds a year would be, in real terms, an increase to a dancing master's earnings. And with a large school and many pupils, he would not be wasting his time, either. Admittedly the potential shared valet was currently Jim, the teenage son of the Baxters, who learned the trade as he went along, but he would improve.

"And if you had a separate wing for the male teachers, where perhaps I might preside, there could be no question of impropriety, nor could the girls cause them too much grief," Graeme said.

Elinor laughed.

"I do not know how true it is, that old proverbial story of girls falling in love with visiting masters and plaguing the life out of them," she said.

"True enough for it to have become proverbial," said Graeme. "At least, so one must suppose. Rather like the predilections young girls are said to have for the military."

"I have never, myself, quite understood the attraction of a gaudy uniform," said Elinor.

"But then, my dear Elinor, you are a woman of extraordinary good sense," said Graeme. "I cannot even entirely fault you for having a partiality for Julian Nettleby."

"That implies something more serious than liking him, and respecting the fact that he has been honest about being a fortune hunter," said Elinor.

"Oh, he was honest about it, was he?" said Graeme, seething gently.

Elinor laughed.

"I am not sure he would have done, had I not already found him and his friends out," she said. "Or perhaps I do him a disservice. He said he felt remorse since he has known me as a person, and had learned to admire me tremendously. I am sure he is aware, however, that even if most of my fortune is tied up, he would have a very comfortable life here as my husband. In his favour, he is kindly, and talks to the children as equals, neither avoiding conversation with them, nor going out of his way to cultivate them, as a means of currying favour."

"He is also well-read, well-educated and clever," said Graeme, "but if you are asking me if you should accept his suit, that is up to you."

"To be honest, I wanted to talk about him to someone with whom I feel comfortable, and able to speak on any subject. You are an exceptional man, Graeme, because you are able to be objective, even though you have always suspected his motives. And I want to put my own thoughts in order."

"If you have to get your thoughts in order, and do not immediately think of him as the man you can see yourself turning to in a crisis in ten or twenty years time, then he is not the right man," said Graeme. "If you love him, and by that, I mean more than feeling a, er, physical attraction, you should know he is the one."

"Oh!" said Elinor. "Can it really be so simple?"

"I would not call it simple," said Graeme. "It's a very profound knowledge, deep inside, that this is a person in whom you can trust to be there, to be capable, to be someone you can bare your soul to."

"Oh!" said Elinor, again, flushing. "I thought it was about quickening pulses and thinking that your beloved can do no wrong, and feeling some kind of glow inside. I have not experienced such feelings, though they are mentioned in novels," she added candidly.

"That sort of reaction is generally a part of the physical side of love, other than thinking that your lover can do no wrong, which is just blind foolishness. Such feelings need to be awakened, sometimes. Such physical feelings can arise between men and women, and may be mistaken for love, when lust, to give it its brutal name is all that there may be between a couple.

And though the carnal desires are a part of love, they are not on their own a substitute. We are back," he added dryly, "to the foolish partiality to red jackets and the many frames of soldiers."

"Dear me," said Elinor. "I am pleased that you have been so frank and open with me about this, Doc – Graeme – for it may be something we encounter with the girls, who declare and believe that they are in love, when in reality they are but affected by lust. It is good to know that you do not treat me as a foolish woman who should be protected from such things."

"You need very little protecting in most respects," said Graeme. "I mean that in a good way," he added hastily.

Elinor chuckled.

"What, are you afraid I shall tease you about two-edged compliments again?" she asked.

"Something like that," said Graeme.

"Miss Fairbrother, I'm not happy about Lucy," said Mrs. Ashley, coming in to where the staff breakfasted. "She has what looks at first like a touch of a cold, but I don't like the way she's so flushed and complaining of a sore throat. I've put her straight to bed."

"Dr. Macfarlane and I will be with you directly," said Elinor, catching Graeme's eye.

He rose immediately from the breakfast table, and nodded to Elinor to remain seated.

"If it's what it sounds like, I do not think you should be exposed to infection," he said to her.

"If it is what it sounds like, I had it when I was no older than Lucy," retorted Elinor.

"Well, that's proof if any was needed that your heart is strong," said Graeme, dryly. "A sickly child would likely not have survived it; or the complications that can follow."

Elinor followed him to the room Lucy shared with

Phoebe, where the little girl was tossing and sobbing feverishly. Her neck and face were flushed.

Graeme pressed a thumbnail to the redness and it blanched.

"Open your mouth," he said. "Oh, yes, covered with spots. There can be no doubt of it; she has scarlet fever."

"I feared that was what it sounded light," said Elinor. "Where can she have contracted it?"

"There were children on Eel-Pie Island," said Graeme. "I suspect one of them may have been infectious."

"I recall Libby bathing me with cold water-soaked rags to keep me cool; it hurt so to be touched," said Elinor. "Is there another way?"

"Yes. I don't believe in bathing for it; keep the windows open enough for air to circulate," said Graeme. "A light covering on her bed, and have cook make up a drink of honey, flavoured with lemons, and sage in it for her sore throat. There are fancy draughts, but you cannot beat honey, sage and lemon to fight infection to soothe a throat. She must be kept quiet. We do not want Rheumatic Fever to rear its ugly head in a week or two."

"Dear me, and the girls must be isolated," said Elinor. "I must write to the Cohens to tell them that Rachel and Phoebe cannot come home this weekend."

"Find out if any of the girls have already had it," said Graeme. "We need to know who else may be at risk."

Elinor addressed all the girls, including Cleo, and told them quietly that Lucy had scarlet fever, and if any of them had already had it, perhaps they might be kind enough to sit with Lucy, when adults were busy elsewhere.

"You mean if any of the rest of us go down with it,"

said Daisy, shrewdly. "I have a sore throat and I don't feel well, so I fear I'm one of your patients."

"I've had it, Miss Fairbrother," said Hannah, "Papa and I used to do a lot of pastoral visiting and I think I've had everything catching. I never take anything badly."

"Invaluable child! Just what I need," said Elinor.

Hannah looked pleased. She was getting on much better with the others, but still craved praise.

Elinor wrote to the Cohens, explaining that the girls must be isolated; and received a visit from both Mr. and Mrs. Cohen within an hour of the note being delivered.

"Miss Fairbrother, we felt it only proper to relieve you of Rachel and Phoebe right away; two less to nurse, at the worst, or to have underfoot if they avoid it," said Mr. Cohen.

"I am happy to nurse sick children; Simon had it as a child, and I know what to do," said Mrs. Cohen. "It killed several children in the street in that outbreak, so I am aware of the risks. And we should like our own to be close to us, for prayers…."

"Well…" said Elinor.

"Naturally we shall isolate the family until the danger is past," said Mr. Cohen. "And if you need us to take Hannah, too, we shall."

"That must be up to Hannah," said Elinor. "She is immune; she has had it."

Hannah, when asked, was torn.

"Oh, Mr. Cohen, Mrs. Cohen, thank you, but I must do what I can to help Miss Fairbrother, as I am unlikely to catch it again," she said. "I can read to Lucy, you see."

Mrs. Cohen kissed her.

"You are a good child," she said. "Will it offend you, and Miss Fairbrother if we pray for you all?"

"Not at all," said Elinor. "I'll take prayers from any

loving persons. We may need all we can get. Be aware, Phoebe has been sharing a room with Lucy; and if it does not offend you, we shall include you and your two girls in our prayers."

"God is beyond the differences of our worship, we too are grateful," said Mr. Cohen.

Elinor soon thought she would be glad of prayer; for it was not long before all the girls but Hannah exhibited some signs of the fever, to a greater or lesser extent. And she reflected that it was probably because they all petted Lucy as much as having been exposed to sickness in the eating house. And there was no guarantee that recovery would mean freedom from worry, for Graeme had told her seriously that often enough scarlet fever patients developed Rheumatic Fever in a few weeks, after the danger of the initial illness was past!

Chapter 22

Elinor had to admit that she was grateful to be relieved of two little girls; and to have Hannah to sit with Lucy.

"It's a lot to ask of you, my dear," Elinor said. "But having someone who can see if there are any changes is of great help. It means that Miss Freemantle and Mrs. Ashley and I can nurse the others, secure in the knowledge that Lucy is being watched."

"She's iller than the others, isn't she?" asked Hannah.

"Yes, Hannah. And it may be scary."

"I can help," said Hannah. "I'm not fond of little children, but I am good with sick people. I've sat with dying people for Papa before now."

"You are a good brave girl," said Elinor, who thought privately that a pastor who left the pastoral care of those of his parishioners who were dying to a little girl had something of Chaucer's unclean shepherd about him.

"I was not frightened of death before Papa died," said Hannah, "but now I find it holds more fears for me. Will Lucy die?"

"I don't know, my dear," said Elinor, honestly. "But with you to watch her, and run for Doctor Macfarlane if she shows signs of distress, there is every reason to hope."

"In the outbreak when I was ill, several people seemed to get well, and then a few weeks later they were ill again, and one died, and one was a confirmed invalid, and could not work," said Hannah. "And one went back to work, but was always tired and ill, and when he was fifteen he just died."

"Be assured that we shall care for all the girls most tenderly, and do our best not to let them die," said

Elinor. "And if any are permanently affected they might live out their lives here in peace."

"Papa said it was God's will. Is it blasphemous to think it cannot be God's will for children younger than me to have to work, and to die of it when they are sick?" asked Hannah. "For I think it was the rigours of making bricks that killed Johnnie Tomkins, and he had been making bricks since he was eight."

"I do not think it is God's will for children to work," said Elinor. "I am hoping one day to expand the orphanage to take children of lower estate, who may be trained according to their skills to work as adults in a suitable occupation, so they need not be forced into apprenticeships as climbing boys, or go into factories or down the mines. It will not relieve all, but we must all play our part," she added.

Hannah nodded seriously.

"And as I am good with such people, perhaps Dr. Macfarlane will teach me to physic them," she said. "It seems foolish that ladies cannot be doctors. I've presided over more births than the local midwife, who is always drunk. And our parishioners are not the kind who would have an accoucher," she added.

"I'm inclined to think many accouchers kill more mothers and babies than they save, from what I have heard," said Elinor, dryly, thinking that it was an odd sort of conversation to be having with a child of eleven. However, it was a chance to know Hannah a bit better. No wonder she had quaintly elderly ways at times, not an indication that she had inappropriate adult knowledge from improper carnal knowledge but from her knowledge as a midwife and death-bed comforter to her father's parishioners.

"Well, the women in the Parish work, so they are quick, like the Hebrew women," said Hannah. "But if they drink too much, I have noticed the babies often do not succeed, or are sickly, and dull-witted when they are bigger. And often the women are so thin they do not recover from birth, and that cannot be God's will either," she said defiantly.

Elinor sighed.

"There are many ills in society," she said, "and we can but do our best to redress what we can."

Hannah gave her a beaming smile.

"I am glad you did not just say, 'the poor are always with us'," she said. "I never quite understood how Jesus could be selfish like that."

"Partly it is the proof of His humanity, that he was afraid of the future He knew lay ahead, and he felt in need in extra care. Just as you need the extra care Mr. and Mrs. Cohen gave you," said Elinor, thinking on her feet, "and partly that He knew that it was necessary for that poor woman – it is implied that it is Mary Magdalene – to show her devotions in the only way she could think of. It was compassion for the individual as well."

"Oh!" said Hannah. "I see… I think. Shall I make you a cup of tea? I have tired you by chattering."

Elinor smiled.

"How kind of you! No, I shall wait a little while and have one with Miss Freemantle and Dr. Macfarlane, and we shall compare notes on all our patients."

She kissed Hannah, and continued her rounds to check on the other children.

"It's only Lucy who is really ill," said Graeme. "I was worried about Felicity for a while, but Philippa climbed into bed with her and held her hand. Not usually a recommended treatment, but it seemed to calm Felicity in her fever, and that really is what is important."

"It is very worrying to know that there is still the chance of rheumatic fever afterwards," said Elinor.

"We can permit them something of a holiday until all

danger is past," said Libby. "I amused you well enough with gentle walks and nature study, and by telling you stories that educated you as well. We may play charades and other gentle games when the weather is inclement."

"That should be suitable," said Graeme. "I have a colleague who has a theory that rheumatic fever is precipitated in some wise from a sore throat of the putrid kind, such as may be experienced in Scarlet Fever."

"It seems extraordinary that a putrid sore throat should lead to an illness that affects the joints and the heart," said Elinor.

"The human body is extraordinary," said Graeme. "Doctors do not, by any stretch of the imagination, know all there is to be known. Though some seem to have the arrrrogance to think that they do," he added, rolling the r's in the word 'arrogance' so it sounded like thunder. "It's why I do not discount folk remedies, because hundreds of years of trial and error cannot be entirely wrong."

"And it is why you are a better doctor than so many, for your open mind," said Elinor. "I do not know what we should do without you."

Graeme managed a half-mocking bow.

"Glad to be of service," he said.

Elinor was very glad of Graeme's calm strength in the next few days. Felicity worsened again, and Cleo was also rather sick for a full day round, and Lucy was very unwell indeed. Hannah was a tower of strength, sitting with the little girl for several hours at a time, which permitted Elinor to snatch some sleep, so she could take the night watch. It was, after all, Libby's responsibility to care for the majority, and Elinor pointed out that she might be best employed sitting with Lucy whilst Hannah rested, or took healthful walks outside. Libby reluctantly concurred. Elinor was not strong enough to run herself ragged with the others, and Lucy did need extra watching.

Lucy tossed and turned, crying out and muttering in fever dreams, permanently restless. Elinor tried to take more time with her, but Hannah insisted that the dreams did not scare or distress her. It was worse at night, anyway, for the candles, even good beeswax ones, could not but add a smell to the atmosphere, and make the room hot. Elinor tried to reduce the number of candles, but she had to be able to see, though she might keep them at the other end of the room. She set them well away from the little girl's bed, as well as adjusting a fire screen to keep the brightness from Lucy's face. The candles burned unevenly, guttering and wavering in the draught that Graeme had decreed to gently cool the little girl, where she lay on the bed with nothing but her nightgown and a part of the sheet over her feet and lower legs. Graeme said this would prevent the cold air getting into her knees, and stave off the chance of rheumatic fever. Every half an hour, Elinor roused the restless little figure to induce her to take some honey water. Fortunately cook had found an old feeding cup from Elinor's own infancy, which had prevented too many spills.

Elinor did her best to do mending, between tending to Lucy's needs though with the flickering candles it was hard, and gave her a headache. She put it away in favour of knitting, that could be done by feel.

Knitting was a soothing, even soporific, exercise, and Elinor's fingers moved slower and slower as sleep overtook her.

Suddenly she jerked awake with a start, and wondered what was different. Then she realised! There was no fevered muttering from the little bed!

Elinor got up hastily and picked up the candle in the carrying sconce she used, to go over to Lucy, noting absently that the wick needed trimming, but that must wait.

She bent over the still form of the child, dread clutching at her heart for this, the tiniest of her charges.

Lucy was shining with sweat and her nightgown was dark with wetness. The fever had broken, and Lucy breathed easily.

Elinor was still standing, bemused, when the tall figure of Graeme Macfarlane came in.

"My dear! Oh Elinor!" he was across the room in a stride to catch her in his arms.

She leaned on him, and her body shook with sobs; but she must tell him.

"The fever broke. She's alive! I don't know why I'm crying!" she choked out.

"Hallelujah!" cried Graeme, kissing Elinor swiftly on the cheek.

"Indeed!" managed Elinor. "Graeme! I find I have singed your hair!" she stepped back in consternation, having forgotten the bedroom candle as she leaned into the comfort of his embrace.

"Losh, it's a conflagration anyhow," said Graeme, relieving her of the wavering candle. "And now not the contrary thing has drowned itself in wax and has gone out," he added, as the little flame flickered once more, apologetically, then failed.

Elinor fell to her knees.

"We must give thanks!" she said.

"Pray later," snapped Graeme, "the wind has changed and has chill in it. Strip her while I close the window, and I'll hold her whilst you strip that bottom sheet too. No point letting her catch her death of cold now the fever's gone."

Elinor meekly rose and stripped the little nightgown, towelling down the wet body before putting on a clean one.

"You are always so peremptory," she complained.

"It gets things done without argument," said Graeme. "When you've sorted out her sheets we'll walk down to the family chapel in the woods if you like, and give thanks there. The rest are doing fine."

"Even Felicity and Cleo?" asked Elinor.

"Cleo has a mother's love to fight for her, and has turned the corner, and if you think that stubborn child, Philippa, will permit her twin to come to harm, then you underestimate her tenacity," said Graeme. "Felicity doesn't dare not get well!"

Elinor laughed. It was a trifle hysterical, but it did her the world of good.

The little family chapel was by way of being something of a conceit on the part of a previous Fairbrother. Elinor was not sure if it was her great grandfather, or his father. It had been a part of the landscaping of the grounds, and was decidedly picturesque. However, it was consecrated, and the last three generations of Fairbrothers were mouldering gently in its crypt, though the family had no chaplain at the moment. Nor, indeed, did Elinor find a need for one, as it was but a short drive to the village for Sunday service, and it did the girls no harm to meet the local people. Elinor gasped, and Graeme caught her elbow, concerned lest she had stumbled.

"Graeme ... the village! They must be warned, for we went to church after the boat trip!" she cried.

"I will ride down," said Graeme, "but I think it unlikely that the girls were infectious by then. Why, Lucy did not begin sneezing until Tuesday."

"Of course. But I pray you, do warn them," said Elinor. "It is not impossible that one of the visitors who caused the disease also passed through the village, or met with someone from the village. The innkeeper has juvenile daughters, anyone stopping there for a drink or meal might have spread it."

Graeme nodded.

"I shall pass on your concern," he said. "The Reverend White may be a little vague, but he has plenty of sense when it comes to the wellbeing of his people."

"Unlike the late Reverend Loring," said Elinor dryly, and relayed her conversation with Hannah.

"Hmmm," said Graeme. "An enigmatic man. He cared enough to send his daughter... I believe he dabbled in politics, and was keen to find a way to compromise between the people and the government. He preached against Cobbett, so I believe."

"That endears me to him even less," said Elinor, who took *'The Political Register'* along with her other periodicals.

"Oh, Cobbett dresses up his plaint as well as any actor or Member of Parliament, but I repeat myself," said Graeme. "If he were less vehement, he might get further."

"He cares so deeply," said Elinor. "And he's no hypocrite, which is why neither he nor Cochrane got elected; they would not buy votes."

"I never said I don't admire him, for I do," said Graeme. "But a man need not be a bad person to oppose him. Many were upset by his campaigning to emancipate Catholics."

"And our Hannah had a rather rigid religious background," said Elinor. "I should send the servants to brush the chapel out, I think; it is so little used. Save," she giggled, "in a way Papa disapproved of. It was the only time I've seen the Reverend White angry."

"Truly? Tell me more!" said Graeme.

"Well, some vagabond woman had crept in there to give birth, and when Papa and Mr. White happened upon her and her baby, Papa wanted to drive her out with a whipping to see her on her way, and I pleaded for him not to do so. But Mr. White fairly shouted at him, about how he dared call himself a Christian! For, he said, besides ordinary Christian charity, where better for a mother with nowhere to lay her head to choose to birth her son, even as our Lord's mother had to birth where she might. Papa fed the woman for a week, he was so ashamed of himself," she added.

"What a nice story!" said Graeme, much moved, as they knelt in the dusty little chapel to pray in thankfulness.

Chapter 23

Lord Milverton was wondering why there had been very little traffic from Swanley Court over the last few days, and was gratified when the red-haired doctor rode down to the rectory to speak to the vicar. Perhaps he might accost the doctor on the way back. Lord Milverton sauntered forth accordingly.

Graeme was emerging from the rectory with Timothy White shaking his hand as he saw him out. Milverton heard the vicar saying,

"… no cases as yet, so it is to be hoped that it has passed us by entirely."

"I hope and pray so," said Graeme. He took his leave, and doffed politely in answer to Milverton's raised hat.

"Trouble?" asked Milverton.

Graeme regarded him. In the time he had been the resident doctor, he felt he knew most of the local notables who attended church. This was not one of them. Of course he might be a local who did not attend church; he looked fashionable enough, and many men of fashion did not even bother to pay lip service to church. Or he might be a visitor. But Graeme rather objected to being accosted in the street.

"I can't say I recognise you," he said. A neutral enough phrase.

Milverton laughed.

"Oh, I don't suppose you do! I'm Milverton; I'm staying in the neighbourhood, and everyone has heard of the charitable work of Miss Fairbrother."

Staying in the neighbourhood implied that he was the guest of someone local, and Milverton thought it a master touch. The stiff-rumped doctor thawed slightly.

"No trouble that you need worry about," said Graeme, "Merely that we took the girls out, and they have caught scarlet fever. I wanted to make sure we had not brought it to the village, and nor had anyone infectious passed through."

"Scarlet Fever?" Milverton was briefly alarmed, then relaxed. "It's a childish complaint, isn't it?"

"Almost invariably," said Graeme. "You have nothing to fear from it. But if there are any children where you are staying, I would ask that you be aware, and pass on a warning that it's been at Eel-Pie Island."

Milverton nodded curtly.

"I'll be aware. No children that I know of," he added, changing his initial thought of 'brats' to 'children'. The innkeeper's younger offspring were not children in his mind, but peasants. "So are you expecting many funerals?" he asked. A woman distracted by grieving for a dead brat would be the devil's own nuisance, though why she might be so fond of these brats and be likely to grieve for them he could not understand. It was not as though they were of her lineage, and were only girls in any case.

"Losh, man, no," said Graeme. "I'm a doctor; I'd be sore affronted if any of my little patients died. Though I'll be honest that one caused us some concern for a while," he added.

"Well, well! Glad you've no tragedy on your hands," said Milverton. "Be a while before everyone is in fine trig again, I suppose?"

"A month or so," said Graeme. "To see that no complications ensue. If you were fishing to be introduced to Miss Fairbrother, she'll be distracted until then," he added with a degree of malicious pleasure, in case the fellow had angled for an invitation with connections just to meet the heiress.

"I? Why would I? I have no interest in philanthropic institutions," said Milverton, who could recognise a protectively jealous man when he saw one. Besides, there were more ways to abduct an heiress than by seduction. It was an irritation that neither she nor the brats would be around for a while; he may as well go back to the amusements of the town for a few weeks. A pity; it meant he had to pay his shot at the inn if he hoped to return, but that could not be helped. It was probably too much to suppose that the innkeeper would hold a room and let his bill run until he needed to return, as might be done if he were a frequent visitor.

"Are you staying long?" asked Graeme.

"I? no, I'm off home later today," said Lord Milverton. "It's too noisy in the country, nothing but roosters and cows and their vulgar noises."

Graeme laughed.

The man was no suitor for Elinor's hand, he decided. He was too old, in any case, and no lover of the countryside!

The girls were soon on the mend, though it was two weeks before Rachel and Phoebe returned to school. Rachel had avoided the disease entirely, but Phoebe had suffered a sharp attack, and was quite wan still, when she returned to school. Hannah was ready to help Rachel to see to hers and Lucy's needs, and Graeme had to order both of the fit children out into the grounds to run about and play, lest they overtire themselves in misplaced zeal. It may be said that Philippa and Felicity muttered mutinously over their own confinement, as they watched their dormitory fellows play battledore and shuttlecock outside, while those not fully recovered must sit quietly. However, when Elinor taxed them with whether they felt able to play, the twins had to admit that the thought of so much effort was enough to almost reduce them to unwonted tears.

The twins were, however, fit enough to make apple-pie beds for Hannah and Rachel, and explain, when those two maidens yelled in anguish over finding their bedsheets trapped and trapping them, that it was in revenge for enjoying themselves.

Wonder of wonders, it was Hannah who threw the first pillow in answer to that piece of unfairness, in what became a splendid little pillow fight. Philippa eventually called pax, because Felicity had sat down suddenly on the floor, looking rather pulled. Hannah and Rachel, contrite, cleared everything up, including the burst pillow, whose contents they emptied willy-nilly out of the window. [Later, the discoveries of feathers led to one stable boy having his ears boxed by Baxter for encouraging his wild friends to engage in cock-fighting near the school; the assertion by Mrs. Baxter that thieves had been at the hen-coop; and the half-believed fears on the part of one of the kitchen girls that witchcraft was being practised. Elinor had her own suspicions, especially as Hannah was later seen mending the ticking with a careful patch, but was too pleased that the girls felt better to reprimand them.]

Meanwhile, Hannah whispered,

"Sorry, Felicity!"

Felicity looked up, eyes a bit too bright in her peaked face, but she giggled.

"Oh what fun that was!" she said. "We must do it again when we are all well! But please, Hannah, will you fetch me a glass of water?"

The carafe set to refresh any thirst for the girls was, for a wonder, undamaged, and even fairly free of feathers, and Hannah quickly complied. Elinor had decreed that honey water flavoured with lemon was to continue to be the order of the day until all sickness was past, and Felicity drank the soothing mixture gratefully.

"Are you feeling better, twin?" asked Philippa, sharply.

Felicity nodded.

"Yes, thank you," she said. "I just needed to rest."

Philippa gave a brief nod.

"You twins are amazing, knowing how each other

feels," marvelled Rachel.

"I knew it had to stop," said Philippa. "I knew if it didn't there would be bad things that would come of it. Thanks for listening."

The whole episode forged bonds of friendship that would last a lifetime.

Lucy continued to be much weakened from her illness, and slept a great deal. She found it too much effort to try to read, and Daisy and Abigail, who were well on the way to recovery, took turns reading to her, to relieve Hannah.

It was Philippa's idea, though most of the execution of it was carried out by Hannah and Rachel, to produce a Lilliputian Theatre.

A vegetable box hastily furnished with curtains, scenery painted by Felicity, and the slatted sides forming natural wings, made the theatre. Old magazines were begged by the girls, and furnished fashion-plate figures, to be cut out and glued to pasteboard, and mounted on spills for the girls to manipulate from the other ends of the tightly rolled paper spills. The figures poked through the slats might then be made to move on stage. To be sure, there were a disproportionate number of actresses compared to the actors, but Elinor assisted by drawing some gentlemen. The other disadvantage was that the actors must either come on, or exit, backwards, for all the world, giggled Philippa, as though they were leaving the presence of royalty.

Lucy, however, was delighted, and she and Phoebe, who constituted the audience, giggled at the antics of the actors at the behests of their little playwrights.

"It may not be Sheridan," murmured Graeme, "but it has a naïve charm."

"Sheridan's wit is balanced equally with his malice in the way his characters are drawn," said Elinor, "and I think I like the innocent and gentle stories our little girls come up with far better when it is aimed at the tender ears of our smallest ones."

Daisy was voted to be the one to ask Miss Fairbrother and Miss Freemantle if the Lilliputian Theatre might give a subscription performance to selected invited individuals for the benefit of the Middlesex Hospital at Mary-Bone,

"Since we are lucky to be so well cared for, ourselves," said Daisy, earnestly.

Elinor was perhaps a little dubious about this, but it was no very great thing on her part to organise, and might be a fillip to her charges. They would invite only those who might be expected to have no very great expectations of the efforts of children. Libby frowned in thought, briefly, and then concurred.

The children planned to do scenes from Midsummer Night's Dream, rather than their own play, and were soon occupied in dressing their actors and actresses in scraps of gauze and lace that they supposed made good fairy costumes.

The project was very nearly doomed from its inception through a quarrel amongst the producers.

"Of course, the 'Dream' is the greatest piece of nonsense ever," said Daisy, without thinking. "It has the mythological traditions of everywhere that Shakespeare could think of, thrown into a tub together and stirred. The whole thing is held together with brass pins and a firm faith in the ignorance of the audience."

"You are talking fustian!" cried Abigail. "Nothing the Bard has written is nonsense; he's incapable of bad writing!"

"He wrote for money, Abigail," said Daisy, "Which means he had to turn out plays on a regular basis, or starve. You can't write your best when you write under such circumstances, it stands to reason."

Two fractious children still pulled from illness were

soon shrieking at each other as the argument descended to personal insults. It was finally broken up by Graeme, who heard the rumpus, and promptly sent both girls to bed. He gave them long enough to undress and then proceeded to dose them with a vile-tasting mixture of valerian and asafoetida.

"Are ye no' ashamed of yerselves?" he demanded, in very Scots idiom. "Heaven forfend that the Bard should make such a falling out! He was a genius, forebye, but he had his bad days, and I'm not an admirer of the 'Dream' myself, though his language lifts anything he touched. As for the way ye were screeching like Billingsgate fishwives, could ye no' have managed to insult each other with Shakespearian language and spoken such insults as 'the devil damn ye black, ye cream faced loon', or 'Oh most pernicious woman! Oh villain, villain, smiling devil villain,' or similar?"

"The first is in the Scottish play sir; is it not bad luck to quote it?" ventured Abigail, rather thickly through a vile-tasting mouth.

"Not to a Scot," said Graeme, serenely. "And have you not made your own bad luck in this falling out? Now make up your quarrel or I fear I may have to dose you until your tempers mend!" and he stalked out.

Abigail managed a giggle.

"Doesn't he just 'suck melancholy out of a song as a weasel sucks eggs'?" she declared.

Daisy giggled too.

"I'd love to see him play Macduff," she said.

"It would be good," agreed Abigail.

"I'm sorry I was nasty to you," said Daisy, "but I'm not sorry that I think Shakespeare wrote rubbish at times. Dr. Macfarlane does have a point, though," she added thoughtfully. "He wrote rubbish most awfully well."

"I love the language," said Abigail, simply.

Elinor, checking on her big girls after she had

laughed over Graeme's handling of them, found them both cuddled up together in Daisy's bed, in perfect amity.

She ejected both Arbuthnot the rat and Columbine the kitten-cat, both of whom had settled with surprised gratification to find warm sleeping bodies during the daytime.

With the increase in good relations between the two producers, the little set of scenes was put together, and local notables were invited to attend.

Lady Herongate arrived, escorted by Mr. Nettleby.

"I presume all contagion is past?" demanded the formidable old lady.

"Oh, quite gone," said Elinor. "It is a complaint only usually caught by children in any case."

"Ha! Well at least you do not make some sly comment that suggests I have entered my second childhood to be at risk," said Lady Herongate.

"I would not trouble you, my dear Miss Fairbrother, when you had enough trouble already, or I should have visited," said Mr. Nettleby.

Elinor read in his eyes a half-apology for cowardice in remaining distant from infection; and sighed. A man who was afraid of childhood illnesses was not a man to be associated with orphans.

"I quite understand, Mr. Nettleby," she said.

Julian Nettleby was quite sure that she did. However, he did take her to one side, leaving Libby to welcome others, to impart information.

"A bit of news," he said. "Ned Atherton has been seen in conversation with Milverton – Arthur, Lord Milverton, you know, gamester and rake. And it was Milverton who first told Abby Rivers about you."

"I see," said Elinor. "Well, actually, I do not, not precisely. I will discuss this later with Libby and Graeme."

Mr. Nettleby concealed a sigh. She used Macfarlane's given name quite naturally. Well, he might take a tour of Greece or somewhere. It would take his mind off love, and besides, it was cheap to live there.

The Lilliputian Theatre was much enjoyed because of, rather than despite, the lack of polish to the performance, and an impromptu collection ensured that the Middlesex Hospital would have a donation of almost twenty guineas. The girls were very grateful, and said so as they handed out sandwiches and tea.

"So long as you don't plan to poison us with sandwiches!" laughed Mr. Nettleby.

"Oh, sir, I pray you will not spread that story!" cried Daisy.

He winked, and touched his lips.

"Mumchance shall I be," he said. "Besides, I'm going travelling, no chance to blab!"

"We shall miss you, Mr. Nettleby," said Daisy. Mr. Nettleby thought her a nice child to sound so much as though she meant it.

Chapter 24

"Did you say Milverton?" cried Graeme, when Elinor finally had the chance to share Mr. Nettleby's intelligence.

"Indeed; do you know him?" asked Elinor.

"Know him? I'd not go that far, but I met him in the village," said Graeme, and proceeded to recount his encounter.

"But what can he do?" said Libby. "We shall not permit dear Elinor to be alone in such a place that affords him the chance of carrying her off, if such he plans."

"And because we are forewarned, we may do so," said Graeme. "Elinor, Mr. Nettleby plans to travel. Would it be improper to pay him to be your agent to investigate foreign markets? I'd say he deserves your thanks for his loyal friendship, even though he does not expect a fortune."

"He plans to travel?" Elinor was startled.

"He told me he thought to visit Greece," said Graeme.

"Oh!" said Elinor. "Dear me, we must not tell Daisy, she would very likely dress as a boy and ask to be taken as his tiger!"

"Will you miss him?" asked Graeme.

"Of course I shall miss him!" said Elinor. "He is a most pleasant companion … you mean, will I miss him in a way that brings me grief and heartache? No. I shall miss a friend. I cannot be in love with him," she concluded, a little sadly. "Moreover, he hid from the scarlet fever."

"Well, he's a good man for all that," said Graeme. "Will you make him an allowance?"

"As my agent and to keep notes of his travels for the edification of the girls? Willingly" said Elinor. "I'll see

Mr. Embury to arrange it."

Lord Milverton became aware, shortly thereafter, that the school had received visitors, when it was mentioned in his presence that some young sprig's mother had enjoyed herself being entertained by 'that parcel of genteel orphans out at Richmond'.

He removed himself from Town back to the inn, and the accommodating Mary, to whom he spun a lying tale about a dead brother, and the illegitimate child he had left, and his own determination to help her out now her father was No More.

He had to work around Mary's native shrewdness, in wondering why he had not mentioned this before, and pitched her so much gammon he wondered if his story might get up on trotters and walk away as he declared that he had been foolishly too proud to ask for help in tracing his poor little niece.

Mary's native shrewdness broke down before several golden guineas, as many expert kisses, and enough flattery larded on to baste the said gammon. She proceeded to furnish Lord Milverton with a fairly accurate description of all the girls, whom she had seen, of course, in church. Milverton was delighted. There was a babe of no more than six or seven summers who would be most likely to wring the tender heart of a foolishly fond woman.

Mary had very little free time, as the oldest daughter, she was expected to mend for and feed her siblings in addition to working full time in the inn. However, she was able to tell Arthur, as Lord Milverton insisted that she call him in private, that one might easily cross a stile up Farmer Beeson's lane, and go through the woods to see the children at play after lessons in the afternoon. Mary was accustomed to go to Farmer Beeson's farm for her father, to purchase butter, milk and cheese, for the inn, and had often watched jealously the games these girls played. Girls scarcely younger than she was, and only orphans. Mary's father was not so kind a man that she had not spun fantasies that she had really been sired by one of the gentry; and spurned by him might be one of those orphans of genteel birth and no fortune, pampered so by Miss Freemantle. She said as much to Arthur, pointing out that her mother was considered a lovely lass, and plenty of gentry passed through the inn. It may be said that Lord Milverton privately sneered at such fantasies but encouraged Mary in her despite for the orphans.

Mary did have the occasional qualms of conscience over her private jealousies, and especially over despising Miss Fairbrother, who had sent her game from her own table and fruit from her conservatories, on hearing that Mary had been sick the year before. The game had ended up being served to guests, and Mary had not had any of it, but she appreciated that Miss Fairbrother had meant well. And Miss Fairbrother would be delighted if one of her orphans turned out to have such a distinguished uncle! Hence, Mary did everything she could to please her Arthur, secure in the hinted belief that the position of nursemaid to his niece was hers as soon as he achieved his goal, and a position too as his mistress. She duly reported on the habits of the orphans so Arthur might observe them for himself, and see whether or not this was his brother's child, so he might approach Miss Fairbrother properly, and not raise the hopes of any child unduly.

Lord Milverton observed the little girls playing tag, and curbed his impatience until they should approach the spinney in which he had concealed himself. Milverton was no devotee of the sporting life, waiting in coverts until birds were put up to shoot, and this was scarcely less tedious and unpleasant, to his way of thinking. The great outdoors so beloved of romantics was full of mud and dirt, insects and bird droppings. It was very untidy and disorganised. In Milverton's opinion, apart from those necessary evils, farms, for the production of food, the countryside would be better for having all the vegetation burned away, and paved over. The beauties of Elinor's skilfully landscaped estate passed him by entirely.

The beauty of an easy lever upon the heiress, however, did raise some emotion of satisfaction in his breast, as the smallest girl ran close to the spinney. In an instant, Milverton erupted from his place of concealment, trying to ignore his disgust at the shower of leaves that descended on his neck and head, and seized Lucy Lamming by the arm.

Lucy screamed. Milverton hoisted her over his shoulder and headed for the wood, through which he might cut back to his carriage. He tugged the letter he had written to Elinor from his pocket, to drop on the ground. The woman was bound to act, under the threats he had written on what might happen to a small child.

Lord Milverton was used to females of the kind of simpering debutants, or servile servants. He was not used to furious twelve-year-olds flinging themselves upon him. Felicity fastened her teeth into his thigh, while Philippa sank hers into his wrist, both girls clinging on to him. Philippa, indeed, lifted her feet from the ground to wrap her legs around the leg her twin was not biting, both adding to the weight he carried and impeding him.

Milverton fell, heavily, and Lucy cried out in pain.

Being the weekend, Phoebe and Rachel were not in evidence, but Abigail, Hannah and Cleo were quickly upon him, and Daisy hobbling up as fast as she might. Cleo's mother, Mrs. Ashley, was running from where she had been keeping a distant supervisory eye on the children.

Milverton was trapped. But he had one more ace up

his sleeve. He drew his pistol. He had to let go of the brat, but better that than capture.

"Let me go, or I'll shoot!" he said.

The girls fell back in fear. Abigail picked up Lucy and cradled her gently. Milverton backed away until he felt safe to turn and run as best he might with one pulled hamstring from the weight of Philippa and lacerations on the other thigh from Felicity's teeth. He was cursing himself that he had not managed to hang on to the brat and had not thought to threaten to shoot her if they did not let him leave with her. Who would have thought that a pack of brats could cause so much trouble! Well, he would have to find another way, and when he was safely married to the heiress, these brats would most certainly suffer!

Daisy picked up the missive left for Elinor. It was unsealed, and after a moment's hesitation, she opened it and glanced at the contents.

Mrs. Ashley caught up with Daisy in time to steady the girl as she swayed, almost fainting.

"Daisy, what is it?" she demanded.

"This note – to Miss Fairbrother!" said Daisy.

"You naughty girl! Don't you know how discourteous it is to read someone else's mail?" scolded Mrs. Ashley.

"It'd be more discourteous to let Miss Fairbrother read this without preparation," said Daisy. "She's still not very strong, and it might kill her."

In which Daisy showed herself to have a better appreciation of a shock than had Milverton, across whose mind had never crossed the thought that his missive might actually kill a woman with the heart condition he supposed her to have.

Mrs. Ashley also hesitated, then glanced at the note and paled.

"Dear me!" she said. "Miss Fairbrother must see it, of course, but to be prepared for it would be a good idea. Thank the Good Lord that Lucy is safe. You girls must all come within."

Graeme listened to the confused babble of young voices explaining what had happened as he examined Lucy, and deftly set and immobilised the arm Lord Milverton had broken by landing on it. Elinor held the sobbing Lucy in her lap.

"Abigail, I am going to give Lucy some laudanum," said Graeme. "Then I would like you and Daisy to put her to bed. I think you should all have a hot cup of chocolate and lie down. Such excitement must have exercised all your minds unduly."

He ignored Felicity's muttered comment to her twin that anyone would think they were as precious as society misses. It was an excitable sort of age that they were at, as well as being barely over a nasty illness, and hysteria should not be permitted. The unusual treat of hot chocolate would calm the nerves, and help them to take a nap, which exercised nerves on top of recently pulled bodies would not hurt.

The girls might resent being sent to lie down, but they were obedient enough, and only Daisy hesitated, knowing the contents of the letter, and knowing she could never tell the others. Mrs. Ashley kissed her on the cheek.

"I'll see you have a drop of laudanum in your chocolate, my dear," she said. "Then you may forget what you saw for a while in sleep, so you may be restored to talk about it later."

"Thank you, Mrs. Ashley, you are very good," said Daisy, well aware that her sleep for many nights would be long coming, and filled with nightmares when it overtook her.

"What is this?" asked Elinor, sharply. "Doctor, I

can put Lucy to bed, Abigail and Daisy need not."

"No, dear Miss Fairbrother; there is a note you and Miss Freemantle need to know about, that Daisy has also seen," said Mrs. Ashley. "It is most unpleasant, and it is providential that those twins are such hoydens. The letter is to you, but I think the doctor should read it out."

"Very well," said Elinor.

Graeme opened the door after the last of the girls had filed out, and the order had been given to the kitchen for chocolate, to make sure that none of the girls were lingering; then shut it again and took up the missive.

"'*Dear Miss Fairbrother*'," he read, "'*I have your youngest charge. She…*'" He paused. "Dear G-d, you say little Daisy read this? And understood it?" he asked Mrs. Ashley.

"She certainly seemed to comprehend it," said Mrs. Ashley. "I believe her grandparents were accounted philanthropists, so she may have overheard more than a young girl should know."

Graeme made a noise of disgust.

"Graeme, Libby and I need to know what has been said," said Elinor.

"Yes, you do," said Graeme, grimly. "He goes on, '*she will remain alive and well, so long as you meet my carriage, ready to marry me, on the North Road at the turnoff to Coppice Farm. If you do not meet me there by midnight, I shall sell her to a brothel whose clients like children.*'"

Libby gave a little cry, and Elinor went ashen.

"It will have brought back to poor Daisy that awful woman who tried to abduct her," she said. "What an evil man! And a clever one, for I could do nothing but comply."

"And with no guarantee he had not killed her, and would not sell her in any case," said Graeme, harshly. "We should have taken him and his coach, my dear

Elinor; half your outdoor staff are related to the local poachers. He would never have known he was being crept up on until it was too late."

"You are right," said Elinor. "It would have been too tame to let him get away with it, but how well he knows a woman's weakness when a child she cares for is threatened! This letter must go to Bow Street, of course."

"If you will pay for one of them to investigate, rather let an officer of Bow Street be sent for," said Libby. "For even if he can avoid being convicted, since he is a Lord, and Lucy but the bastard daughter of a soldier, at least he might be made uncomfortable in gaol, whilst avoiding a trial."

"He should not go scot free just because of his birth!" cried Elinor.

"No, but Libby is right. He probably would, you know," said Graeme. "And it's worth trying to get him convicted."

"I will go to Daisy," said Elinor.

"With luck, she is asleep from the laudanum," said Mrs. Ashley. "The girls must play indoors until this monster is apprehended."

"Yes, of course," said Elinor. "If I were only safely married to someone, this could not happen, but oh dear! I should need a perfect paragon not to mind that the money is to go to the children."

"Oh I make no doubt you will find him," said Libby, dryly, reflecting that her clever one-time charge had missed several points.

Chapter 25

"You read the note," said Abigail to Daisy.

"Yes, and I don't want to talk about it," said Daisy. "He threatened to hurt Lucy and I don't even want to think about what he threatened."

Abigail shrugged.

"Well, I'm here if you want to talk," she said. Daisy was so self-sufficient, Abigail doubted she would want to talk, but one had to make the offer.

"You're too innocent," said Daisy, "but thanks anyway."

Daisy had extra lessons with Libby, and as one took place the next morning she considered talking to Libby about how she felt. She was not entirely surprised to find Libby and Elinor both waiting for her.

"I'm sorry to have been rude in reading the letter," Daisy said, "But I'm not sorry I read it, as I'm glad I could warn Mrs. Ashley not to just give it to you, Miss Fairbrother."

"I am sorry that you saw such filth directed at me," said Elinor. "I take it that you understood what was meant."

"The vicar really did not censor my reading," said Daisy. "Suetonius, you know, and others."

"Ah," said Libby. "Rather, er, warmer works for a young girl than even the most liberal parents generally permit, indeed warmer than that ghastly work 'The Monk', which no mother in her right mind would permit a young girl to read; far too shocking."

"Also badly written, no grammarian can ever encourage its perusal," said Elinor. "Miss Freemantle would not permit me to read Suetonius; she considered it would exercise my mind too much and place strain on my heart from some of the less salubrious incidents."

"Ah, Caligula, and such; yes it's not very nice. I

never minded it so much though, because they are all dead," said Daisy. "It's very different when it's a real person."

"The twelve Caesars were real people," said Libby, chiding gently.

"She means they are not people one might meet, or that one knows, because they are so far removed from modern people, didn't you, Daisy?" asked Elinor.

Daisy nodded. She so admired Miss Fairbrother for understanding what she could not put into to words.

"It's hard to think of them as real," she said. "Oh Miss Fairbrother! If you were only married to Dr. Macfarlane, nobody could try to coerce you at all!"

Elinor stared, then a slow blush spread over her face.

"What makes you think that Dr. Macfarlane would ever want to marry me?" she asked, lightly.

"Well, when Abigail mentioned that he was quite spoony on you, Miss Fairbrother, I looked more closely, and she's quite right. And you do like him too, don't you?"

Elinor flushed more, and Libby groaned.

"Spoony? What an ugly term, to be sure, Daisy, I did hope you girls might have more extensive vocabularies than to resort to such horrid slang," said Libby.

Daisy chuckled wickedly.

"So I should not say that Dr. Macfarlane plainly thinks that Miss Fairbrother is corky?" she said.

"Thank you, Daisy, if that is a compliment, and please, I pray you, do not ever again use a word like 'corky' to describe me," said Elinor, aghast. "And do not change the subject; Miss Freemantle and I are hoping that if you feel a need to talk about what was in that horrid note that you will feel yourself able to come to either of us."

"Thank you, ma'am," said Daisy, seriously. "I don't suppose there's much to talk about; if such places truly exist, it is horrible, and I will have nightmares, but if you have told Bow Street about it, as I am sure you have, then surely they will investigate."

Libby and Elinor exchanged a quick look. It was said that Bow Street was riddled with corruption, and that dens of vice and iniquity of the more exotic kinds were too well frequented by the rich and aristocratic members of the *haut ton* to be investigated by officers of the law. However, there was no point worrying Daisy about that.

"I have sent for a Bow Street Runner to pursue Lord Milverton," said Elinor.

"Oh good," said Daisy. "He really is quite loathsome; and Felicity says he tastes as though he does not wash very often, too."

"Dear me," said Elinor, avoiding meeting Libby's eye in case they dissolved into laughter over that non-sequitur. "Well, my dear, Lucy is in no danger, and I am sure that the matter will be resolved very soon."

On due consideration, Daisy took herself to Dr. Macfarlane's study.

"I fear that knowing what that monster had planned for Lucy is likely to give me nightmares," she said, abruptly. "May I have a sleeping draught to take in case of need?"

"I dislike giving sleeping draughts," said Graeme, "Though you are a girl I do actually trust only to take one at need, Daisy. If you promise me that you will only take it if hot milky drinks at bedtime fail you, you may have it."

"Oh, thank you, doctor," said Daisy. "Of course, what would really make us all safe and so sleeping better would be if Miss Fairbrother was married. Have you some strong moral scruple that means you haven't come up to scratch?"

"*What* a vulgarity!" said Graeme, startled. "Well,

young lady, apart from the fact that Miss Fairbrother is my employer, which makes it most improper to consider approaching her romantically, there is also the fundamental requirement that she should welcome my suit. And if she did not, it would then become impossible for me to remain here; it would be too embarrassing, and the reason I tell you this rather than boxing your ears and sending you about your impudent business is that I think your tact might be nurtured by understanding."

"Oh, but she would welcome your suit!" said Daisy, earnestly. "Why, I've seen the way she looks at you!"

"And what do you know about it?" said Graeme, sufficiently touched and amused that Daisy should care, not to take offence.

"Oh, you look at each other like old married couples, like my grandparents, only you seem to have missed out on the preliminary romance," said Daisy.

"Upon my word! If I didn't know you meant well, I'd call you down for impudence!" said Graeme. "I am not a romantic man, young Daisy; and I'd caution you about how you speak, lest it be, hrm, taken the wrong way."

Daisy blushed.

"Oh, I suppose it could be; I'm sorry," she said. "But we all love Miss Fairbrother and respect you no end, and it would be nice to have it settled."

"Well! This business with Milverton must be settled first," said Graeme. "Go away, Daisy; you shall have your draught, but I want no more of your infernal cheek today!"

"No, doctor. Thank you," said Daisy, meekly enough.

She had started the train of thought and hopefully the doctor would stop being so slow about courting Elinor. And he had let her say more than she thought he would.

Graeme had much to consider. He had loved Elinor to distraction almost from the first meeting. Her vivacity, her compassion, her willingness to embrace new ideas, her bravery, all attracted him as much as, or even more than, her beauty. Beauty was an ephemeral thing, save in those with the gift of contentment, and he could imagine Elinor being quite lovely in old age for her serenity. He examined their relationship; and it did seem that Elinor was not indifferent to him. Whether she would consider marriage to a doctor who had only the most limited financial independence might be another matter, for he would not wish her to think him the fortune hunter he warned her against so often! Graeme examined his reluctance to woo Elinor openly, and discovered that it was his own pride, and fear of being thought a fortune hunter, that held him back.

He went in search of Elinor, and discovered that an individual from Bow Street had arrived. The man was a rough-looking fellow, who was frowning and tutting over the letter from Milverton.

"Oh, Dr. Macfarlane, this is Mr. Nuttley, who is from Bow Street," said Elinor.

"Ar, glad there be a man about the place," said Mr. Nuttley. "Serious business, this is, serious business. I was just about to tell Miss Fairbrother and Miss Freemantle that it's difficult, because *tech*nically, you see, there ain't been no crime committed. Not *technically*," he added.

"You mean, you can't do anything?" said Graeme in horror.

"Now, I didn't say that, Doctor. Didn't say that at all," said Mr. Nuttley. "See, there ain't been no kidnapping, but there is demanding with menaces. And he did attempt to snatch the liddle girl. Assault with intent, that is, and the letter making clear what his intent was, and actual bodily harm to the liddle maid with her arm broke and all."

"So he can be arrested?" asked Graeme, sharply.

"Oh, aye, he can be arrested. Whether he manages to get off or not, now that's another matter. But there's enough to arrest him," said Mr. Nuttley. "Got daughters, I have," he added.

Graeme nodded. A man with daughters would pursue a child-spoiler, or one who was prepared to sell a child to such, with utmost vigour.

Mr. Nuttley took his leave, with the intent of making enquiries first at the inn.

"Elinor!" said Graeme. "May I speak with you in private?"

"I have marking to do; excuse me," said Libby, getting up and leaving. "And about time too," she added.

Graeme pulled a rueful face as she went.

"Is a' the worrrld concairrrrned aboot the matters of ithers?" he demanded, rhetorically.

"More than likely, Graeme," said Elinor. "If I duly unravelled a most awfully *Scots* phrase. What can I do for you?"

"Marry me!" said Graeme.

"Graeme, if you think it's a good basis for marriage to do so merely because some of the children think it is a good idea, or in order to be safe, you must think me very hen-hearted!" said Elinor.

"Havers!" said Graeme. "If you think I'd propose merely to please interfering children, ye do not ken me verra weel."

"You really are being awfully Scots," said Elinor, wondering why she felt rather breathless.

"Emotion does that to me," said Graeme.

"Graeme ... Are you saying that you care for me?" said Elinor.

"I thought that's what I was trying to say," said Graeme, reaching out a hand.

Elinor took it, finding that her fingers were shaking; as was the rest of her. He was so dependable!

The door burst open.

"Oh Doctor Macfarlane, do come quick! Philippa has fallen and there's blood *everywhere*!" declared Phoebe.

Graeme bit off a few choice words regarding Philippa's timing, and looked ruefully at Elinor, before following Phoebe. Naturally Elinor came too, reflecting that one of Graeme's endearing features was that he would always put the children's needs before his private desires.

Blood everywhere was not an exaggeration, as Philippa sat, rather dazed, on the ground in the schoolroom, her twin holding the top of her nose firmly, Daisy dropping cold water down the back of her neck, and most of the rest staring in horrified fascination.

"What happened?" said Elinor, fighting to sound crisp and matter of fact. Graeme smiled approval on her as he moved to examine Philippa.

Philippa tried to speak.

"*Hush*!" said Felicity. "If you please, Philippa was rescuing Hannah and a spider from each other."

"That almost makes sense," said Elinor, "but how did she come to fall, and from where?"

"It's my fault, Miss Fairbrother," said Hannah. "The spider ran up the curtains and I was so frightened it would come down on me on a silken thread, as that's where I sit, so Philippa put a chair on the desk to collect it and put outside, only the chair slipped."

"Well, you do bear some responsibility, but by no means all," said Elinor. "A fear is a fear, and whilst the bravest may overcome it, I quite understand your terrors. Philippa did not have to choose so precarious a means to reach the spider, but could have asked for a step ladder; asking for a ladder seems to be something she is in the habit of eschewing! However! Is she badly hurt, doctor?"

"Och, the wee hellion is fine," said Graeme, cheerfully. "The de'il takes care of his own! A few bruises, a nose bleed, and she'll avoid having a fat lip for having put her tooth clean through it. A wee scar she'll have there, but it'll nay show, forebye."

"Dthe chair backg caught by chid ad dose od the way down," said Philippa thickly.

"Oh, Philippa!" sighed Elinor. "I cannot fault your compassion, but I do wish you would learn to think before you act! You are well punished for your thoughtlessness, but I think perhaps you should go to bed now! I will have a hot bath drawn for you, for your aches, and to wash off the blood, and you shall have a cold compress for your nose, and tea and supper on a tray. No, do *not* protest!" she added, as Philippa opened her mouth to display her teeth all red with blood from her lip. "You are too ghastly an object and will put the others off eating," Elinor added firmly. "And Hannah, for your part in this affair, you shall run to the kitchen for a bucket and mop and see if you cannot remove that puddle of blood."

Hannah nodded, and ran!

Elinor watched Graeme carry Philippa upstairs; it was not necessary to make the child feel in any way an object of pity, in need of resting after a nasty shock. Fortunately, Philippa was an equable and obedient child. And a good-hearted one, if occasionally peagoose-brained.

Libby had to be told, of course, and Mrs. Ashley. And if Graeme had sighed that the moment had been lost to him, both he and Elinor might hope to recapture it another time.

Chapter 26

"Am I to wish you happy, my dear?" asked Libby.

"I'm not sure," said Elinor.

"Not sure! Are you telling me he did not manage to, er, come up to scratch, as Daisy put it?"

"Well, yes, and no," said Elinor. "I thought he was only being chivalrous, to stop any more fortune hunters causing trouble, but I believe he truly does hold me in some regard."

Libby gave vent to the sort of sniff she would have told Elinor or any of the girls off for producing.

"The man is head over heels in love with you," she said. "Anyone might see it. Did he not tell you?"

"He never had a chance to say so, because there was Philippa," said Elinor.

"I suppose *that* was almost inevitable," sighed Libby. "What has she done now?"

Elinor filled in Libby on what had happened. Libby shook her head.

"Those twins!" she said. "Well, you must give poor Graeme every opportunity of telling you how he feels," she added firmly.

"Yes, indeed," said Elinor. "Dear me, it makes me feel quite nervous, and odd inside, as though I had tried to go without breakfast!"

"I expect that is to do with the physical side of attraction, my dear," said Libby.

"I hope not; it is not altogether pleasant," said Elinor.

"Doubtless the feeling is partly nervousness that what has awakened may be unfulfilled after so rude an interruption," said Libby, "and one cannot expect a man to renew easily a romantic stance after dealing with the snotty, tear-filled blood of a child with a nosebleed."

"No, indeed; monstrous unfair," agreed Elinor.

Next morning, Elinor planned to ask Graeme if he would care to walk with her in the grounds, but before she could do so, the youngest tap-boy from the inn was to be heard shouting at the butler.

"You rancid old gundiguts! Miss Fairbrother be a kind lady wot will come to Mary, you see if she don't!"

"Baxter, what does the boy want?" asked Elinor.

"He wants a good hiding, if you ask me, for coming to the front door," said Baxter, his usual plummy tones slipping a little in irritation. "Apparently the ale-draper's eldest daughter is all upset by yon Robin Redbreast, and in an excess of sensibility as would do credit to an Earl's daughter she wants, of all things, you to go to her! Stands to reason, that isn't what you'd be wanting to do, Miss; sending her food to tempt an invalid is one thing, treating her megrims like they were important is something else!"

"Oh dear," said Elinor. "But on the other hand, Baxter, perhaps she knows something about Milverton that she was scared to tell the Bow Street Runner, if he made a bumble-broth of asking her. Girls of that age can be so very silly. Perhaps I had better go and see her. Have John Coachman bring the gig round; that will suffice just to go into the village."

"They didn't ought to expect you to minister to them, it's presuming on your good nature, it is, Miss Elinor!" said Baxter, severely.

"I can't leave a young girl in distress, Baxter," said Elinor. "Suppose Milverton has hurt her?"

"Then you'll want the doctor to her," said Baxter. "He'll take care of you. Sooner he marries you the better, I say, and I'll have John put up the carriage and see that Dr. Macfarlane is told."

Elinor opened her mouth to protest this assumption about her private life and shut it again. Her servants were determined to protect her, and if they expected Graeme to marry her, that was much better than having them decide to disapprove of him as her husband. And it would be nice to have Graeme's support.

"What's all this about the tavern wench?" demanded Graeme, when they were out of earshot of any servants, being ensconced in the carriage.

"I'm not sure, precisely, but her little brother said she was very upset," said Elinor. "And if the Runner has upset her with clumsy questions, why, it's my responsibility to put right what a man in my employ may have done. And of course, I also fear that Milverton may have taken advantage of her, and has hurt her."

"Not impossible at all," said Graeme. "You do accept the realities of life, my dear Elinor."

"There is no point ignoring them, Graeme," said Elinor, blushing at the endearment. "I may not recognise all the realities that there are, but I do not blink at those I do recognise."

"I admire your moral courage," said Graeme. "A doctor must face unpleasant things, but many ladies prefer not to. Even those married to doctors."

"I think anyone who takes on waifs and strays must be prepared to face the unpleasant," said Elinor, "and the husband of a practical philanthropist should not hide in being a gentleman any more than the wife of a doctor should hide in being a lady."

"Well said, my dear!" said Graeme, taking her hand. "*DAMN*!" as the carriage came to a halt outside the inn.

"We appear to be doomed to extensive disruption of such serious discussion," said Elinor.

"Och, weel, with children around, that's a'most inevitable," said Graeme, rising to help Elinor out. "I'll stay in the taproom until or unless you need me; even if she is hurt, a woman will do more good for her at first."

Elinor nodded.

"I concur," she agreed.

The landlord looked at Elinor in some relief.

"Oh, Miss Fairbrother, that silly chit of mine didn't ought to have asked you to come, but I'm main glad you have, for she's doing nothing but weep and wail."

"Dear me!" said Elinor. "Was it the Bow Street Runner that upset her?"

"Well, I don't say as how the Robin Redbreast didn't set her off," said the landlord. "She's taken to her bed, hollerin' that her Arthur ain't done no wrong, and I asks you, Miss Fairbrother, ain't it the height of impidence, calling Milord by his first name?"

"Indeed!" said Elinor. "She considers that threatening a six-year-old with terrible things to be nothing wrong?"

The landlord scratched his chin where he had missed a patch of stubble with his razor.

"I don't know what he'm done nor what her think he'm done," he asseverated. "Her be up in the attics, Miss, if you be kind enough to go to her. I ain't going up them stairs to give her the whipping she deserves, she can stay there til she starves, and you may tell her so."

Elinor merely nodded curtly, and made her way up the old, creaking stairs to Mary's room. She knew which one it was, having been before, with fruit. She knocked, and went straight in without awaiting an invitation. Being asked to come constituted the same, after all.

Mary was curled up on the bed, her face red and blotchy, her nightrail none too clean, and her nightcap awry. She looked up.

"Oh Miss! Someone has been and set Bow Street on Arthur, just because he wanted to help his dear brother's daughter!" she cried.

"Mary, if it is helping a child younger than your brother Ben to write that he plans to sell her into a brothel if her guardian does not do what he wants, it's an odd sort of help," said Elinor. "It was I who put Bow Street onto Milverton after he was foiled trying to kidnap a child who is no relation of his at all, and indeed whose father may very well be living. If he told you that he was Lucy's uncle, he has told you a farrago of lies. And if he *were* her uncle, what was to stop him coming to see me directly and honestly? Do you seriously think I would deny him the chance to meet her? Has he bedded you?" she asked, bluntly.

Mary cried louder.

"Oh, my Arthur could not be wicked like you say! It is a mistake! He said I might be her nursemaid and … and his mistress!"

Elinor resisted the urge to slap the foolish face.

"Mary, if you knew of his plans to snatch a child, you have been a very wicked girl; but because I think you believed Milverton's lies, I am not going to give you in charge for conspiracy," said Elinor. "You have always been a good girl. And when you think about it, you will see how foolish you have been to even consider such a thing, instead of advising anyone to approach me openly. Milverton wrote me a foul and filthy letter, threatening just what would happen to Lucy if I did not agree to marry him and elope with him.. Yes, my girl; he used you to try to marry me for my fortune. Fortunately the other girls helped Lucy to get away, though not before he broke her arm. But his note was then to no avail as she was safely home."

Mary stared.

"He said he was going to *marry* you?" she cried, more exercised in her mind over this than over a dreadful fate for a child she did not know. Mary had no illusions that any man of fashion would prefer her to a diamond of the first water like Miss Elinor Fairbrother.

"That was his intent," said Elinor, coldly.

"*Ooh* the *rat*!" cried Mary.

"I could think of harder names myself," said Elinor.

"He did lie with you then?"

"Oh Miss Elinor! I been sick in the mornings!" cried Mary. "I be certain I be with child!"

"It is something of a risk that is run when one permits a man to one's bed," said Elinor, dryly. "Have you ever lain with anyone else?"

"Oh *no*!" said Mary. "A few kisses, but … no, not the whole way!"

"Well, I doubt he can provide for a child," said Elinor. "But if you come to term, and do not in the meantime ask the village midwife to help you, as you may very well wish to do, and I will say nothing of that matter to anyone, if it is a girl I will take her into the orphanage, and if it is a boy, I will arrange for him to be farmed out suitably and raised according to the estate of a gentleman."

Mary howled.

"Da will beat me!" she wailed.

"He will not," said Elinor. "I will forbid him from doing so. And you must quickly make up your mind whether you wish to consult Dame Agnes whether she knows any herbs to bring down the courses as you are … late … with your menstruation."

"Ooh, I couldn't," said Mary.

"It's your choice," said Elinor. "But if Milverton tries to contact you again, you must let someone know."

"Oh I will! He has deceived me!" cried Mary.

"You won't be the first, I don't suppose," said Elinor. "Now get up, and wash and dress, and go about your duties. You've been a very silly girl, but I will see that you are looked after."

Mary sobbed, but obediently got out of bed.

Elinor went back down.

"Mary has been deceived and seduced by that fellow Milverton," she told the ale-draper crisply, "and if you shout at me, as your purpling face suggests you might, I will call upon Dr. Macfarlane to knock you down. You are *not* to beat that girl; do you understand?"

"How's she going to do her duty with a brat?" said the innkeeper, sullenly.

"I will make arrangements for her child," said Elinor. "The child will be gently born, and will be brought up accordingly. If indeed she does not lose the baby anyway, as may easily happen to anyone. Mary is aware what a silly and wicked girl she has been. I have given her a good telling off. She needs no more on the subject. I would keep her hard at work, if I was you, to keep her mind off brooding, though be aware she is not well in the mornings. I am sadly disappointed in you that you have not kept a closer eye on your daughter, such that Milverton was able to seduce her. It does not speak well for your abilities."

"I can't be watching her all day long," grumbled the landlord, now on the defensive.

"No? Ah well, plainly you cannot control your own household," said Elinor. "If you had been a kindlier father who cared for your daughters as more than just unpaid slavies, you might perhaps have noticed how a silly young girl in love behaves differently. I hope you will be more careful with your other daughters."

"Yes, Ma'am," said the innkeeper sullenly.

"Very well, you may carry on," said Elinor.

Graeme was watching in amusement.

"You handled that very cannily," he said, when the landlord had returned to the taproom. "One would never realise how gentle you are."

"Mine host is a hard man, and a hard father," said Elinor. "His offspring expect, and get, more blows than comfits. He'd be likely to beat the poor girl for her foolishness and hope it made her miscarry. And I do confess I wanted to slap her for maundering on about her 'poor Arthur', but beating she does not deserve. I suspect he has to be a plausible man if he is a rake."

"I found him moderately plausible, and he was

certainly not trying to seduce me," said Graeme. "That is, I disliked him, but could not put a finger on why I might do so. A simple country girl would be easily deceived by him if he set out to charm her, I am sure. I will, of course, extend my professional services to her, though I'm no accoucher."

"Your patients are probably safer for you not being an accoucher," said Elinor, dryly. "For you will apply common sense, not fashionable theory."

Graeme laughed.

"There is that," he said. "Poor silly girl."

"Indeed," agreed Elinor. "I have assured her that her child will be cared for, and I left her getting dressed to resume her duties. I think that she has learned her lesson about trusting too well and unwisely. Shall we return home?"

"Aye; and then perhaps we might have a few moments of privacy," said Graeme.

"I should not place money on it," said Elinor. "However, perhaps we might take a turn about the grounds, to minimise the risk of interruption."

"An excellent plan," said Graeme, "so long as that Milverton fellow is not still skulking about and tries to snatch you himself. He will, however, have to go through me," he added, holding the door for her to precede him from the inn.

Milverton had come to the conclusion that the inn was now the last place that he would be looked for; and Mary would surely help him. He had had his coachman cover with mud the conspicuous emblazoned panels on his coach, so the crest was at least not obvious. He fondly hoped that no busy-body would remark upon it, because if nothing else, he could not afford to lose the clothes he had left in the inn.

He was just alighting from the coach when he saw Elinor Fairbrother come out of the inn.

With two steps he was able to grab her by the arm, and taking her by surprise managed to throw her into his carriage, thrusting shut the door on the red doctor. With her fortune he could buy new clothes, and as his wife she could not testify against him, which perhaps was as attractive as her fortune!

Perhaps his day was going to go well after all!

Graeme, shocked, and knocked back by the heavy door, wrenched it open and almost threw himself at the coach as Milvertons' shout had the coachman start the horses at a trot. The door was shut by the time Graeme reached it, and the doctor did not think he could safely jump on the back of a moving coach.

However, John Coachman was there, with Elinor's fast and comfortable modern carriage, likely to be able to easily keep up with Milverton's older and elegant but cumbersome coach, inherited from his father. Graeme leaped up beside John.

"Follow that carriage!" he said.

"Yes *sir*," said John, grimly.

Chapter 27

"*Now* I have you, and you are going to marry me," gloated Milverton. "And demme if you ain't truly lovely, and I'll even enjoy getting an heir on you."

Elinor was pale at the best of times, and felt quite faint for this ill-treatment, but her mind was racing.

She gave a little gasp and clutched at her chest, gasping for air.

"Oh! The pain!" she cried. "My heart! Oh my heart! The pain is tearing me apart!" she slumped and collapsed to the floor, arching and writhing as though in agony, and then with a little jerk, she lay still.

"Bloody hell!" swore Milverton. "Here, wench, you can't die on me, I haven't got me hands on your thousands yet!"

Elinor breathed a silent sigh of relief. She had wondered if her histrionics had been too hurried for verisimilitude, but she had gambled on Milverton not having seen anyone die of a heart attack. Elinor herself knew only too much about it. However, judging from the very real panic in his tone, Milverton was quite convinced. She felt him take her reticule from her wrist and let her arm fall back with a loud thump, which bruised it but added to the illusion. What was he doing? Ah, searching for her vinaigrette, she saw, observing him through her eyelashes. Well, before he plied it, she must act.

Milverton bent over his apparently dead bride and began to take the top off the little box of salts. Elinor stuck two fingers right up his nose.

Even the strongest of men will flinch in like circumstances, and Elinor grimly seized the opportunity to grab his neckcloth, and twisted with all her might.

Milverton fought back, slapping her as hard as he could when he found out that pushing her away was somewhat less comfortable for him than for her; a man is at some disadvantage when three slender fingers are inside his shirt collar, their knuckles on his adam's apple, and the whole hand engaged in twisting the already too tight cravat. Elinor did not have fingers that were as strong as the laundry-maid, accustomed to wringing wet washing, but she was by no means incapable, and knew how to wring washing. Having managed to get a second hand on the cravat, she was treating it like washing.

It seemed likely to Elinor that Milverton might yet succeed in punching her into oblivion before he passed out from lack of air, though his poor colour was quite encouraging, but then the coach lurched sideways and descended. Elinor held on, grimly.

"Ever heard of the so-called sport of 'hunting the squirrel', John?" said Graeme, as they pursued the heavier carriage.

John gave a fierce grin.

"Ar, that's when a sporting gent tips the carriage of some old gager into the ditch," he said.

"Ten guineas says you can get that carriage into a ditch before he reaches the North Road," said Graeme.

John gave a spit over the side of the carriage.

"I don't need no golden incentive to rescue Miss Fairbrother," he said.

"I know. But a wager…" said Graeme.

"Ten guineas it is then, if I get him into Cummin's ditch," said John.

Farmer Cummins had one of the deepest ditches in the vicinity, but it was set well back, so did not usually pose a problem.

"I don't actually care whose ditch you use, so long as the coach is off the road," said Graeme. "Then you deal with his coachman."

"I cut my eye teeth before yesterday," said John. "Still, reckon you must be well shook up that he has your lady-love, sir, else you'd know you was teaching your granddam to suck eggs."

"No doubt," said Graeme, wishing, as Elinor had wished earlier, that the servants had not settled his private affairs before he had managed to do so properly for himself.

John took a steep corner with style and panache, accelerating smoothly out of the curve, and onto the outside of the big coach as they approached the boundaries of Cummin's Farm; and cursed to see a haywain ahead on the straight.

"We'm likely to be a bit hasty," said John, laconically, cracking the whip, and edging his leaders to the left.

The wheel of the smaller carriage barely clipped the wheel of the larger, but at that speed it was enough, and then John was pulling to the left, judging nicely to avoid the plunging hooves of Milverton's horses, to pass in a hair's breadth between them and the oxen on the haywain that was being shouted to a halt by the bucolic in charge of it.

"Be you out of your head, John Coachman?" cried that worthy.

"Them ow' villain be kidnapping my mistress!" cried John.

"Ar, well, that be-ant no cause to be a danger on the roads," said the wain driver, severely. "You could of enacted them shenanigans on the Great North Road where there's only the Mail and Gentry-fools."

John treated this remark with the contempt it deserved.

Graeme leaped down as soon as the carriage was safely stopped, and did not bother to check if John was doing likewise. John knew a b from a battledore, and was likely right behind him to deal with Milverton's preoccupied coachman, thrown clear, and trying to cut the traces of the flailing horses. The coach had lurched to one side, and then subsided, together with the edge of the ditch. It was half turned over, and buried in mud. Graeme wrenched the door open.

Elinor had lost her grip as the coach tumbled, and was thrown up against the lower side of the coach with Milverton on top of her. He was half dazed from being half throttled, but she would not have long to think. If only this was not an accident, but presaged the arrival of Graeme!

Seeing the familiar red hair at the door made her almost swoon with relief; and Graeme was in the coach in a single bound, and by some miracle of prestidigitation on his part, Milverton was flying out of it.

"My darling!" cried Graeme. "How badly has he hurt you?"

"Not as much as I think I hurt him," said Elinor, candidly. "Oh dear Graeme, I wish you will get me out of this horrid coach, there is slime coming through the window, and between that and the bruises, I fear nobody could tell the difference between me and Philippa in a scrape."

"Havers," said Graeme. "Ye're the most beautiful woman in the worrrrld, forebye, and I'd no' want tae kiss wee Philippa."

"Oh Graeme!" sighed Elinor, in satisfaction, as he matched deeds to words and swept her up into his arms.

It may be said that Graeme kissed his lady most thoroughly before he even tried to help her out of the listing coach; and Elinor, well content with this hastiness, kissed him back, and discovered that the odd feelings inside her were distinctly pleasurable when they were accompanied by a masterful pair of lips on hers. She wrapped her arms around him.

Graeme lifted his head.

"Wumman!" he said. "I'll no' take 'no' for an answer, and let the world think I am a fortune hunter if they choose!"

"Well I don't, and as it's me saying 'yes', then that's all that matters," said Elinor. She wrinkled her nose. It was unromantic to talk business, but one must reassure him that he could be shown not to be a fortune hunter, and hope that he might kiss her again once thus soothed. "We can always have a settlement wherein I retain control of such of my fortune as is not tied up, if you please; and that will have to be re-worked if marriage changes things. Though as it was a deed of gift, I think it does not."

"Embury can sort it out," said Graeme, who was less worried about how people saw him than Elinor realised. "It's what you pay him for. Can you manage to scramble down if I set you out of the door?"

"Why, Graeme, after you have taken all the trouble to see that I am not a feeble creature any longer, I should feel ashamed if I might not!" said Elinor.

It was an effort; she was much bruised, and she was glad of Graeme's strong arms about her when he followed her out.

The coachman lay on the verge, his nose pouring blood, and John standing over him grimly. Of Milverton there was no sign.

"Where's that damned villain?" demanded Graeme.

"Sorry, sir," said John. "I was engaged with this jobberknoll here, and the bas… the noble lord managed to make off with one of the horses."

"Oh dear! Now we must fear him returning!" said Elinor. "Oh Graeme, let us get married as soon as possible!"

"I'll undertake to find the Bishop of Norchester for a special licence as soon as I have you safely home," said Graeme. "And tell your inefficient Runner where his prey was last seen."

"Be fair; could anyone expect him to return to the inn?" said Elinor.

Graeme grunted.

"I suppose not," he said. "Elinor, your face is all bruises! If you wanted to wait to be wed …."

"If you think I care, so long as you love me anyway, you are sadly mistaken," said Elinor. "Dear me, and what a lack of sensibility I have; I would rather have a cup of tea and some macaroons than swoon."

"I love you for your lack of sensibility," said Graeme, kissing her again.

As he was apparently quite indifferent to this lack of feminine attraction, as well as to the fact that she was by no means a beauty at the moment, Elinor gave in to his fervour.

Milverton had run out of options, and was making for the coast as fast as the horse could carry him unsaddled. The sale of a prime piece of blood would at least probably cover passage and a few immediate necessities to take ship for somewhere like Jamaica, where he must hope, being well educated, to do something so sordid as to take a job as secretary to a plantation owner. Or perhaps America would be a better option, where in banning titles they had made them more attractive in visitors. And where simple settlers might be easily gulled at cards by a man of address and title.

He would take the first ship he might to America, with that express purpose.

That would do nicely.

Elinor, restored to Libby and the girls, was made much of, and put to bed after a hot bath by Libby and Mrs. Ashley. Despatching John to find Mr. Nuttley, Graeme set out himself to London, in the hopes of catching the Bishop of Norchester in residence there for the Season.

It may be said that the girls all took turns reading to Elinor, to keep her occupied, which did their skills at reading aloud no harm either.   And Daisy and Abigail were most satisfied of all of the girls when Elinor told them all that they were to be her bridesmaids shortly when she married Dr. Macfarlane. If the little ones had no idea what had been in the wind, Abigail and Daisy were very pleased that two of their favourite people had finally seen what was what!

And if Daisy was convinced it was because of the heavy hints she had dropped, neither Graeme nor Elinor ever enlightened her.

The happiness of the bride made up a great deal for the bruises on one side of her face, and as the tale had spread around the village, not one of those who turned out to wish her well – and for the anticipated feast – was so foolish as to assume her bruises came from her bridegroom.

Mr. Nuttley managed, it may be said, to trace Milverton to the coast, and to his embarkation, but not before Milord had embarked for Virginia.   It was, however, closure to Mrs. Elinor Macfarlane!

The pupils of Swanley Court

Abigail Meersham, b 1794
Olive complexion but high colour on cheeks, soft brown hair. Greenish eyes.
Founder pupil leaves November 1810
Orphaned at 14, when her parents drowned in a bathing accident at Brighton.   Quiet, bookish, Shakespeare lover. Kind to the little ones, capable, sense of humour.

Margaret [Daisy] Ellis b1795
Perfect complexion, golden curls and blue eyes.   Club foot.
Daisy entered the school a sad and angry child, but found peace and contentment with the kindness of her preceptresses and doctor.   Her parents were out in India as her father worked for the East India Company, and then ventured on his own account.   They died out there of some disease.   When Daisy's grandfather died, her grandmother was not well, and was offered a home by her sister-in-law providing she did not bring That Child. Daisy had been highly educated by the local vicar who arranged her transfer to Swanley Court. Daisy, having been immobile for years, is something of a bluestocking. She also has a flair for business, as her father was said to have had before investing all his money in some mysterious venture that was not revealed before he died.

The Goyder Twins b. 1797
Founder pupils
Red-gold hair.   Orphaned by a rather feckless father whom they hardly knew, who shot himself over his debts.   They are more bereaved by the death not long before of their beloved governess, Miss Philpot, or 'Fippy', whose death shortly preceded that of first their mother, who faded away, and then their father's suicide. They are naturally mischievous and have dealt with their

bereavement with different bad behaviour.

Felicity Goyder
Felicity subsumed her grief into being a vain and selfish little madam. However, she has responded well to compassion, and if inclined to vanity, is a normal, mischievous child, no more thoughtless than any other. She is claustrophobic. Felicity has ambitions to be a modiste and is an enthusiastic dress designer.

Philippa Goyder
Philippa has a passion for rescuing animals in need, which has been known to extend to human children. Her compassion is infinite but not always wise. She is a bit of a chatterbox when not being quiet to help her current waifs.

Hannah Loring b. 1798
Founder pupil.
Pale, rather lank brown hair, both complexion and hair improve with country living.
The daughter of a vicar who died whilst trying to prevent a riot. Hannah, whose mother had died when she was little, resented his death whilst helping other people not her. She was the most obnoxious pi brat at first. Once able to deal with her grief, she rapidly settled down and because a much nicer child.

Rachel Cohen b. 1798
Sort of a founder pupil
Solemn, piquant little face, dark curls.
Rachel is not an orphan, she is the sister of Rabbi Simon Cohen who helped out with Phoebe [see below]. She is an obedient and quiet child who takes her duties as Phoebe's surrogate sister very seriously. She likes having a younger sister-figure, being the youngest in her family.

Cleopatra [Cleo] Ashley b. 1799
Joins orphanage shortly after it opens
Blonde hair, pale complexion, light blue eyes, skinny like a piece of chewed string but muscles like whipcord. The daughter of the school nursery nurse, Cleo was born right after the Battle of the Nile, at which her mother was a decorated nurse, for having been working on the orlop deck with the surgeon right up until she gave birth. Cleo grew up on board ship, until her father's death in battle at Trafalgar. He was a Gunner, so Mrs. Ashley had a reasonable pension once she had fought for it. Cleo loves words and is something of a poet. She and her mother also support the Chartist movement and are quite radical. Cleo is not a lady, but she loves learning, and the preceptresses do not see why she should not learn.

Phoebe Goldstone b. 1801
Founder pupil.
Dark brown hair, peachy complexion
Phoebe's parents died when their coach overturned, as they moved to a smaller house, her father having lost all his money on the 'change. Phoebe was thrown clear. She was taken in by a kindly Stage-coachman, though he thought it 'not right' for a little lady to be reared by lowly folk such as himself and his wife, and gladly passed her into Philippa Goyder's care as the twins were on their way to the school. It transpired that Phoebe is nominally Jewish, which has led to the school's association with a Rabbi and his family.

Lucy Regina Lamming [Sanderville] b 1803
Founder pupil
Chestnut curls
Lucy was born out of wedlock to a vicar's daughter by a soldier, whose full name and regiment her grandparents

did not know, so were unable to contact him when Lucy's mother, Amabel, died in childbed. When Lucy's grandfather died, the new vicar would have turned the 'bastard child' and her sick grandmother out onto the street had not the village folk cried shame on him. As soon as her grandmother died, he drove straight to Swanley Court to dump her [though it may be said he also hoped to court the supposedly dying heiress who founded it.]

Sarah's other books
Sarah writes predominantly Regency Romances:

The Brandon Scandals Series
    The Hasty Proposal
    The Reprobate's Redemption
    The Advertised Bride
    The Wandering Widow
    The Braithwaite Letters
    Heiress in Hiding

Wild Western Brandon Scandals
    Colonel Brandon's Quest

The Charity School Series
    Elinor's Endowment
    Ophelia's Opportunity
    Abigail's Adventure
    Marianne's Misanthrope
    Emma's Education/Grace's Gift
    Anne's Achievement
    Daisy's Destiny
    Libby's Luck
    Julia's Journey
    Penelope's Pups

    Spinoffs:
The Moorwick Tales
Fantasia on a House Party

Rookwood series
    The Unwilling Viscount
    The Enterprising Emigrée

The Wynddell Papers
    Lord Wynddell's Bride

The Seven Stepsisters series
Elizabeth
Diana
Minerva[WIP]
Flora [WIP]
Catherine [WIP]
Jane [WIP]
Anne [WIP]

One off Regencies
Vanities and Vexations [Jane Austen sequel]
Cousin Prudence [Jane Austen sequel]
Friends and Fortunes
None so Blind
Belles and Bucks [short stories]

The Georgian Gambles series
The Valiant Viscount [formerly The Pugilist Peer]
Ace of Schemes

Other
William Price and the 'Thrush', naval adventure and
Jane Austen tribute
William Price sails North
William Price on land
William Price and the 'Thetis' [wip]

100 years of Cat Days: 365 anecdotes

Sarah also writes historical mysteries

Regency period 'Jane, Bow Street Consultant 'series,
a Jane Austen tribute
    Death of a Fop
    Jane and the Bow Street Runner [3 novellas]
    Jane and the Opera Dancer
    Jane and the Christmas Masquerades [2 novellas]
    Jane and the Hidden Hoard
    Jane and the Burning Question [short stories]
    Jane and the Sins of Society
    Jane and the Actresses
    Jane and the Careless Corpse

Spinoffs:
The Armitage Chronicles

'Felicia and Robin' series set in the Renaissance
    Poison for a Poison Tongue
    The Mary Rose Mystery
    Died True Blue
    Frauds, Fools and Fairies
    The Bishop of Brangling
    The Hazard Chase
    Heretics, Hatreds and Histories
    The Midsummer Mysteries
    The Colour of Murder
    Falsehood most Foul
    The Monkshithe Mysteries
    Toll the Dead Man's bells
    Wells, Wool and Wickedness
    The Missing Hostage
    The Convenient Saint and Other stories
    Sell-sword Summer
    Buried in the past
    The Crail Caper [coming soon]

Children's stories
Tabitha Tabs the Farm kitten
A School for Ordinary Princesses [sequel to Frances Hodgson Burnett's 'A Little Princess.]

The Royal Draxiers series
Bess and the Dragons
Bess and the Queen
Bess and the Succession
Bess and the Paying Scholars
Bess and the Gunpowder Plot [wip]
Bess and the Necromancer [wip]

Non-Fiction
Writing Regency Romances by dice
The Regency Miss's Survival Guide to Bath
Names in Europe from the Etruscans to 1600

Fantasy
Falconburg Divided [book 1 of the Falconburg brothers series]
Falconburg Rising [book 2 of the Falconburg brothers series]
Falconburg Ascendant [book 3 of the Falconburg brothers series, WIP]

Scarlet Pimpernel spinoffs
The Redemption of Chauvelin
Chauvelin and the League
Chauvelin and the Lost Children